Rain Must Fall

Deb Rotuno

RR Books

Published by RR Books

First edition, October 2016

The characters and events in this book are fictitious.
Any similarity to real persons, living or dead,
is coincidental and not intended by the author.

ISBN: 978-1-5393-6653-9

10 9 8 7 6 5 4 3 2 1

Cover Design & Interior Book Design by Coreen Montagna

Printed in the United States of America

This is for everyone who told me I could do it.

PRØLOGUE

April 10, 2016

HURRICANE BEATRICE SETS COURSE FOR DISNEY WORLD

Tropical Storm Beatrice has gained speed and strength as it sits off the west coast of Florida. It shows no signs of slowing down, and its path seems set to barrel through the Sunshine State.

As a precaution, state officials, upon the order of President Parker, have ordered military backup and security to be brought in to not only secure military bases but to help with clean-up once the storm passes by. Troops from all over the country are being ordered into the tropical state.

The Red Cross is asking for volunteers in the medical and construction professions to lend a helping hand.

April 15, 2016

CATEGORY 5 STORM DESTROYS MOST OF CENTRAL FLORIDA, MILITARY BASE IN CRUMBLES

Due to the sustaining hundred-and-fifty-mile-per-hour winds, several beaches, towns, and ports along the west coast of Florida were destroyed. Hurricane Beatrice's strength built over the course of two days, stirring up waves in the Gulf of Mexico that rivaled that of a tsunami. Tampa Bay—mainly Bayshore, Davis Island, and MacDill Air Force Base—are in crumbles. The military base is now partially under water, with very little hope of salvaging any of the buildings. Most aircraft were evacuated several days prior, and the ones unable to fly were damaged or underwater.

From Panama City, south to Port Charlotte, the damage is unimaginable. Power and phone-line outages are scattered throughout central Florida, and communication is down at Dexter Air Force Base on the east coast. While the Atlantic side of the state didn't have any high waves or flooding, they did receive high winds and several tornados.

There are rumors of security breaches at Dexter AFB, which is in conjunction with a military research laboratory, but government officials say the base is under control.

May 2, 2016

REPORTS OF UNTREATABLE FLU-LIKE SYMPTOMS FROM JAPAN, GREAT BRITAIN, AND THE US

The CDC—the Center for Disease Control—has issued a warning of a new global flu. It's been reported that a highly contagious virus is making its way around the world. The new strain has caused a few deaths in Japan, Great Britain, Brazil, and the US. Citizens are being warned to cancel any travel plans and to stock up on supplies.

"Staying home and out of the public is the best way to avoid catching this new influenza," states a member of the CDC, who wishes to remain anonymous. "It spreads quickly. The symptoms are high fever, nausea, even death."

May 5, 2016

ALL AIR TRAVEL TEMPORARILY SHUTS DOWN TO CONTAIN VIRUS

Airline officials called a press conference yesterday, stating that all flights in and out of the US are canceled, with no date in sight as to when they will resume.

Military officials stated that due to the damage inflicted by Hurricane Beatrice and the recent influenza scare, the entire state of Florida is quarantined. No flights are allowed in or out of the state, and roadblocks are stopping any traffic. People are being urged to stay home.

May 7, 2016

PRESIDENT PARKER SUCCUMBS TO VIRUS, VP NOW IN COMMAND

Vice President Hawkins was sworn in as Commander in Chief yesterday, due to the untimely death of President Parker. No statements or autopsy reports have been issued, but according to anonymous tips, President Parker took ill with the flu that has claimed the lives of reported thousands around the globe.

The Department of Defense has stated that contact with the governments of Japan, China, Great Britain, and Russia is down. According to satellite images, there are power outages across the globe.

Religious groups, including the Vatican, have issued a worldwide statement that the end of days is near.

May 10, 2016

RUMORS OF VIRUS BEING A LEAKED BIOWEAPON CAUSES UPROAR IN DC

Thousands of protestors outside the White House fence were urged to go home at gunpoint. Martial law has been in effect for several days in various cities around the country. Most communication has been lost, and power is out in the larger cities, from New York to Los Angeles.

Congress, Homeland Security, and the Department of Defense refuse to answer for what has now been dubbed the "Zombie Apocalypse." The massive flu virus is rumored to be an escaped bioweapon that had been housed at Dexter AFB.

Scientists have stated that the virus starts as flu-like symptoms, only to destroy the brain tissue. The result is something out of a horror movie. Most states have reported more deaths, fires, and these reanimated bodies, but since communication is down in over 85% of the country, there are no updates.

Looting, riots, and fires have all but destroyed our city of Portland. Due to the fluctuating power issues, the Oregonian cannot continue to publish. We wish everyone the best, and may God have mercy on our souls.

JACK

Clear Lake, Oregon
5 Months & 10 Days after Hurricane Beatrice

I flipped the page of my son's scrapbook, my heart hurting. He was so much like his mother in some ways that I couldn't help but smile, despite the circumstances. He may have looked like me, but he was smart and meticulous like my Sara.

Swallowing thickly, I gazed around the cabin. Nothing looked disturbed. They'd fortified the windows and doors, and there were enough supplies in the cabinets and stacked on the floor to get them through another week or so.

I flipped another page or two, noting some tears, some vacant spots where something had been ripped off the paper. I sighed at the poem he'd stashed in there, not to mention a few pictures, some ticket stubs from a Trail Blazers game I'd taken him to, and a pass to the Oregon Zoo. Freddie loved the damn zoo.

Setting the book down on the bed that had obviously been used by my son, I scoped out the rest of the cabin. Melted candles stood cold on the mantel next to pictures of my wife and me. There were lanterns scattered about the place, although they were low on oil. Two makeshift beds were set up in the spare room. The master bedroom hardly looked touched, which made panic rise up in me concerning my wife. She'd done exactly as I'd asked her, but…

I'd spent the last several months trying to get to her, only to arrive to empty cabins. The entire camp looked abandoned in a hurry. Vehicles and RVs were parked in various places, but there was no sign of life, no movement; not even the fucking birds chirped.

However, the sound of rain pelted down on the roof, which caused my skin to crawl. Rain was never fucking good, and neither was the setting sun. The combination of the two would bring a long fucking night, and I wasn't sure my group had any more fight left in them from the last hundred miles we'd traveled, especially after seeing our small town of Sandy.

I stepped into the living room of the cabin I'd dreamed about more over the last few months than anything else. There was a part of my soul that was ripping in half, that was crumbling to the wood floor at my feet. My wife, my son weren't here, and there was no way to know where they'd gone or even if they were still alive. That last thought almost brought me to my knees just as the door flew open and the sound of the telltale groans, growls, and snapping of teeth met my ears.

"Get your ass outside!" Joel snapped, looking exhausted like the rest of us, but there was a spark in his eye. "We got a swarm moving through, and they're focused on your dad's cabin."

My eyes narrowed as I pulled out my weapon. "They smell something?"

He smiled slowly, and it was evil and hopeful and determined all at the same time. "Doc says there's a bomb shelter under that bad boy. Didjoo know that?"

"Wha... Well, yeah, but I forgot about it..." I darted out the door and into the rainy night with him close on my heels.

The sheer size of the swarm of foul, dead beasts brought me up short. There had to be well over two hundred of the putrid bastards.

"Holy fuck! They're migrating from Portland," I breathed, shaking my head. They hadn't noticed us yet, and they were scoping out my dad's cabin like ants with a bowl of sugar. "Oh, they smell something, all right..."

Joel and I moved slowly, quietly, until we reached the rest of our group parked at the edge of Clear Lake. They were from every walk of life, ranged in ages from toddler to the elderly, not to mention the giant Rottweiler panting in my face from the back of Dad's pickup truck. We'd accumulated, lost, and accumulated even more people the entire way from the east side of the country to the west. They were good people merely trying to stay alive in a world that was determined to kill us all. And the dog…Fuck me if Sasha wasn't a loyal-as-hell and deadly member of our group and had been since we set off on this fucked-up journey.

Scratching her ear, I took a deep breath and let it out. "Sasha, draw 'em out. Everyone else? Get someplace high and safe. Make sure to take enough ammo with you inside the cabins. Go, go, go," I ordered quietly, turning to Joel once everyone started to move. "You and me? We're getting inside my dad's cabin. As soon as Sasha draws them away, we'll move in."

Joel grinned, though I noted it was weary as he wiped rain off his face and nodded. "Sasha, separate!" he ordered, and the large dog launched herself off the back end of the truck, hitting the ground at full speed. Her growl was low, menacing, as she bared her teeth.

She moved quickly, smart enough to stay just out of reach of those not-so-dead bastards. The swarm banging around the cabin shifted their attention to her—something moving, something edible, something attainable. They moved quickly, their senses sharpening not only with the rain but with the night falling.

My personal ammo was low, so I opted for my long knife, slipping slowly along the edge of the lake. Joel opted for his Marine sword—a weapon he'd grabbed at Dexter Air Force Base. What had once been a ceremonial symbol, something for show, had now become his favorite weapon. It was quiet, saved ammo, and did the job from a safe distance.

Gunfire erupted across the camp, from the inside of my cabin, from the four-wheeler that was racing around the lake. But finally I noticed that some was coming from the windows of my dad's cabin.

"Watch for friendly fire," I grunted as I slammed my knife through the eye of the closest biter. His teeth snapped once before he fell to the ground with a wet thump.

We worked our way slowly, and I lost count of the kills I'd made by the time I dodged the gunfire coming out the windows. It was the arguing on the other side of the windows that made me finally speak.

"Derek! Hold your fire!"

Everything came to a standstill for a split second, but then I heard the shuffling of feet, raised voices, and finally, the lock on the door clicked. A rifle barrel was pointed in my face the second the door flew open. I froze at the same time Joel aimed his .45 inside the cabin.

"Everyone...*stop!*"

When the rifle barrel was lowered from my face, I saw Derek glaring at the man with his finger on the trigger. Brody Fucking Matthews sneered back at me, and I knew under other circumstances, he'd have pulled the trigger, whether I was a zombie or not. That bastard hated me. But it was the gasp behind him that caught all our attentions.

"Sara," I breathed, finally setting eyes on one of the most important people, one of two whom I'd been fighting to get to these last long fucking weeks.

Her gun dropped to the wood floor and her hands covered her mouth as tears welled up in the prettiest blue eyes I'd ever seen. It looked like her knees were about to give out, and despite how weary I was, I was inside and across the room in a blur, catching her up in my arms.

"Jack?" she sobbed, wrapping herself around me. "I knew it, I knew it! I knew you were coming..."

Groaning, I held her closer, but she fought me, cupping my face. "You're here. You're real."

I couldn't speak. I didn't think that moment would ever come, so I could only nod, kissing her fingers as she muttered about waiting, about having to leave, about things that didn't make sense.

"Where's Freddie?" I asked, but Sara's gaze locked behind me at the same time the fight from outside met the front door.

She scrambled down from my arms as the door collapsed inward. It was then that I noticed where she was standing—over the trap door in the floor. However, an explosion ripped through the night sky, sending all of us to the floor. Covering Sara with my body, I took the brunt of it, but a sharp pain caused my vision to blur.

My last thought as I locked gazes with my wife was that at least I'd been able to see her one more time.

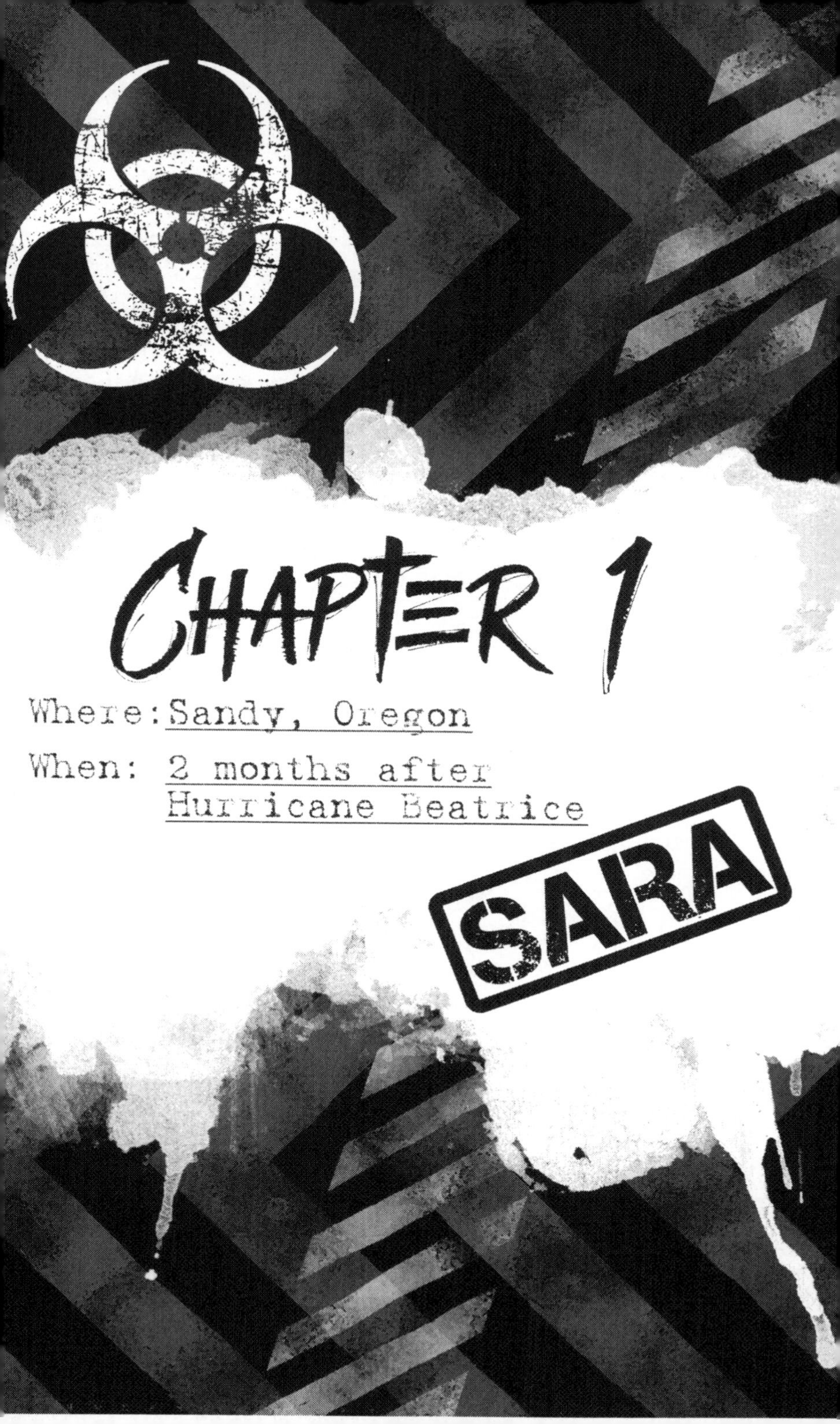
CHAPTER 1
Where: Sandy, Oregon
When: 2 months after Hurricane Beatrice
SARA

SARA

Sandy, Oregon
2 Months after Hurricane Beatrice

I pulled the truck into the driveway and turned off the engine. My hands gripped the steering wheel as I took in my home, a lump forming in my throat at how it was almost unrecognizable.

My beautiful home that was once pale yellow with white shutters now looked like something in a ghost town, with the first-floor windows boarded up. My street was clear, but that didn't mean it would stay that way. My hedges and flowers were destroyed by trampling feet from securing the place and from those…other things.

"Mom?"

I turned to look at my son. He'd already seen too much since all this madness started, and I was damned certain he'd see more before it was all over. At least, I hoped he'd see the end of it.

At seven, Freddie was the clone of his father. From the thick, dark hair that topped his head, to the silly-sweet smile he'd give me when he was in trouble, all the way down to his long legs. It didn't end there. Even the way he fidgeted was like his dad—cracking the knuckles of his fingers, bending the long digits in ways that looked almost painful, although they both were double-jointed, so they assured me it didn't hurt.

Watching him at that moment, I'd never missed my husband more. I wouldn't be making these decisions alone, and we sure as hell wouldn't have to worry about our safety.

"Ready, Freddie?" I teased him, trying to keep it light, but we were about to abandon the only home he'd ever known for a place he hadn't seen in a few years.

"Yeah, but..." He pointed out the window. "Grandpa Hank's here. Is he still pissed we're leaving?"

I snorted. "Probably. And don't say pissed."

"Dad says it."

Grinning in spite of it all, I nodded and opened the truck door. "Yeah, well...your dad says a lot of things he shouldn't. C'mon, buddy. We've got to get loaded up."

The stench in the air wasn't as bad as it had been a few days before, when Sandy had been hit with the worst of it all, so stepping out into the midday sun was bearable. Watching my father kneel down to Freddie's level, I shook my head at their whispered secrets to each other.

I started for the front door, leaving the two of them, but stopped when my dad called me.

"Sara, wait!"

I turned at the top of the porch steps, narrowing my eyes and waiting for another fight, but he merely grasped my son's shoulder for a moment.

"Freddie, you need to go upstairs to your room and pack your duffel bag. Make sure you take plenty of socks and undies."

"Okay, Grandpa."

I handed Freddie the key as he ran by, only to fold my arms across my chest. "*Now* you're telling him to pack? Dad, four weeks ago, you told me I was crazy for heading up there."

My dad held up his hands in a surrendering gesture. "Four weeks ago, my town was safe and under martial law. Now, most of the town is either gone, dead, or...or..."

"Turned." The word I supplied was correct, but it landed between us almost with a heavy thud.

He sighed wearily but nodded, reaching for his baseball cap to readjust it. He still hadn't addressed the real reason I was pissed, so I stepped forward, speaking low enough that my son wouldn't hear me.

"You also said I was crazy for thinking Jack was still alive." My lip twitched, but my eyes burned with tears I couldn't shed—wouldn't shed. Not yet.

"Jesus, Sara…I didn't mean it that way. Just…he's so far away, and I just…Oh, baby girl, I just don't want you to hold on to false hope."

I was shaking my head the entire time he spoke. "No. I'm not listening to this."

I started to turn around, but my dad grabbed my wrist gently and turned me to face him. "You haven't heard a word since…"

"Dad, *no one* has heard anything…*anywhere*. But he knew something was fishy. *He knew.* He said his gut told him something was about to go down, and he was right. He said if it did, then we were to get out, get away from people. He knew it the day the hurricane hit Florida."

Dad nodded, scrubbing his face with a shaky hand, only to pull his cap off again to rub his short, gray hair. "Sara, he's all the way across the country. You can't possibly think—"

"Please." It was all I had. It was all I could beg from him. "Please, don't. I *need* to hold on to this…for now. I have to…for my sanity, for my son. I need to trust Jack on this, if only to get us someplace safe. He made me swear, Daddy. I can't break that promise."

The tears that burned my eyes welled up and spilled over, and I found myself wrapped up in my father's arms.

"Well, he wasn't wrong, Sara. In fact, it's the smartest plan," Dad admitted against my forehead. Cupping my face, he pulled me back so he could look me in the eyes. "Portland is…" He sighed deeply, shaking his head. "Portland's on fire, sweetheart. Whatever security the military was providing is no longer functioning. The streets are a war zone, between survivors fighting for supplies and food and those…those *things* hunting down the survivors. All power, communication, and highways in and out of the city are completely shut down. It won't be long before people and the infected start making their way out of the damn city and into the country."

Things. No one wanted to call them what they were. They'd been given every other name in the book but what they truly were: the undead, biters, the infected, monsters. Unfortunately, they were people we knew, people we'd grown up with, people we'd laughed with, dated, loved. They were friends, family, neighbors, and coworkers. But they'd changed. They'd died, but they'd come back as something from a nightmare, from a horror movie. They were now…zombies. It had all happened so damn fast that some days, it didn't even seem real.

"Then leaving is imperative, Dad. Please, come with us," I begged him, gripping his SFD shirt.

He looked pained at the request but kissed my forehead again. "I can't. Not yet." When I started to argue, he bent his knees so we were eye to eye. "I'm responsible for these people, Sara. You know that. I have to make sure every last one is either moving on, dead—*really*, dead—or safe enough to leave behind. Shit, kiddo, I've got the old folks' home still completely filled to capacity. I can't just leave them."

I nodded, hating that he felt he had to stay, but growing up with my father as Sandy's fire captain helped me understand. The people of Sandy loved him, depended on him.

Nodding again, I kissed his cheek.

"You won't be alone, Sara," he told me. "And I need to ask a favor of you."

My brow wrinkled in curiosity. "What favor?"

"I need you to take some people with you. There are plenty of cabins up there. You'll need the safety in numbers for the trip, and you'll help me by getting a few more people out of this town."

"Who?"

"Millie and Josh Larson…and…Brody and Leo Matthews."

I groaned, rubbing my eyes with the heels of my hands. "A middle-aged woman, a kid, an asshole, and a man in a wheelchair. Jesus, Dad, are you trying to get us killed?"

I heard a familiar chuckle behind me, and when I turned toward the sound, I smirked at the laid-back form that was leaning against my father's truck.

"Aw, now Sara…You and I both know you're not counting the positives. Millie's a damn good cook, and Josh is pretty quick on his feet. Leo's a helluva damn shot with a rifle in his hand, but yeah, Brody's an asshole. There's no getting around that one," Derek drawled, pushing off the truck and walking to me. When I chuckled, his easy grin curled the corners of his mouth. "Besides, you're not the only one who made Jack a promise," he added, raising an eyebrow at me. "My cousin made me swear on a stack of Bibles, my mother's grave, and my own soul that I'd keep you and Freddie safe. I plan to keep that promise."

"He's coming," I vowed weakly.

"If I was a betting man, then my money would be on Jack," my dad stated with a nod. "Believe me, I want that to be true. I can't fathom what would happen—"

"Hank," Derek warned, shooting my dad a sharp glare, but his hazel eyes were softer when they looked back to me. "Anyway, I'm going with you, which means we need to leave at first light tomorrow. Can you be packed up by then?"

Nodding, I said, "I was planning on it."

"Good, then we'll start with the supplies Hank brought you." He pointed toward the tarp-covered truck bed. "You go get what you need out of the house. We'll pull out first thing in the morning," he stated, shoving his hands in his pockets. "And Sara, be prepared for a long ride…and an even longer camping stay at the cabin. It won't be a smooth journey. The highway will be a cemetery, and I'm hearing rumors that those rotting bastards are traveling in packs now, so… we'll have to be armed and move carefully and quickly."

Swallowing thickly at the mere thought of it, I nodded. "Thanks, D."

"He'd do it for me," he muttered before walking to my dad's truck to start unloading and organizing. I caught sight of gas cans, bags of charcoal, bottles of water, and several boxes.

Turning back to my dad, I tried one more time. "Please, come with us."

"I'll meet you there. Give me time, Sara, and I'll be right behind you. Now…let's get you loaded and the house packed up."

Eastbound, OR-126

The rumble of Derek's Jeep engine slowed, and he tossed a signal over his shoulder for us to pull over. The sound of rocks and gravel popping underneath the large tires of Jack's truck was reminiscent of the sound of bones breaking. They sounded almost identical, except maybe drier.

What normally would have been a little less than three hours' drive had taken us almost two full days, and we weren't anywhere near close to the turn-off we needed. The 126 was just like Derek had predicted. It had been a graveyard—sometimes a quiet one, and sometimes a threatening one. We'd had a close call or two, but glancing into my side-view mirror, I could see we were all hanging in there.

I shut off the engine to save gas and watched as Derek scouted ahead. There were woods and trees all around us, but all seemed still. Up ahead, as far as I could see to the bend in the highway, were stopped cars, trucks, and RVs.

Turning to Freddie, who'd been pretty quiet since our last stop, I nudged his shoulder. "Hanging in there?"

He nodded, reaching up to push his hair off his forehead, but his brow was furrowed and his mouth was in a tight line when he turned to face me. "I could help, you know," he stated, practically glaring my way with eyes so familiar they made my heart hurt.

I wanted to laugh at his temper, but I couldn't. The thought of my baby with a gun in his hand scared the living shit out of me. But this was a new world—a dangerous one at that—which made my head shake back and forth slowly.

"Grandpa Hank said I needed to learn. Even Derek says so. And Dad said—"

"Frederick Jackson Chambers!" I snapped, my eyes closing for a moment. I took a deep breath and let it out. "I know your dad said he'd teach you to hunt when he got back." Cupping his face, I tilted my head at him. "Gimme a break, kid. I know this isn't easy. I know you want to help. You're strong and brave like your daddy, but let me think about it, okay?"

"Yeah, but..."

Squishing his face to shut him up, I said, "I'm not saying no, Freddie. I'm merely asking for time to think about it. If I say yes—and I mean *if*—then I want to do it in a controlled environment at the cabin. Not out here in the middle of nowhere, where something could go crazy. Got me?" I asked, releasing my hand from his face and running my fingers through his hair.

He smirked at me, but at least he didn't roll his eyes. "'Kay."

When he sulked, facing out the passenger window, I nudged him again. "Hey," I whispered, leaning my head to the side so that it was resting against the headrest. "You *do* help, Freddie. You've got sharp eyes, and you..."

Movement off the side of the road caught my eye, and my nostrils flared.

"There's more than one," Freddie whispered, tapping the window lightly. "I see...four, maybe five?"

"Okay. Don't move, and stay quiet," I ordered him, grabbing for my gun on the dashboard. I waited until he nodded before reaching for the door. Silently, I slipped down out of the truck, barely making a sound when the door clicked closed.

Behind me was an extra car that hadn't been in the original plan. By the time Derek had pulled up to my house two mornings ago, there'd been an extra vehicle in the caravan. A middle-aged couple, Martin and Carol North, were driving the older truck with a topper on the back. Behind them was Millie and Josh's RV. It was older, but it was tall enough we could use it as a lookout spot. The last vehicle was Brody Matthews' truck.

Dodging between Brody's truck and the back of the RV, I climbed up the ladder to the top of the RV, finding Josh already there with binoculars in hand.

"Seven, Sara," he whispered, giving me the binoculars to see for myself. "Seven, and if we shoot one, we'll draw them all here."

"I know," I whispered back, "but if we stay here much longer, they'll smell us. Luckily, for the moment, we're downwind."

Josh groaned but nodded. He was a sharp kid. He was pushing fifteen, with long hair and a happy smile. He was the only child Millie still had living at home, and he watched over her like a hawk. Just like the rest of us, they'd lost contact with the rest of their family. He had two older sisters away at college, and no one had heard from them.

Josh was also wicked fast on his feet. He was good at scouting out supplies we might need in some of the traffic jams we'd driven through. And having grown up in Estacada, just outside of Sandy, he'd learned to hunt, so he wasn't half bad with a gun in his hand.

I could hear Derek's Jeep coming closer, and I sighed, looking back at Josh. "We're not going to have a choice. His engine will draw them in, and I have a feeling we're gonna stop for the night."

"Damn it," he groaned, setting the binoculars down and reaching for his rifle. "You want up here? I can take Brody with me on the ground."

Shaking my head, I waved him away and made my way to the ladder. "I'll take the ground. Just watch my back," I said on the way down, finally dropping to the asphalt.

Pulling my gun from the waistband of my jeans, I waved Brody out of his truck.

"How many?"

"About seven…give or take."

We stepped to the shoulder of the road, about the time one of the creatures stepped out of the woods. I grimaced at it, noting its slow gait. One arm was hanging misshapen by its side, while the other hand opened and closed stretched out in front of it. Its jaw was askew, and the flesh was now a purplish-black.

"Fuck me, they stink," Brody muttered, shaking his head and raising his shotgun to his shoulder to aim.

I could still hear Derek's Jeep coming, but this would most likely be over before he arrived. I raised my gun and aimed, popping off the first round.

There were a few things that drew the zombies in: loud noise, the scent of humans, and movement. Despite their corpse-like state, their senses were still sharp, if not sharper than when they were human. They never tired, never wore out, but kept going until they found a food source. Nighttime made them much more active and feral, but the rain made all of those things a thousand times worse. Something about the rain enhanced every smell, every noise, and every movement. The night Sandy fell, the rain never let up.

My shot took down the first one, which caused the rest of his small pack to turn our way. Five more emerged from the woods almost at the same time, and Brody popped off three rounds, while I took the other two.

"We got more!" Josh cried out, his rifle sounding off above our heads as what looked like ten more stepped from the trees.

I took the left, and Brody took the right, clearing most of them before they could even set foot out of the shade of the pines. The pack was way bigger than we'd estimated, and they kept coming, one right after the other. I heard a vehicle door open and close, and Martin joined us with his own weapon. As fast as we could take them out, the quicker they'd spill out of the trees.

Derek's tires squealed to a stop, the engine cutting off completely at the same time I heard Freddie's cry.

"Mom! Behind you!"

Swinging around, I fired my last two bullets in my clip at the two closest to me, but there was another coming. I reached for another clip as fast as I could, but as soon as I aimed, an arrow flew by my head, lodging right in the middle of the forehead of what looked like an old woman. I let out a breath, giving a quick nod to Derek, who was reloading his compound bow as he stayed standing in the topless Jeep. He'd used that bow for hunting deer at one point, and now it was used for defense. He lifted it quickly, nailing two more at the same time—one right behind the other—essentially skewering them through the middle of their heads.

"I leave you for ten minutes!" he teased above the din of gunfire, jumping down to the ground.

Shaking my head, I smirked but took out the last straggler near me. "Yeah, well, you know what Jack always said…"

Derek's laugh was low and easy. "Yeah, that you were trouble from the get-go."

Grinning, I nodded, ignoring the pain in my chest from missing my husband as I scanned the woods for movement. Derek's arrow flew silently into the shade of the trees, and a body thumped down to the ground.

"Clear!" Josh called out.

Derek walked past me, taking his spent arrows back. He couldn't afford to leave any behind; he only had so many, though I was pretty sure he had plans to make more once we got to the cabin.

"We'll stay here tonight," he said, gesturing around us, only to point up the highway. "We've got a long day ahead tomorrow, and there's no rerouting. We've got no choice but to push and tow cars out of the way. We'll use Jack's truck and Martin's to do it. Plus, there may be some fuel to siphon."

"All right," I sighed, suddenly very tired, but my temper rose to the surface when I heard Brody's usual complaints.

"Who the hell put you in charge?"

I rounded on him. "My father, Brody. If you don't like it, feel free to turn back and go ask him about it. I have no problem continuing on without you."

"So sweet, ice princess," he drawled, grinning my way. "You'd leave me with my handicapped father—"

"Oh, no…no, no, no. Leo is more than welcome to come with us, but you?" I said with a grin, pointing a finger in his chest. "You, on the other hand, not so much."

"You need to let the past go, Sara," he sneered, shaking his head.

I laughed, turning away from him. "You're the one who picked a drunken fight with a combat soldier, so don't cry to me about it."

Brody's hand landed on my shoulder, and I spun around to face him, waiting for the old, misguided argument. "He was touching my girlfriend."

"Oh, Brody…I wasn't your girlfriend. You'd made sure of that the moment you cheated on me. And this is almost *ten years later*. I married the man who so skillfully handed you your ass on a silver platter. If you can't deal with me—or Derek—then go back. Otherwise, shut your mouth and try to find a way to be helpful. This isn't about the past; it's about right fucking now. I know it goes against your nature to not look out for number one, but give us all a break."

He started forward, but his father stopped him.

"Brody, if she shoots you, I wouldn't blame her. Now get over here and help me out of this godforsaken truck!" Leo ordered, and Brody's sneer twitched a little before he walked to his father. "She's doing *us* the favor, son, so keep your mouth closed."

I walked to Derek, who was smiling crookedly as he cleaned his arrows. "Want me to mistake him for a biter? I can shoot him in the middle of the night. No one would suspect a thing…"

Chuckling, I shook my head. "No, let's just set up camp here for the night. I'll take first watch on the RV once we've eaten."

Derek looked like he wanted to say something, but he merely nodded, smiling, and ruffled my hair. "By the way, Jack would've already shot his ass."

Snorting into a laugh, I nodded. "Don't I know it." My laugh trailed off, and I locked eyes with my husband's cousin. "God, I miss him."

Derek nodded solemnly. "Yeah, me too. Me too."

Mount Hood National Forest

Four days and twelve hours. That's what it took to travel a little over a hundred and fifty miles. We'd run into three packs of zombies moving down the highway, more car accidents than I could count, one set of dangerous-looking men traveling south—they'd moved on quickly once they'd caught sight of our weapons—and we'd acquired two extra mouths to feed.

I glanced into the rearview mirror at the two sleeping forms in the backseat of Jack's crew-cab truck. The mother and daughter were exhausted. They'd been trapped in their camper in the last pile-up we'd had to navigate on the 26, for what I'd assumed was several days. They'd been down to their last bit of food and ammo when we'd stumbled upon them and a pack of zombies moving through.

Tina Chase, who looked to be somewhere around my age of twenty-nine—maybe a little older—and her daughter, Janie, who was eleven, had no place else to go. Tina's husband, Jerry, had turned. In fact, it had been his changed form trying to rip through their camper door when we'd pulled up. Derek had put a knife through his head.

"Mom, where are we?" Freddie asked softly.

"NF-770," I told him, tapping the map in his hand with one hand while steering with the other. "We're smack-dab in the middle of the Mount Hood National Forest."

The national forest road was surprisingly empty and free of traffic, which was both comforting and a worry at the same time. It made for easy driving and at a faster speed, but it also meant we were almost to Clear Lake, which meant we'd be on our own for who knew how long.

"How many cabins are there?" Tina asked softly from the backseat.

"Four," I told her, starting to slow down to look for the private drive, though Derek was leading the way just fine. "My father owns one, which Millie, Josh, Leo, and Brody are taking. Derek has one, and the Norths are going to stay with him. My husband and I own one, and you can stay with us. You and Janie can take the spare room."

"And the fourth is Grandpa Rich's, right?" Freddie piped up.

"That's right," I sighed deeply, taking the narrow private road.

The other half of my family had been clear across the country when everything started. My husband and his company, including our good friend, Joel Woods, were called into Florida when the path of Hurricane Beatrice was dead-set on hitting land. Jack's father was a former Army surgeon, as was his mother, Dottie, although she specialized in disease control. All of them had shipped out almost two months prior to go help where needed. My husband's company had been extra security in and around the base, not to mention being there to keep the peace if things had gotten out of hand. And they had. Way out of hand. We hadn't heard a word from them since the hurricane. A little over two months was all it had taken to destroy the world, the US government, and all we'd ever known.

Shaking my head to clear it of the last frantic conversation I'd had with Jack, I smiled in the mirror. "We'll open up the fourth cabin if we need to, but for now, you guys can stay with Freddie and me."

Derek's brake lights glowed bright red in the shade of all the trees surrounding us as he pulled to the side. He jumped out of the Jeep to unlock the chained gate, pushing it wide open so we could all pull through.

I stopped beside him. "You want me to wait?"

"No, I'll be right behind you." He glanced up for a moment. "And we may have just enough sunlight left to actually sleep indoors tonight," he added with a grin. "We'll have to secure windows and doors, store food, but we should just make it by nightfall."

"Let's hope so," I told him, and he patted the truck before waving me on.

The private drive wound through the woods for another mile or so but emptied out into a clearing that always made me smile, made my heart beat faster. So many memories at this place. I could imagine my husband's face as I pulled up in front of our cabin. Jack loved it here, but even more he loved to tease me about this place. We'd made love for the first time in the small log home in front of me after he'd returned from Afghanistan. We'd been crazy in love with each other, and that hadn't changed a bit over the course of ten years—eight of those married and seven as parents. It was this place where we knew we'd be together for the rest of our lives. He'd been about to ship out for another tour—this time to Iraq—but we knew we were it. Every time we'd come back here, he'd wear the sexiest of crooked grins, always raising an eyebrow at me.

Rubbing my face to stop the tears, I sent a silent plea to whoever would listen to send my husband—and the other members of my family—home, before opening the truck door.

We just barely got the three cabins fortified by the time night fell. Luckily, there were no interruptions with zombie packs, and the night was looking to stay clear of rain. Tina was a huge help inside my cabin. She stored the food, set up the beds, and even started a fire while the rest of us barricaded windows, sorted ammo, and parked the vehicles strategically around us. The youngest of us gathered firewood, helped Millie prepare dinner, and unloaded clothes and supplies. By the time the older woman actually fed us, the entire lot of us were exhausted; even the kids were falling asleep at the table, so Tina and I guided our sleepy ones to my cabin.

"Go brush your teeth, buddy," I told Freddie, and when he started to complain, I shook my head. "Frederick Jackson, do not argue with me."

Tina's chuckle met my ears when I muttered about how much he was like Jack.

"He's his dad made over," I said, pointing to the framed pictures on the fireplace mantel, which were visible because of the handful of candles and a lantern.

"Oh, wow, you're right," she said with a soft laugh, holding up a picture of the two of us. "Handsome."

Smiling, I nodded. Jack was truly handsome. With warm brown eyes, dark-brown hair, and a smile that could wipe away the worst of days, Jack was beautiful—inside and out. The picture she held up was from our second honeymoon, which we'd spent here for four days—the first had been spent at a hotel just before he shipped out. He'd wanted to marry me before he left, and it was fast and perfect. But the picture she was holding was of our real honeymoon. He'd come home safe from Iraq, and I'd just graduated from college with my accounting degree. It was the two of us laughing, playing, and Jack had turned the camera on us. We were hopes, dreams, and happiness incarnate.

She smiled my way, but it fell quickly when she looked back at the picture of Jack and me. "Can I ask…?"

"He's Army, so he was sent to Florida just before Beatrice hit," I answered softly, my chest aching.

I could tell she couldn't quite decide what to say. I knew how it sounded. The entire world had been thrown into hell, and Jack was pretty much on the other side of the planet. He was technically at ground zero, where all this originated. I knew the odds, but I couldn't face them just yet. My heart wouldn't let me.

Movement caught my eye, and I saw my son standing in the doorway. Smiling his way and picking up a lantern, I shooed him into his room. "C'mon, kiddo. You'll need some sleep. I hear a rumor that Leo's taking you guys fishing tomorrow."

He smiled, but it didn't reach his eyes as he crawled under the covers. In his hand was the scrapbook he'd been keeping for the last two months. I wasn't sure why he had an obsession with the virus. My guess was that he'd figured out where his dad and grandparents had gone. He had to have put two and two together from the news. I didn't have the heart to stop him.

"Can I see?" I asked, and he set it in my hands.

The meltdown of society was all right there in the headlines.

HURRICANE BEATRICE SETS COURSE FOR DISNEY WORLD

CATEGORY FIVE STORM DESTROYED MOST OF CENTRAL FLORIDA, MILITARY BASE IN CRUMBLES

REPORTS OF UNTREATABLE FLU-LIKE SYMPTOMS FROM JAPAN, GREAT BRITAIN, AND US

ALL AIR TRAVEL TEMPORARILY SHUTS DOWN TO CONTAIN VIRUS

PRESIDENT PARKER SUCCUMBS TO VIRUS, VP NOW IN COMMAND

RUMORS OF VIRUS BEING A LEAKED BIOWEAPON CAUSES UPROAR IN DC

The rest of the articles started to dwindle down, but I could see that Freddie had stashed a few things in there that were important to him—pictures, ticket stubs, Jack's old dog tags. I trailed my finger down those, feeling the raised letters, the dents and dings in them.

Freddie settled in against me, and I wrapped an arm around him, dropping repeated kisses to the top of his head. Turning the page, my heart lodged in my throat. Somewhere, Freddie had found a copy of the poem Jack always quoted us when things looked bad, when there seemed to be no light at the end of the tunnel. He'd quoted it to me over the phone and in letters more times than I could count when we'd been separated due to his job.

"Read it," Freddie asked softly. "Please, Mom."

I kissed his head again, leaving my lips there when I spoke. "Okay. *The Rainy Day* by Henry Wadsworth Longfellow…"

The day is cold, and dark, and dreary;
It rains, and the wind is never weary;
The vine still clings to the mouldering wall,
But at every gust the dead leaves fall,
And the day is dark and dreary.

My life is cold, and dark, and dreary;
It rains, and the wind is never weary;
My thoughts still cling to the mouldering Past,
But the hopes of youth fall thick in the blast,
And the days are dark and dreary.

Be still, sad heart! And cease repining;
Behind the clouds is the sun still shining;
Thy fate is the common fate of all,
Into each life some rain must fall,
Some days must be dark and dreary.

We were both quiet, absorbing the words Jack had tried so hard to instill in us, but this seemed the darkest and dreariest of times. The harshest yet.

"Mom?"

"Hmm?"

"You think Dad'll come?" he asked through a long, deep yawn, looking so much like Jack that my heart nearly shattered right there in the small bed of the old cabin.

Brushing his thick hair off his brow and thinking he needed a trim, I kissed his forehead, breathing in deeply the scent of little boy and grass and a slight musty scent that filled the cabin, which had been closed up for too long.

"I really hope so, kiddo."

"He promised, right?"

Smiling a shaky smile, I nodded, kissing his forehead again, but I had to squeeze my eyes closed to fight the tears. My son would never see my fear. I had to stay strong, had to keep going, if only for him.

"That's right; he did promise, and he's never broken a promise to us. Ever."

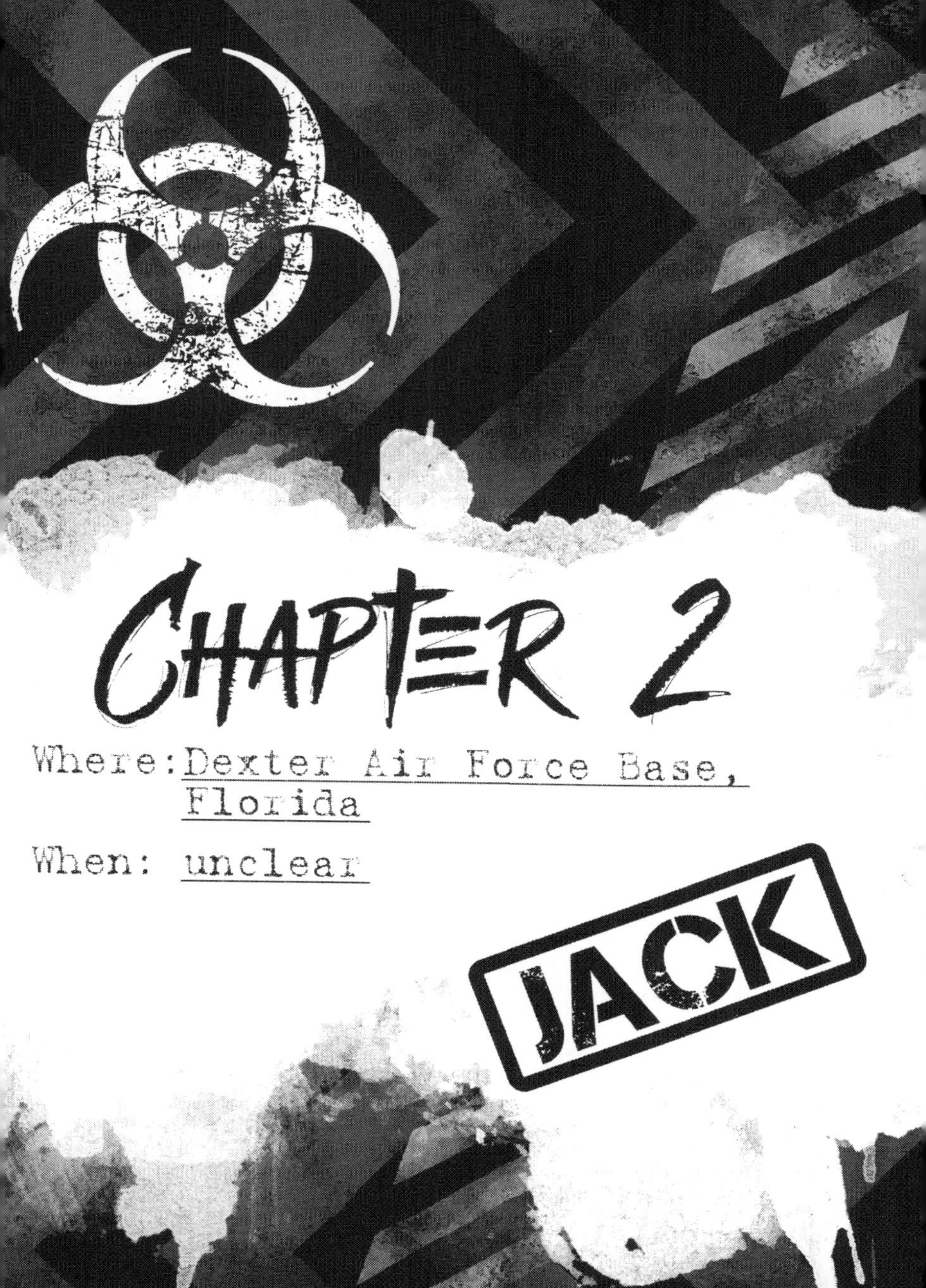

CHAPTER 2

Where: Dexter Air Force Base, Florida

When: unclear

JACK

JACK

Dexter Air Force Base, Florida

"*We have a security breach, Chambers!*"

"Parts of the base are already flooding…"

"We've lost power, and the backup generators need to be…"

"Shut this wing down! Shut it down now!"

The sounds around me sounded far away—breaking glass, alarms, gunfire. That last sound made me flinch as I tried my damnedest to come up out of the fog I was in, but pain shot through every inch of my right side. It felt like flames licking at my skin, from the inside out.

I tried to claw my way up out of blackness as familiar voices, sounds, and smells wafted all around me, but the pain was too much. Stars exploded behind my eyes, blooming into stark white, and I sank into it.

"Fever, contusions, concussion…"

"I don't have a choice!"

"Both of them…we're gonna lose both of them…"

The voices around me were so familiar that my heart hurt. I fought the fire, the pain, the cloud of fog in my head. There was an urgent feel around me, like I needed to get my ass up and be somewhere, but I couldn't focus on it. My head pounded, my leg throbbed, and my chest felt like someone was sitting on it. Still, I fought it all.

"Son, you need to calm down…"

"Jack, can you hear me?"

"Give him something for the pain…"

The pain skyrocketed from my head to my feet. As quickly and as forcefully as the pain slammed into me, the feeling of tingling bliss felt like a cool blanket that started in my head as the aching calmed enough for me to let go.

"Jack, what're you saying?"

"Listen, Shortcake. I think…I think there's some hefty shit about to go down. This storm caused a helluva lot of panic around here. I want you safe. I need you and Freddie someplace safe."

"Baby, you're scaring me…"

"I know, Sara, but I need you to listen. Something tells me there's more than just some flooding and broken windows. The higher-ups are freaking out. I need you to promise me…even if you don't hear from me, 'cause comms are sketchy. I had a bitch of a time calling you. But you get Freddie, your dad, and Derek out of there and up to the cabins. Promise me, Shortcake!"

"I promise, Jack, but—"

"No, no…no buts, baby. Please do as I ask. I'm begging you. I've heard shit around here that makes me fucking nervous…"

"What about you?"

"Don't you sweat me, Sara. I'll get to you, no matter what. Tell me you know that."

"I do, Jack. You know I do, but you're too far away. And that storm…"

"Tell me you love me, Shortcake. That's all that matters to me. If you say that, then I'll go AWOL to get to you and Freddie."

"Oh God…Jack, I love you. Please, please be safe."

"I love you, too, baby. Cabins, Sara. I'll find you there."

"Jack, wait! You're cutting out…"

That voice. I needed more of it. I needed it like the air I was breathing. It felt instinctual, but I couldn't pinpoint why. And the fogginess in my brain couldn't put a face to the voice, though all I could do was fixate on finding it.

The dream faded, and the voice was replaced with beeps and echoes. My head gave a dull throb, but at least the fire in my veins had stopped. I chased the dream, but it left me in a puff of smoke as soon as the bright lights of the room filtered in.

"Take it easy, son," I heard to my right, but I couldn't open my eyes just yet.

"Bright," I rasped, trying to swallow, but my throat was too dry.

"Okay, hang on."

The lights dimmed a little, and I was able to barely crack my eyes open. The figure beside me was blurry but felt familiar.

"Son, can you hear me?"

"Yeah," I groaned, trying to reach for my face, but my arms were restricted. "What the fuck?"

I struggled against the restraints, feeling cool hands on my face. "Jackson Alan, you need to calm down now."

I froze, panic coursing through me. "M-Mom?"

"Shh, please stay calm. You've been in an accident, and you needed fluids. I had to put an IV in your arm, but you kept pulling it out."

Sagging back to the pillow behind me, I groaned in frustration. "Where am I?"

"You're in a medical facility..." Her voice trailed off, and I tried to look her way again, but she was still blurry.

"Hospital? What the hell happened?"

"Not..." She sighed, and I felt her fingers on my wrist, only to brush my hair from my forehead. "It doesn't matter right now where you are, but, Jack, there's been an accident. Don't you remember?"

She released one of my bound wrists, and I rubbed my face, shaking my head. "I remember the storm, alarms going off..." Squeezing my eyes closed, I fought the throb in my head. Finally, I was able to open my eyes all the way. When I saw my mother's face, it shocked me. "Mom?"

She looked...exhausted, terrified, and pissed off, all at the same time. She was pale, not the vibrant woman I knew. She leaned forward, dropping a kiss to my forehead, a sob escaping her.

"I thought...for a moment there...Christ, Jack...I thought I'd lost you."

My agitation grew by leaps and bounds because I couldn't think. I couldn't remember why she'd be that upset.

"Mom...Mom! Help me sit up. Tell me!"

The head of my bed raised up slowly, and I shook my head again but wrapped a weak arm around her when she hugged me. She smelled like antiseptic and sweat and smoke—no, not smoke... Gunpowder, which set me on edge. She didn't smell like my mother, not the way I remembered.

She pulled back, swiping at her tears. "There's so much to tell you. You've been out for...a while."

"Okay, well...start with why I'm in a hospital bed. Where's Dad? And Joel? And my company?"

My mother seemed to steel herself. "Jack, the only way for me to do this is to ask you what you remember. You know...name, rank... all that."

I snorted weakly but nodded. "Staff Sergeant Jackson Chambers, from Sandy, Oregon." Something about that statement made me antsy, nervous. I paused, rubbing my temple. "Why...do I feel I have someplace to be?" I muttered to myself but looked to my mother, whose brow was furrowed. "Anyway, my company was shipped to Florida...Security detail for a storm that hit. I remember the base flooded and parts of the north section collapsed, but..." I shook my head and looked up at her. "Is Dad here in the hospital? What about Joel?"

"Joel's in the next room. He's...hanging in there. He'll be okay, but it was touch and go for a bit. But, sweetheart, the rest of your company...they didn't make it. There was an incident."

"I know. The storm."

"No, son. *After* the storm."

I stared at her for a moment and then shook my head. "I don't know!" I rubbed my face with my left hand, letting it fall to my lap. My fingers balled up into a fist on my thigh, the gold ring on my finger glinting in the dim light. My heart hurt, my chest felt tight, and I opened my hand to look closer, my thumb running over it on the inside as my dream echoed in my head.

"Oh God...Jack, I love you. Please, please be safe."

"I love you, too, baby. Cabins, Sara. I'll find you there."

My breathing picked up. "Mom…Where's Sara? And Freddie? Do they know?"

My mother inhaled sharply, but she didn't answer me right away.

"Yes? No?" I rubbed my temple, squeezing my eyes closed tightly for a second or two. "I thought I heard her, but had to have been a dream…" Glancing around, I looked for a phone. "I need to call her, let her know I'm okay. Where's my cell phone?"

Mom placed her hand on top of mine, saying, "It won't work, sweetheart. Communication is down everywhere."

"What? The storm?"

She flinched but nodded. "The storm caused a huge chain of events, Jack."

My temper flared out of my control. "Jesus Christ, Mom! Would you stop talking in riddles? Tell me what the fuck is going on! Is the storm over?"

She flinched but turned when my door opened. My dad strolled in, not looking any better than my mother.

"Jackson, you need to calm the hell down before you hurt yourself."

"Dad, tell me…And while you're at it, tell me why I can't think straight and why I can remember some shit and not others," I snapped, reaching across my body to pull at the Velcro on my right wrist. "And while you're doing that, get all this shit off me!"

My dad's hand landed flat in the middle of my chest. "Only if you calm down, son. I mean it. This won't be an easy conversation, but you need to hear it. Promise me you'll stay calm, and I'll explain everything."

His voice, his face, his furrowed brow told me that he wasn't to be fucked with, but his unshaven face, the dark circles under his eyes, and the state of his clothing told me there was a bigger picture here and I needed to let him lead.

"Okay," I whispered, looking between them. "Can I get up?"

They glanced at one another, but my dad nodded. "Yeah, let me get this IV out of you."

An uncomfortable silence fell over the room, and I squinted a little when my mother turned the lights back up so my father could get to work. He carefully removed the needle in my arm, wrapping it up with gauze and tape. He stepped to the cabinet and pulled out a pair of scrub pants and a white T-shirt, setting them on my lap.

"I'll help you dress. You're gonna be sore, Jack, so just let me help you. You're not the only one who needs to be…briefed. Joel's awake too."

I nodded, setting the clothes aside and carefully pushing myself up off the bed. My right leg was sore, and my limbs felt weak. There was a bandage wrapped around my calf, just below my knee.

"Damn, how long have I been out?" I asked him, pulling the shirt on over my head.

"Ten days. Some of that we kept you under to help you heal."

My eyebrows shot up. "You're joking…"

"No, son, I'm not." He held my arm while I pulled the loose pants up over my underwear. "Sit for just a second, please."

Nodding, I did as he said and sat on the edge of the bed. He stood in front of me, shining a light in and out of each of my eyes. He stayed quiet as he checked me over, finally placing both his hands on my shoulders.

"You were in the north section of the base when it collapsed. Some debris fell on you, which is where your concussion came from. There was an explosion, and shrapnel lodged in your leg. It wasn't too deep, and I was able to repair it, but you'll have to give yourself time to heal completely."

When I nodded, he smiled a little, but I noticed it didn't reach his eyes.

"You said you had a hard time remembering stuff," he stated, and I nodded again. "Like what? Tell me."

"Um, I remember getting to Florida, the storm…I know why I was here. I remember calling Sara after the storm, but I can't remember why I was so urgent. I can't remember how I got hurt…or how I lost my company."

My dad's face was clear of any expression, but he nodded. "You had a pretty bad concussion, Jack. So your memories may be spotty for a little bit." He smiled, patting the side of my face. "Do you remember what you said to Sara?"

Frowning, I nodded. "Yeah, that if something happened, to get to the cabin, but I don't know why I'd say that…or I can't remember."

"That's okay. It'll come, and we'll help you."

"Maybe if I could just talk to them..."

"No, son. You can't. The phones are down—both landlines and cell service."

"Damn, how bad was this storm?"

"It's not the storm, Jack. It's what the storm...unleashed," he stated with a dark look, helping me to my feet. "C'mon. Joel's in the next room asking the same questions you are. I might as well tell you both at the same time."

Suddenly, it occurred to me how quiet the hospital was—no bustling nurses, no overhead pages, nothing.

"Um, where's the staff? Nurses?" I asked him, following him out of my room and down one door.

"Just wait. I'll explain," he sighed wearily.

The next room was identical to mine, from the cabinet to the hospital bed. Joel, however, was sitting up, letting my mother look him over.

"Jack," he greeted with his usual grin, but he looked like I felt—tired, sore, groggy. "What the hell do *you* remember?" He held up his arm, which was wrapped up in a temporary cast.

I snorted. "And I was hoping you'd tell me."

"I got my ass kicked. *That's* what I know." He held up his Velcro cast again for emphasis. "I know you've been out longer than me, but you kinda took the worst of that explosion."

"I don't remember that part. The last thing I remember is calling Sara."

"Oh." Joel looked confused but nodded. "But, dude...that was a few days after the hurricane hit."

"Jesus, how many days have I lost?" I yelled, glancing around the room.

"Like I said, you were unconscious for ten days. The fact that your memory is sketchy isn't exactly a surprise," my dad explained. "It's been four weeks since the storm touched land. It traveled across the state of Florida, right through the center. It moved slowly, destroying just about everything in its wake. It was a category-five storm, which rivaled that of Katrina or Andrew."

"And I was there when you called Sara," Joel stated. "We were barely getting a signal as the storm passed over us. You were freaking out 'cause you'd overheard someone say something about a security breach and Department of Defense." He rolled his eyes to my dad. "Okay, Doc, let's hear it."

My dad pinched the bridge of his nose, sitting down heavily in the chair. "Sit, son. This won't be easy to hear for either of you." He gestured to the chair in the opposite corner, while my mother stood beside him.

We were all silent for a moment. The atmosphere in the room was tense and heavy. Again, I took in my parents' disheveled appearance. Normally they were better put together than what was in front of me. My dad hardly went a day or two without shaving, but he had what looked to be almost a full week of growth on his face. Reaching up to my own face, I had about the same. My mother, on the other hand, was the one who worried me. She was gaunt, her skin sallow, and her hair, while usually perfectly combed, was drawn back in a low ponytail.

Frowning, I waited because I had a feeling I was about to hear some heavy shit.

"This isn't a hospital," Dad finally stated, gesturing a finger around the room. "This is a part of the remaining north section of the base—the laboratory that survived the storm."

There wasn't a window in the room, so I couldn't exactly verify that piece of information. I nodded for him to go on.

He closed his eyes, shaking his head, but looked up to my mother. "This…this is really your area of expertise, so maybe you should explain."

My mother nodded and stood up straight. She ran a shaky hand over her face before saying, "Dexter Air Force Base houses one of the laboratories that works with communicable diseases. It also studies bioweapons. You and your company were brought in here to secure this location, should the storm cause damage, but as Hurricane Beatrice hit the warm waters of the gulf, it grew in speed and power, beyond anything anyone was expecting. Tampa, St. Petersburg, and Clearwater are gone…simply flooded out. MacDill Air Force Base is no longer standing—well, it's standing, but it's standing under water. What didn't flood was destroyed with winds and heavy rain, never mind the tornadoes.

"It was the latter that hit here," she continued, starting to pace, but she pointed to the floor. "It took out the power, the phone lines, and the north side of the base…this side." Her eyes filled with tears, and it was all I could do not to go to her, but my dad's hand slipped into hers. "Jack, Joel…when the building collapsed, it not only shut down the containment for the laboratory's storage, but it shattered several vials—no, not several…most of the vials of an experiment the military was trying to contain. In doing so, a virus was unleashed into the base."

Joel and I locked gazes for a moment, both of us confused, but I had to ask a question. "Okay, so…we're in some sort of quarantine? And how were you here? I mean, I knew you had clearance to be on base, but…" I waved a hand around me to indicate this specific place, and I didn't mention the fact that I was a little unnerved that I'd still seen no signs of others—nurses, faculty, officers. No one.

My dad sat forward, his face solemn. "You know Major Mathis and I were good friends," he said, and when Joel and I nodded, he went on. "Well, he allowed us to wait out the storm here on base, said that we could help, should anyone get hurt. We obviously agreed. We had no problem helping out. We weren't far from you, from this section, when the explosion went off. So we…" He grinned a little, locking gazes with me. "You're our son, so…" He shrugged a shoulder. "Mathis allowed us in here to get to you, to your company."

Mom pointed to Joel and me, saying, "You two were the tail of your company. You were the last in the group to step foot inside the north section. Up until that point, you'd been patrolling other areas of the base. However, you were the last team brought into contain—" She stopped, her face going even paler than before. "Um, there was no getting to your men. Two very lucky things happened at the same time. The explosion created a barrier between you and the farthest part of the building. It severed you away from the…the worst part of it."

"And the second thing?" Joel asked, looking between my parents. "I mean, I remember the patrols when the power went down. Don't you, Jack?"

"Barely," I groaned, rubbing my face, but I looked to Dad to answer Joel's question.

Dad smiled ruefully. "The second thing was we were able to get to you two, get you out of there and into another wing. We've closed off this portion of the building, focused the generators on our area."

I sat forward, rubbing my face with both hands, only to rest my elbows on my knees. "Okay, um…I get all that. And…well, thank you. Both of you."

"Definitely," Joel concurred, nodding like a kid.

"But I have a question." I held up a finger. "You…" I pointed to Dad. "You said the storm 'unleashed' something. The collapse of the building wasn't the worst part, was it?"

Both my parents shook their heads slowly.

Mom stepped forward, her hands shaking a little as she ran her fingers through my hair like she'd done my whole life—just like Sara did to Freddie—and my heart literally *ached* to see my family, to see my sweet, gorgeous wife and my little boy. They had to be worried sick about me, with so much time since our last call. And remembering that call made me nervous; that couldn't have made things any easier for my Sara. Shaking my head to clear it, I focused on my mother.

"The virus that was in storage was set free."

That statement landed heavily in the room, and Joel and I looked to one another with wide, shocked eyes.

"Um, so…we're sick?" Joel asked.

"No, you're fine," Dad stated, standing up from the chair and looking to my mother. "We'll have to show them in order for them to understand."

She nodded, turning to the cabinet next to Joel. She handed him the same thing to put on as my dad had given me.

"Put this on," she said and then turned to me.

"This virus is like nothing I've ever seen, not in…reality. It's been discussed for decades, and there have been theories on it, but the truth is much worse than the Hollywood version."

Joel snorted as my mother helped him dress due to his encased arm. "What? Aliens have landed?"

"Uh, no." My dad's answer was firm and without the humor Joel usually brought to a room, despite the tenseness that filled it.

"Aw…and here I was hoping for those egg-laying, acidy-spit drooling things Sigourney Weaver so epically battled," he added, and I chuckled, shaking my head.

"Only *you* would wish for acidy-spit," I told him, standing up gingerly on my sore leg when he finally had the scrub pants on.

My father led us out of the room, but it was my mother who was spewing medical facts and statistics.

"The growth rate of this virus is unlike anything I've ever seen. Those at the center of the original source—the stored vials—were sick within…seconds. Probably less than a minute. The explosion caused it to go airborne, and what normally would've killed them… well, didn't. The tissues reanimated." She stopped at the end of the hallway, turning to face us. "The problem wasn't that the virus was set free; it was the fact that several of the people working in the lab panicked and got out."

My eyes narrowed. "Got out…as in…*out,* out?" I jerked a thumb behind me in a useless gesture, but they knew what I meant. "As in off base?"

"Yes," they both said.

"And if my calculations are correct, if what we heard before communications went down is true, then the virus will spread…everywhere. Very, very quickly."

Again, I noted the silence and the lack of people in the hallway, but I merely waved her on.

Mom turned to open the door in front of her, and we entered another hallway, only the lights were dimmer, flickering. At the end of that corridor was a set of double doors. What normally would be push-to-open doors were barricaded with mop and broom handles. What caused the hair to stand up on the back of my neck was the rather large pile of automatic weapons leaning against the wall off to the side.

I reached for the broom handle, and both my mother and father yelled, "No!"

I froze, glancing back at them, but my dad's hand slipped up the wall to a light switch, flicking it up. The windows in the double doors lit up with more flickering lights, but something told me I didn't want to look. Dad jerked his chin toward the window.

"Oh my fucking hell," Joel groaned, taking the left window, his eyes wide and his mouth hanging open in shock.

I stepped to the right-side window, narrowing my eyes down another hallway. I could see the damage the storm had caused, not to mention the explosion. But it was the movement that truly caught my attention. I could see people, but they didn't look real…or alive. With distorted faces, missing limbs, and destroyed clothing, they all looked like something out of a movie.

"Oh, shit..." I breathed, my forehead thumping softly to the glass in front of me as memories flooded me. "We were sent in, Joel. Remember? We were sent to contain this section. We were told to shoot to kill, that it was a breach in security."

He huffed and nodded, turning to look my way. "We were ordered to kill, to contain...but these were..."

"Innocents."

"Well, they aren't human anymore," my mother stated firmly behind us, reaching between us to bang on the door. "They're killing machines."

What happened next made me sick. The ten or twelve...things on the other side of the door suddenly shifted, almost as one—like a flock of birds. They shuffled, walked, dragged themselves toward us, and I took a tentative step backward. The stench that met my nose was putrid and foul. It was death and rot and decomposition. But it was fucking moving.

They hit the door, teeth snapping, with grunts and growls. They smeared a black slime—which I realized was dead blood, old blood—against the window. They pushed and shoved each other, practically ripping limbs off rotting bodies, in order to get to the doors...to us.

"Jesus Fucking Christ," Joel breathed, stepping back, finally rounding on my parents. "Night of the living fucking dead? Are you fucking kidding me?"

I placed a hand on his chest but swallowed back bile and nausea as I recognized names on military uniforms, men I'd known, men who'd once had my back. When I felt I could speak, I asked, "What are they?"

"People. Or they were," my dad replied, wearing a disgusted expression as the banging and clawing at the door continued uninterrupted behind me. "They're not now. The brain...reanimates, but only the brain stem. There's no more thought, no more emotion, no more...*person* inside. They only want one thing."

"What's that?" Joel whispered.

"To feed. On flesh." My mother's voice was barely heard over my labored breathing.

It was all too much. With my head pounding and the snarls behind me, my temper unraveled.

"Tell me I'm fucking dreaming!" I snapped, pointing behind me. "Someone tell me this shit isn't real, because…" I pointed to my mother, but she shook her head. "I gotta get outta here. I gotta get home."

I started to walk by them, but my father stopped me, gripping my T-shirt and pulling me into the closest room. He shoved me to the window, tapping it harshly.

"There's no leaving, Jackson!" he snapped, tapping the window again. "We're trapped. We shut this section down in order to keep you two safe, and in doing so, we've cornered ourselves. We've been lucky so far because there's a store of MREs on this level, but those won't last forever."

Looking out the window, my mouth gaped at the sight of an entire base filled with those mindless, foul…things. They were shuffling by the fence, wandering in and around the parking lot, and bumping into one another. I saw wrecked cars, crumpled fences, and dead bodies everywhere. Movement at the gate caught my eye, and I locked on to what looked to be one of the K-9s wandering around. It was a Rottweiler, a fairly large one, but it had missed a meal or two. It jumped back, ears flattened to its head as one of those things moved toward it. Several shifted at once, again like a flock of birds. They moved quicker than I was expecting, and the dog didn't stand a chance. I swore I could hear the howl from that third-floor window as they landed on it like a football tackle for a fumbled ball. Fur, limbs, and what I imagined to be intestines were fought over. When one of those beasts looked up, he was covered in blood.

Gagging, I dropped to a knee, crying out when the wound on my leg protested and felt like it was ripped.

"We can't leave," my dad whispered, kneeling beside me and helping me to a sitting position.

When I leaned back against the wall, I gazed up at him. "We can't stay here, either."

I blinked when the power came on in the room. My mother stepped to one of the tables, picking up a stack of papers.

"Jack, Joel," she called, and we both looked over at her, Joel barely dragging his gaze away from the window. "This virus has been loose for almost a full month. In that time, reports of an incurable flu have been reported…all over the world."

"How's that possible?" I asked.

"Think of where you are," she urged, pointing toward the window. "This is one of the biggest vacation capitals on the planet. People from everywhere come here—beaches, Disney World, whatever. It's here. A few lab techs got through, not to mention however many they infected along the way. You were sent to contain, but really, you were sent to destroy them. That didn't happen. They infected your company before you two were even removed from the rubble of the explosion—which, by the way, was a result of a truck slamming into the building due to the tornado. Those techs were bitten or scratched, something that starts a chain of events that is unstoppable. Flu-like symptoms—fever, chills, nausea. That's the slow side. It takes hardly any time killing, only to reanimate within minutes of the heart stopping."

My dad stood up. "However, if they bite you? Feed on you? You also…change. There's something in their bite…a venom or bacteria that starts the process. Minutes…seconds, boys. That's all it takes. Do the math, factor in time, distance, and speed. Add in the numbers of human beings in Florida alone."

"Can they be fucking killed?" I asked, my lip twitching in hatred and disgust.

"Oh yeah," Dad stated, walking back to the double doors.

Joel helped me to my feet, and we followed in silence. My father unsheathed a military length knife, barely flinching at the gnashing of teeth and surly growls on the other side of the glass. With a swift, precise aim, Dad slipped the knife blade between the doors right between the eyes of the closest of those nasty bastards. It ceased all movement instantly, dropping to the floor, which only allowed more to shift closer to the doors.

"That's the motor functions—walking, blinking, breathing, reaching," Mom explained, tapping the screen and then a file folder in front of her.

Dad raised his knife again and the struggling, snapping teeth, and shaking all came to a standstill when the blade went through the forehead and into the brain of a guy in a white lab coat.

"The brain. That's the key," I stated, looking at them as they nodded. "A sudden injury to the brain or sever the brain stem…That's how you do it."

They nodded again.

"How fast will this travel?"

Dad sighed but answered, "It's already everywhere, son. The last news report was that even the president had caught it and that Vice President Hawkins took over. This base, most of the surrounding town is destroyed. Jack…boys, listen to me. They've already shut down air travel. Some places are under martial law. There are power outages everywhere, not to mention phones—both landlines and cell—aren't functioning. If your mother's math is correct, then most of the world will be destroyed within…a…a week or two."

"There's no more military," Mom added. "Not here, anyway."

I closed my eyes, and Sara came into my head in such a crystal-clear picture that I almost smiled. My son was next, and my only thought was the promise I'd made…to stay safe, to come home. My temper skyrocketed, making my head pound and my hands squeeze into tight fists. My family—my wife and son—would *not* meet this fucking fate. And now I knew why I'd sent her to the cabin. I'd overheard the words virus, breach, and global terror. I rounded on my parents.

"So…what?" I sneered, tapping the window behind me. "We're just gonna lie the fuck down and let these…these…things win?" My nostrils flared, but I didn't wait for an answer. "Oh, hell no! We're getting the hell out of here. I'm not letting this shit stop me from getting home, from getting to Sara, Freddie, and Derek! Our home, Dad! Your grandchild, your nephew—you know, the one you raised like a son? Imagine Sandy…*like this!*"

My mother's tears streamed down her face, but she shook her head.

"I *promised* Sara," I told them, placing a hand on my chest. "I swore to her that I would find her…that something screwy was going down. I must've seen or heard enough that sent me calling her to tell her to get away from people. I won't let her down. I won't let some freaks of nature stop me from getting to my family."

"Think about what you're saying, Jack," Joel stated, gripping my shoulder. "We can't just…catch a flight home. We're clear across the motherfucking country."

"And?" I asked, looking at him like he was crazy. "That's different than what we do…how? Joel, we dodged terrorists overseas, and they could fucking *think!*" I snapped, tapping the middle of my forehead.

Joel grinned, shrugging a large shoulder. "True that."

"You can't leave in the condition you're in," my dad stated with a finality, pointing between us. "First, you need to be healed—well... you need to be strong and healthy. Second, the wound will draw them to you like flies to shit." He sighed, shaking his head. "Just from observation, I can see that blood, heartbeats draw them in. At night, they're much more active, almost animalistic. Their sight and hearing are enhanced, and they don't tire. Loud noises get their attention. When they set their sights on a...food source, as you saw, then they can move a bit faster. However, the rain makes all that worse; it magnifies their senses."

Nodding, I glared down at the floor, at my traitorous leg that would hold me back. "We're going home. I promised her, Dad." I whispered the last sentence but met his gaze. "I've never broken a promise to her...or Freddie. I don't intend to start now, even if the world is ending."

"Not until you heal," he argued.

I let out a breath, gripping my hair. "Are there any other survivors on this base? Have you seen anyone?"

"Not in this section," my mother answered.

Turning to Joel, I said, "We've got an entire military base at our disposal. That means rations, fuel, weapons, ammo, supplies." I raised an eyebrow at him.

"Okay, so what'choo thinkin'?" he asked, folding his arms across his chest as best he could with that cast.

"I'm thinking...we raid the fuck out of this place before we hit the road. We'll take our time, clear section by section in order to get what we need." I turned to my parents. "We stock up, plan, ration, and I can get us out of here," I vowed.

"Nah, bro, *we* can," Joel added, gripping my shoulder. "But they're right. We need to be ready to hit the ground runnin'. Which means... no casts and no open wounds," he said, pointing to my leg, which had spots of blood on the scrub pants.

"You ripped your stitches open," my mom sighed. "I'll clean you up."

"Wait," I begged, looking to my dad. "Are you with me on this? I gotta know."

Dad smiled sadly and nodded, placing a hand on my shoulder. "C'mon, let's clean you up, and we'll start planning. I'll tell you what I've scoped out already."

"Hey, Jack...You know, driving across the country is one thing, but if everywhere looks like this, then it'll take us forty forevers to get back home," Joel advised, tapping the window overlooking the base.

Joel wouldn't say what he was really thinking, that home, Sandy, Sara, Freddie, all of them could be gone by the time we got there. But I knew my girl. She'd have done as I'd asked, even if the Devil himself had tried to stop her, and I also knew who and what surrounded her: Derek, who was a deadly hunter and born to live off the land; and her father, a firefighter who'd rather die than let anything happen to his family. Her dad had taught her how to handle weapons, how to hunt, and my Sara would lose her mind if something tried to touch Freddie. That thought made me nod his way.

"We're going home," I vowed, but I couldn't think beyond that. I couldn't allow the "what ifs" to get to me, because the mere idea of losing my wife, my son...it was too much.

"Okay," Joel agreed, leading us back out into the hallway. "Then tomorrow, we'll start clearing out this floor and then the rest of the building. We'll work our way down and out into other buildings. We'll make a list of what we need, along with an inventory of what we have...or can see out the damn windows. When we leave this place? I wanna be armed to the teeth, Chambers."

Grinning because I knew him so well, I simply nodded. "Exactly."

CHAPTER 3

Where: Dexter Air Force Base, Florida

When: 6 weeks after Hurricane Beatrice

JACK

JACK

Dexter Air Force Base, Florida
6 Weeks after Hurricane Beatrice

The shuffles, growls, and snapping of teeth on the other side of the doorway made me sigh wearily. Glancing back at Joel, I nodded, then kicked open the door to the stairwell. The stench of rotting flesh hit my nose, but I was slowly growing used to it, which was slightly disturbing, considering I'd only been clearing out one section at a time of the medical facility my parents had locked us in for two weeks.

I was tired of the MREs they'd hoarded. I was tired of headaches from the hit on my head and tired of the pain in my leg, though the latter was getting better. And I was damn sure tired of being holed up like rats in a cage.

Joel and I had slowly cleared the med unit and labs, all but the top floor and roof. It was the roof we needed most. We needed to get up top and survey our surroundings. There were commissaries and hangars, not to mention housing units, we needed to raid for supplies. We also needed to obtain transportation, fuel, and a way to get the fuck off this base.

Using the Sigs my parents had salvaged, Joel and I took out six rather nasty fuckers on the way up the last set of stairs. They were once soldiers, lab techs, and maybe even a civilian or two. It was hard to tell, when they were as torn up and decomposed as they were, but I'd been trying my damnedest to stop seeing them as people. The first time Joel and I had cleared a section—the same section my parents had shown us that first day—we'd both been pissed off, angry, and disgusted by the end of it all.

Reaching the roof door, I looked back at Joel. "Ready?"

He snorted and fidgeted with his temp cast—something I knew he was about five seconds from chucking away, even though my mother threatened him with every grumble. "We have to get up there, whether I'm ready or not. So just...go."

I threw open the door, catching one of the infected by surprise, though it recovered quickly, lunging our way. Joel's gun popped off two rounds, and it fell to the tar rooftop. There were two more up there, and we disposed of them quickly before I made my way to the southern side of the roof.

Reaching into my backpack, I pulled out binoculars and swept our surroundings. Dexter AFB was a fucking mess. Located along the beach, the whole base was long and spread out almost in a grid-like formation. The damage from Beatrice and the damn virus was everywhere. Slow, shuffling swarms of the infected roamed free in the streets, in and out of buildings, and up and down the beach.

There were no planes or choppers. Anything that could have flown prior to the hurricane would've been evacuated to another, safer base. However, my eyes locked on to a parking lot just outside a hangar.

"Bingo," I sang, handing the binoculars to Joel. "Hangar fourteen," I told him. "Hummers, trucks, tanks."

"Tank would be helpful."

"No shit." I huffed a laugh. "But it wouldn't last us long. We need those fucking Hummers. They'll be easier to drive, to fuel up, and they'll handle any kind of terrain."

"Mmm, true," he agreed, scanning the area again, only to hand the binoculars back. "I'm ready to get the hell out of here, but are you sure about...?"

"Don't ask me that again," I snapped, shoving the binoculars into the bag and shouldering it. "Yes, I'm fucking sure. I'm sure I promised Sara and Freddie I'd come home. Yes, I'm sure I'd walk through hell to get to them. And yeah, I'm pretty fucking sure hell ain't got nothin' on what's out there."

Joel studied me but nodded. "You'd better fucking hope Derek is with them."

"He swore he'd watch over them." My brow furrowed, and I shook my head slowly as I glanced down at the ground to watch a few…things—fuck, they were zombies, like out of an idiotic movie, but saying the word sounded ridiculous—wander slowly around the front door of our building. "Though, when I asked him, I was more worried about car trouble or Sara working too late at Shelly's while I was gone, or…or…Freddie getting hurt at the playground. Not…*this shit.*"

"You know, your cousin is kinda badass, so…" Joel's voice trailed off, and he took a deep breath as he ripped open his cast, scratched like hell, only to strap it back on. "I'll be glad when I can take this thing off permanently. How's your leg?"

"Better," I said, yanking up my scrub pants. The stitches were out, and the muscle was slowly strengthening, though I didn't give it much choice. There was shit that needed to be done.

"Rich and Dottie are stalling us," he stated wisely, nodding when I did. "They keep drawing my blood. Yours too, I noticed."

I snorted but showed him the gauze and tape from my mother's last draw. "While the generators are still working, she wants to find a cure."

"Oh Lord…" Joel groaned, shaking his head, but he grinned. "Only your mom, man."

"My dad says there's not one, but he's been studying the file the science bastards had on the virus," I explained. "She has maybe ten more days to two weeks before I think we're safe to pull out of here. With your arm and my leg, we're a liability, not to mention I want to be fully stocked when we go."

"You realize that once we leave here, once supplies run out on the road, we'll be fucked." He pointed north. "Look that way. Look at the beach hotels and the stores and shit. Jack, this virus is everywhere. And all that's on the TV and radio are warnings. Martial law, emergency evacuations, and some bitch on the news on repeat. It's everywhere. You know what that means? It means this virus has spread to every nook and cranny. It means there are survivors willing to kill anything that moves. It means those whackos who planned for the zombie apocalypse were right and they're living the *country-boy-can-survive* dream. This will be dangerous and stupid, and we'll run into more trouble along the way."

"We can't stay here," I argued. "You know that much too. There isn't enough food, and eventually we'll either run out of ammo or those bastards at the front door will smell us. Hell, we may only have a few days left on the generators."

Joel took a deep breath and let it out. "No, dude, I get that. And you're right. If anything, heading home is the better plan, simply because the mountains of Oregon will be easier to hunker down in."

I nodded, rubbing my face. I wanted a shower and a shave, not giving a shit that the water was cold. I was tired and my head was achy, not to mention I was covered in foul-smelling blood from where I'd had to get way too up close and personal with a guy who popped out of a fucking supply closet. Luckily I'd had a knife in my hand. His head went one way while his twisted hands had stayed gripping my shirt until he finally fell to the floor.

"Okay," Joel finally said in acquiescence. He nodded one time when I looked his way. Pointing toward the hangars, he said, "I think two Hummers. We'll snag those first, along with however many cans of gas we can salvage. Once we're mobile, we can start tracking down food, supplies, more medical shit, and…fucking hell, *clothes*. These scrubs aren't cuttin' it."

"Yeah, definitely." I turned to start back toward the roof door. "We'll head out first thing in the morning. Once the sun's up. We'll bring Dad with us in order to load up quicker."

Joel snorted. "Guess we're officially retired from the United States Army, huh?"

Grinning, I shot him a glance over my shoulder. "Not exactly how I planned it," I mumbled, opening the roof door. "This was supposed to be my last leg, you know? Sara was all excited…" My voice trailed off at the mention of her name, and I broke out into a cold sweat. "Jesus, Joel. What do I do if she's…"

Joel's heavy hand landed on my shoulder, turning me to face him. His face was fierce where it usually carried a hint of humor. "Don't. You want to get home. We'll get there, but if you panic now, then it'll be all for nothin'. You have to treat this like you did when we were overseas, man. Each step, each inch we move forward, will be to get back to her. And back then, you'd just found her. Remember?"

Smiling at the memory, I nodded. "Best fight I've ever gotten into," I said with a laugh.

"Oh, but *think*, Jacky!" He beamed dramatically, batting his eyes. "Maybe Matthews is one of those walking nightmares, and even better, maybe Shortcake shot his ass! Oh, to have YouTube back again."

My head fell back with my laugh as we took the stairs to our floor. I couldn't help it. I wasn't sure there was a soul in Sandy who actually liked Brody Matthews, except for Brody himself. Maybe some of the women he still messed with, but not any of my family or friends and for sure not me. Sara's dad, Hank, had stayed friends with Brody's dad, Leo, after the Sandy Fire Department had pulled him out of a car accident years ago. The wreck had taken Leo's wife and the use of his legs. The old man was pretty decent, but his son had walked a fine line with me for a very, very long time.

We made it back downstairs without running into any more infected. We briefed my parents on what the plan was, and I made my way into the staff lounge to shower and change clothes. As night started to settle around us, my heart started to hurt. When I was moving, planning, clearing out those monsters, I was fine, but it was when I was alone or quiet that I thought of my Sara, my son.

Joel's joke about Matthews was funny, but I honestly owed that cheating bastard my life. It was how I'd met Sara. I couldn't help but smile as I stepped under the weak spray of the shower.

Sandy, Oregon
10 Years Prior

"C'mon, Jack," Derek said as he parked the car at one of the few bars in my small-ass hometown. "We'll grab a beer before we head back to the house. Text Joel to meet us here."

"Yeah, okay," I agreed, just happy to see my cousin, who had come to live with us when I was a kid.

He was more like my older brother, having stayed with us through most of his teen years…and mine. He'd then gone off to college right before I'd started my junior year. He'd hated it, but he'd tried, if only for my parents. He'd come home just after I'd joined the Army.

He seemed overly happy, enthusiastic, about being at the bar, but when he looked at me, I could see the truth. It was the same thing with the rest of my family. What no one would say while they looked at me with a frightened look in their eyes was that they were scared shitless about my new orders.

Afghanistan.

Joel and I shipped out in a week for a tour overseas. We'd been given leave to get our families and lives in order. We'd met in basic and had been friends ever since we realized we were from the same area of Oregon. He was from Gresham, not far from my tiny town of Sandy. He wasn't all that close with his family, so I'd brought him home with me. We'd driven over from Fort Warner. My parents and Derek had welcomed him with open arms. As far as they were concerned, he was simply a new member of the family.

The jukebox was pumping some slow, sappy country song when we stepped inside the bar. Derek waved to the old woman pouring beers, and we settled into a booth along the side wall. We weren't the only ones in there. There were a few guys watching a baseball game on the TV over the bar. Three women chattered in the booth opposite us, and two guys about our age had the table in the center.

Just as I was expecting Mrs. Burke to come to us, a young girl walked in from the back room. She didn't look old enough to drink, much less serve alcohol. She was a petite thing, her reddish-brown hair swept up into a long ponytail that swished back and forth as she checked on all the tables before making her way to us. A smirk curled up the corner of her mouth when she saw my cousin.

"Derek, the usual?"

"You know it, Sara," he drawled, giving her a wink.

It was then that I recognized her. "Sara? Sara Stokes? The fire captain's daughter?"

She laughed, and it was a soft, sexy sound. "That's me, Jackson Chambers."

I couldn't stop my eyes from truly taking her in. The last time I'd seen her, I'd been a senior at Sandy High. She'd been a couple of years behind me. She'd been new, and the poor thing had been the center of gossip when she'd come to live with Hank. If I remembered correctly, her mother had been in a fatal car accident. She'd been thinner, not quite skinny, but she'd filled out…just fine. I remembered seeing her in the library occasionally, hiding from the whispers.

Jeans hugged her hips, and the Shelly's Bar T-shirt she was wearing was tied in a knot at her hip.

"You know each other?" Derek asked with a laugh.

"No." Sara chuckled. "Jack was two years ahead of me at SHS." She turned back to me with a soft smile. "What can I get you?"

"Um…whatever's on tap, please."

"Got it," she said, walking away, and my eyes drank in a sweet ass with jeans hugging it beautifully.

Derek's laugh was practically shaking the damn table. "Careful with that one; Mr. Stokes is *mighty* protective of his little girl." He smacked my shoulder before sliding out of the booth. "I'm gonna hit the head and then go outside to call Laurie back. She's pissed I didn't come over."

"'Kay," I answered, my gaze locked on Sara. When she set the beer down in front of me, I thanked her. "So…what are you doing?" I asked, rolling my eyes at the stupidity of the question. "Besides…" I waved a hand around the bar.

She laughed again. "College. In Gresham." She nodded and smiled. "Mrs. Burke is nice enough to work with my class schedule, and when it's slow, she lets me study in this very booth." She tapped the tabletop. "She's also kind enough to overlook the fact that I won't be twenty-one until September, but I help her with her bookkeeping, so she ignores my age."

There was something bold and confident about her now. Her eyes were a very pretty dark blue in the low lights of the room. I could tell she had minimal makeup on, yet her skin and pink cheeks were beautiful, perfect. Suddenly I wanted to know everything about her, but one question popped out of my mouth without thinking.

"You know who I am?" I asked, internally punching myself in the face for sounding like I'd never talked to a girl in my fucking life.

She hummed and nodded. "Ah, yes. You were hard to miss in school—football star, track star, not to mention the crush of every girl I knew."

I groaned, rolling my eyes and waving that shit away. The sports, I understood. The crushes, not so much.

She smiled again but patted my shoulder. "You should know… They moved on. Well, they tried to, anyway," she sighed dramatically, and her teasing was adorable.

"Good," I grunted, smiling at her laughter. "I remember you." I nodded, taking a sip of my beer. When she looked shocked, I said, "I had a girlfriend, Sara. I wasn't blind."

She smirked. "How is Kim?"

"Oh, good, I guess. Last I heard, she was seeing someone at college. Um, Oregon State." I shrugged a shoulder. "We broke up when I joined the Army."

"I heard about that. Your cousin, he's very proud."

Grinning, I nodded.

"He's also worried. You're shipping out?"

I nodded again. "Yeah, a week."

One of the boys behind her called her name, and she nodded their way, but a dark look changed her features entirely.

"Well, it was nice seeing you again, Jack. I'll come back to refill that in a few." She started to step away, but she stopped, giving me an appraising look that was all kinds of sexy. "And…be safe over there, okay?"

She got a little busier when a few more people stepped in, though I caught her gaze once or twice. Derek came back but ended up in a text-fight with his latest girlfriend. Laurie was a pain in the ass, but their on-again, off-again relationship was their business and made me crazy just hearing about it.

Joel texted me back when he was leaving his parents' place, saying he'd meet us at the bar. Derek continued to grumble about Laurie, but my gaze was on the girl working the room with a smile and grace she hadn't had when we were in school.

She stopped by to trade full mugs for our empties but was too busy to chat, though I was beginning to think the boys at the table were doing that shit on purpose. They'd stop her, ask her things I couldn't hear, and she'd merely shake her head, wearing a hard expression.

The place cleared out a little—the women in the other booth had gone, along with the men at the bar—leaving Derek, the guys at the table, and me.

"Crazy bitch," Derek muttered as he glared at his phone.

I snorted. "Just go. Joel should be here by closing. He's got my truck, so I'll ride home with him."

"You sure?"

"Yeah, yeah." I waved him on but looked up when someone new walked into the bar.

The bastard was huge—probably six foot five or six—and he looked like he'd already had a few drinks. He was greeted by the boys at the table.

"Brody!"

If Sara's face was hardened with the boys, then it was pure hellfire when she caught sight of this Brody. Her eyes narrowed, her hands shook, and her mouth thinned into a tight line. She dodged his reach for her, rolling her eyes as she stepped back to our table.

"Another round?" she asked, and gone was the smiling girl. I desperately wanted her back.

"Um, Sara?" Derek started, his gaze glancing from the table to her. "You all right, darlin'?"

She sighed, forcing herself to relax and then smile. "I'm…fine. I'm ready for closing time. I've got a test this week and—"

"Yo, Sara. You gonna get me a beer, or what?"

I huffed a humorless laugh, glancing around her to see the guy they'd called Brody glaring my way. "Buddy, she'll get to you when she's damn well ready."

Sara smiled my way, setting a hand on my shoulder. "It's fine, Jack. Really." She turned to face the table. "The answer to that question would be no, Brody. You're not old enough, though it appears that someone gave you some anyway. Perhaps you should go back to them. I'm sure I know who it was." The last part was mumbled, but we all heard her.

Brody actually had the nerve to look ashamed, and it didn't take me long to put the puzzle together.

"Boyfriend?" I asked softly, and her sad eyes locked to mine.

"Ex."

"He cheated."

She nodded, her nose wrinkling. "Among other things. We've been broken up for a while now…ever since I found out."

My lip curled in hatred, not because Brody was a fucking loser but because she looked so damn betrayed. I glanced over to Derek, who was wearing a calm yet focused expression on his face as Brody stood up from his chair, babbling about apologies and promises and shit Sara wasn't paying a bit of attention to.

It was Sara's flinch that had me reaching out to touch her. Tilting her face gently with my fingers underneath her chin, I asked, "Did he hurt you?"

She shook her head. "Not the way you're thinking. I just…The thought of him touching me…"

Smiling her way, I nodded. "Understood. Then you might want to move to your right in about three seconds." I raised an eyebrow at her, standing the exact moment she stepped to the side, which brought me face to face with the highly inebriated ex-boyfriend. I felt more than saw Derek stand up at the same time. And suddenly, everyone in the bar was on their feet.

I specifically placed myself between Brody and Sara, smiling ruefully up at him. I didn't give a fuck how big he was.

"Didn't you hear me, Sara?" he slurred, trying to step around me, but I was way more aware than he was. "I said, what you saw was bullshit. It wasn't what you thought. Can't we talk? Just talk."

"Go home, Brody," Sara said wearily as she stepped up beside me. "There's nothing to talk about." Turning to me, she placed a hand on my shoulder. "Sit, Jack. You too, Derek. I'll bring another round."

"Thanks," I said, not taking my eyes off her, but I knew he'd reach for her the second she walked by, and he did.

"Don't touch me, Brody. I'm serious," she sneered, rounding on him.

"I just want to talk about this, Sara."

"There's nothing to talk about. Get out."

When he didn't let go, I moved before Derek could, and my hand landed in the middle of Brody's chest, giving him an urging push.

"Let her go," I warned him.

"You wanna quit eye-fucking my girl?" he asked, turning my way, but he still hadn't let go of her arm. "This is between us. Mind your business."

"You realize who her dad is, right?" Derek drawled, standing next to me. "I mean, you can't be that stupid…or drunk. Let her go."

That caught the attention of his friends, and one or two shifted nervously on their feet. Brody's hand slowly released Sara's arm, and Derek urged her to go behind the bar.

"Go home, sleep this shit off, and you'll realize just how badly you fucked up," I told him with a smile, glancing her way, only to meet his gaze with a laugh. "'Cause you *really* fucked up."

I knew he would swing. It was in his posture, in the emotions written all over his face, and in the temper he had no control over. When he did, I ducked, pushing him a little.

"This wouldn't be a fair fight, buddy," I told him, shaking my head. "You're way too drunk…"

"And he's way too trained," Derek tacked on with a laugh, only to groan when the bastard came my way again. "Oh, Jackson…he *is* that stupid."

Brody swung at me again, a sloppy roundhouse punch that wouldn't have done much damage, but I avoided it, finally sweeping my leg beneath his, causing him to fall to his ass. When he scrambled up, he launched everything he had my way. It was over before it truly began. I punched his stomach, just to bring him up short, and then put his ass back on the floor, only this time I dropped a knee to his chest.

"You want a fight? I can give you one," I threatened low in his face. "But I fucking promise you, your ass will still end up on this floor. Only bloody and broken. Get out, and leave her alone. Respect that, or her father will find out exactly what you did here. I'm sure Mrs. Burke is about five seconds from picking up the phone."

"Ah, ah, ah, boys," Derek warned in a sing-song manner. "Not your rodeo. Keep it fair."

When I glanced up to see Derek holding back Brody's friends, Brody took advantage, swinging one more time. He caught me in the mouth, cutting my lip a little.

I was just about to beat the ever-loving piss out of him when a baseball bat appeared. I followed it up to see Sara holding it.

"Brody Matthews, if you don't get up and out of here, not only will I use this, but I'll call my dad, who happens to be having dinner with the police chief and his wife tonight."

Large hands gripped my shoulders, yanking me up off the guy. Turning, I saw Joel standing there.

"You'd have killed him, bro," he warned, shaking his head.

Nodding, I sat down hard in the booth, swiping at my lip and frowning at the blood on my hand. I heard Derek and Joel helping the boys out of the bar, saying something about paying their tab, but my vision was cut off by Sara standing in front of me.

"Be still," she ordered softly, holding a towel with ice in it to my lip. "I don't think you need stitches, but…"

I shook my head, my gaze raking up her body to meet her dark eyes.

"You didn't have to do that, you know," she chided, shaking her head. "He would've gotten tired of me ignoring him and left."

"You didn't want him touching you. He was too drunk to see reason."

She smiled, checking my lip and placing the ice back on. "You always rescue waitresses in bars?"

I laughed, shaking my head. "Only ones I want to get to know better."

"Ah, gotcha. So how'd this plan of yours work out?"

"I don't know. You tell me. Can I see you again before I leave?" I asked her, ignoring Joel and Derek coming back in the door.

She smiled and nodded. "Yeah, I'd like that."

"Damn, you are so pretty," I said, noting that we were eye to eye as she stood between my legs. "And short."

"Hey!" She laughed, smacking playfully at me.

"Hey, Sara," Mrs. Burke called, a smile on her face. "Let's blow this Popsicle stand."

"Closing time," Sara told me, her eyes a touch sad.

"I'll wait. You know, walk you to your car."

"'Kay."

Derek and Joel waited out in the parking lot as I walked the women out the bar. Sara pointed to her car, and I followed her to it.

Shaking my head, I sighed. I had thought joining the Army, getting out of this town, would help me find myself. Turned out, it wasn't *me* I was looking for, and she'd been here all along.

"What's wrong?" she asked.

I laughed a little. "I'm glad I met you, but…"

Sara frowned. "But now you're leaving."

"*Into each life some rain must fall*," I said, quoting the poem my dad loved so much and shrugging a shoulder. "I'll be back. But I'd still like to see you before I go."

Sara reached into her pocket and placed a folded piece of paper in my hand. "It's my e-mail and phone…my address. Call me." She had to stand up on her toes to kiss my cheek, and I chuckled.

"Sure thing, Shortcake."

"Shut up!" She laughed, but I could tell she liked the teasing when her cheeks tinged pink. "And…thank you, Jack."

Nodding, I backed away from her car so she could pull out.

When I joined Derek and Joel, both were wearing shit-eating grins.

"Well, Jacky?" Joel asked me. "Was the fight worth it?"

Holding up her note, I laughed. "Hell, yes."

Dexter Air Force Base, Florida

I stepped out of the shower—and out of that memory—missing Sara more than I could probably articulate. However, if anything made me more determined to get back to her, it was that memory alone.

Smiling to myself, I remembered that week in Sandy. I'd hung out with my parents and Derek, usually along with Joel, but it was the few times I got to see Sara that changed everything. We'd had so much in common, and my attraction to her had grown by leaps and bounds. Our last night together, I'd never wanted to kiss a girl so badly in my damn life. And I did, but with that amazing, deep kiss had come a sense of guilt.

I'd been leaving, heading into a war zone, and despite my confidence, there was the chance I wouldn't come home. And it had been Sara to set everything about us into motion. As we'd swayed to music around closing time at Shelly's Bar, I'd explained how I couldn't promise her anything, but I wanted to, that it wasn't fair to keep her waiting.

Her stunning face had lit up with a soft but sad smile as she'd cupped my jaw. She'd merely said, "Why don't you let me worry about what's fair to me? Hmm? You concentrate on staying safe over there, and I'll be here when you get back."

I'd kissed her stupid, kissed her until I had to go, until she had to close up. Leaving her that first time was the hardest thing I'd ever done. I'd more than wanted to stay, to learn everything about her, and to make love to her in every way imaginable, but those long seven and a half months had made us stronger, closer, better. We'd learned everything about each other through the written word, sporadic phone calls, and amazing care packages.

I'd also learned that she'd been one of the many crushing girls she'd teased me about.

Snorting into a chuckle as I pulled on fresh clothes, I shook my head. God, I loved her. I'd loved her before I'd even left Sandy for Afghanistan, I was pretty damn sure. I'd busted my ass those seven months to get back to her. I'd stayed safe, careful, calling her when I could. At that very moment, I'd have killed to hear her voice. That, more than anything, made my decision to drive across this now fucked-up country to get to her. I was scared about what was out there, but I was absolutely fucking terrified about what could happen to her or Freddie…or both. Failure to make it to Clear Lake was *not* a fucking option.

7 Weeks after Hurricane Beatrice

"Aw, fuck! Go, go, go!" I yelled, hauling ass from the Hummer to the last building—housing—we needed to check. We'd started early that morning, clearing out the commissary, weapons storage, and several hangars of all the camping equipment and supplies we could load up into two very large military-style Hummers. Luckily, there were only four floors in this last building.

Joel, Dad, and I burst through the front doors of the building, Joel slamming them behind us to shut out the swarm that had seen us pull up. Dad and I immediately took out four more just inside the lobby.

"Fuck me!" Joel panted, leaning against the door as the bastards pounded on the other side. "You know what they remind me of?" he grumbled as Dad and I pushed and shoved a huge sofa to barricade the doors. "Tweakers. You know, those people they filmed in order to sway you from drugs back in high school. They'd be all twitchy and shit, picking at their face. They'd lost all sense of reason, they looked like hell, and their teeth were rotting out of their damn head. Only instead of craving crack or meth or whatever, these assholes are craving…*brains*." He leaned on the last word like a fucking B-rated movie.

I locked gazes with my dad, who looked like he wanted to laugh, but I could tell we were both thinking the same thing. When I grinned, my dad laughed softly.

"Then you should be immune, Joel. Go ahead and step outside. Let's test that theory," I taunted him, laughing harder when he simply held up both middle fingers at me before pushing off the door.

We started down the first hallway, my dad still laughing at us. Supplies were stacked in the lobby as we cleared apartment after apartment. We'd decided we would leave Dexter AFB in a week, so we'd been stockpiling everything we could think of. My mother continued to work on a cure that didn't seem possible.

"Zeak," Joel suddenly boomed, wearing a shit-eating grin. "Zombie-tweakers. Zeak. Z-E-A-K. Get it? Like that movie, only spelled different. That's what we should call 'em."

"Fantastic. They have a name," I muttered wryly, rolling my eyes as I motioned for them to start checking each apartment.

The first few floors scored us some bottled water and canned goods, not to mention about six…zeaks that converged on us.

It was the last floor that we had the most trouble. Several children had been turned and had somehow wandered up to the top floor. Killing them was sickening yet necessary. They were faster, if not more feral than their adult counterparts.

When I got to the last apartment, I pressed an ear to the door. Growls, footsteps, and shuffling met my ear, but it sounded different. Pulling back, I held up a finger, and Dad and Joel braced for the door to be kicked in.

I kicked hard, sending the door swinging open. What flew at me was not a zeak, though I panicked all the same. Instead of snarls, rotten flesh, and snapping teeth, I was suddenly knocked to my ass by a large black mass of fur and tongue and whimpers.

"Whoa, whoa, whoa," Joel said through his uncontrollable laughter. "Easy there, big guy…Oh, 'scuse me, *ma'am*."

I sagged in relief at the sight of the big dog as my face was licked over and over. She was enormous, really, though a touch thin. And I grabbed her big face in both hands in order to get a good look at her. She was a black-and-tan Rottweiler, a lot like the one I'd seen destroyed that first day. She was wriggling and panting, wagging the nub of her tail so hard, her entire body was in constant movement. She had a collar, and I turned it in my hand. She was military K-9, though I had no clue how she'd gotten up there.

"Well, Sasha," I sighed, sitting up and shaking my head. "Thanks for scaring the fuck outta me."

My dad peered into the apartment that reeked of piss and shit. The poor thing had been trapped inside for who knew how long.

There was torn-up furniture, bedding, and clothes everywhere; even the doors and carpet had been destroyed by claws and teeth. There were the remnants of what looked like a couple of bags of dog food, but it was gone, along with a bunch of stuff from the cabinets—cereal, pasta, coffee creamer.

"Here, Sasha," Joel crooned, holding out a bottle of water, which she drank from greedily.

"Fuck, she'd have starved," I sighed, scratching her ear.

"We'll have to take her with us," Joel stated, and as much as I knew she could be trouble, I couldn't help but feel for her, especially with the memory of the last Rottweiler I'd seen.

"Whatever. She'll have to learn to move with us," I warned him, though it was halfhearted at best. She was the first sight of something living, something truly *alive*, that we'd seen in all our searching, which kind of made her very special.

"All right, boys," my dad said, unable to not scratch Sasha's ears. "We need to load up what we've found here and get back to the med center."

"What about the zeaks at the front door?" Joel asked as we made our way downstairs.

"I'll take them out from the second-floor window. You two, be at the ready."

Sasha followed Joel and my dad, and I entered the second floor, breaking the window facing out over the front door. The noise alone caught their attention, but they couldn't do shit about it.

There were about ten zeaks milling around the Hummer and a handful more wandering aimlessly across the street. Knowing my gunshots would bring them anyway, I took out the ones across the street first, finally taking out the ones below me.

"Clear!" I yelled down to the street, and the front doors burst open.

I watched them for a few seconds, finally bolting down the stairs to help them finish loading up. Sasha seemed to pace around the Hummer, not exactly in the way, but her ears were perked up and her face was fierce. We were just about finished when she crouched low, her teeth bared and a growl rumbling through her. Her gaze was locked on the corner of the building. She stalked low, and we called her back, but it was the swarm that came rumbling around the corner that threw us all into overdrive.

I was just about to abandon the last few loads, but Sasha did something none of us could've prepared for: she lunged at the swarm. Staying low, fast, and just out of reach, she snapped her teeth at the zeaks, causing their attention to focus on her and not us. She ran circles around them, mixing them up, confusing them, but she'd given us the time to finish loading.

"Sasha! Let's go!" I called her, but she was too busy. I jumped into the passenger side, leaving my door open. "Swing around and pick her up," I told Joel once he'd started the truck.

I popped off several rounds, as did my dad, as Joel squealed around the corner. I took two zeaks out that were closest to Sasha, calling her name again.

She gave one last snarling bark, as if to say *fuck you*, before high-tailing it through my door and plopping herself happily on my lap, despite the fact that she was too big.

"Where in the hell did she learn that?" Joel asked with a laugh, patting her side.

"She was swarming them." Dad chuckled, shaking his head and praising her. However, his smile fell quickly. "Boys, it's time. There's nothing left here. We'll head out in two days."

"What about Mom?" I asked.

His nose wrinkled as he sighed wearily. "She's aware. She'll be bringing that research with her, but she's ready."

I let out a breath of relief. I was ready to get the fuck out of Florida and make some sort of progress heading west. Too much time had already passed away from Sara and Freddie, but my mother had been set on her work, at least until we'd stocked up.

Nodding, I looked back at him gratefully. "Two days."

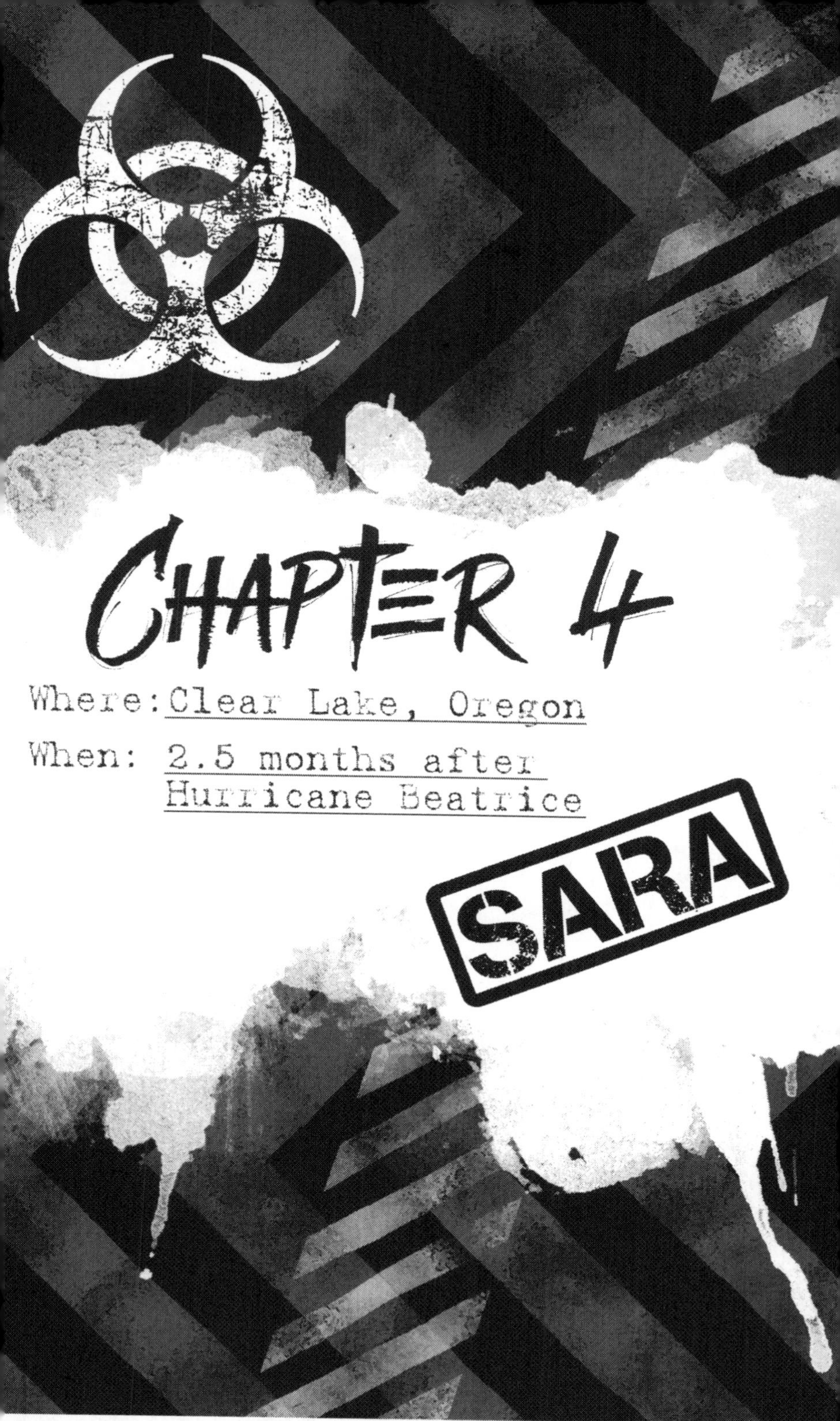

CHAPTER 4

Where: Clear Lake, Oregon

When: 2.5 months after Hurricane Beatrice

SARA

SARA

Clear Lake, Oregon
2.5 Months after Hurricane Beatrice

Crouching low in the forest, I followed Derek's lead. He put a finger to his lips to keep me quiet, but I knew better than to speak. We'd been tracking for days.

The snap of a twig caused both of us to glance up. Derek's grin was relief and amusement all at the same time. We'd been hunting this deer all damn day. However, unlike when I was younger, when my dad and Leo had taught me how to hunt when I'd visit Sandy growing up, hunting now was dangerous. We weren't the only predator in the woods, and new rules applied when we left the campground. There was no staying out past dark, no one went alone, and everyone stayed inside on rainy days.

Today was clear, the weather in our favor, and hopefully we'd be bringing back food that would last us several days.

Derek raised his compound bow, aiming slowly, carefully. The thump of its release was barely audible, but the collapse of the deer was heavy as the arrow hit its mark perfectly.

"C'mon, we need to move quickly," Derek said, grabbing my hand. He whistled lightly, and from across the way, Josh stepped out of his own hiding space. "We need to dress it here, but we need to do it fast, or the scent of blood will bring us trouble."

Josh and Derek worked together to string up the deer, skin it, and finally start wrapping up meat. This had never been my thing—hunting—even though I'd been taught as a kid. I wasn't a fan of killing anything, but life was different now. It was a matter of survival, of being able to feed my son and the rest of us back at camp.

So far, everyone had learned to pitch in. We'd been at Clear Lake for going on three weeks. In that time, there'd been several pack attacks—mainly in the rain or at night—and we'd all worked together just fine. Even Brody, despite his feelings for Derek, had been excellent on setting up a few lookout points on the edge of camp, not to mention providing several days of fish for dinner. He and Leo had taught Freddie and Tina's little girl, Janie, how to fish from shore. As long as they stayed in sight at all times, we were okay with that.

Josh and Derek worked quickly, dividing the load between them as I kept watch around them. It was dangerous releasing the scent of blood into the woods, even more the noise they were making, but we had no choice.

Another snap of a twig caused the hairs to stand up on the back of my neck, and I spun to see what I'd been hoping to avoid: infected. It was a small pack, but that didn't matter because they were blocking our trail back to camp.

"Derek…Josh," I called softly in warning, raising the rifle. "Company." I scanned for a number. "I see six."

"Easy, Sare," Derek soothed, abandoning the deer for his compound bow. He raised, aimed, and took out the closest one, but it sent the others into a frenzy. "Keep your back to a tree. Always, Sara. Got me?"

Nodding, I raised my gun and fired, taking down what looked like it used to be a teenage boy—if I had to guess, probably Josh's age—although I tried not to think of them as people anymore. We cleared the area of all but one, and he was mine to kill. However, his military clothes, dog tags, and dark hair were a little too close to home for me. The hesitation caused the dead man to lunge for me, but I pulled the trigger. I wasn't sure who dropped to the ground quicker, him or me, but I gagged, losing everything I'd eaten that day. Cold sweat broke out across my brow as reality tried so fucking hard to crash down over me.

"Oh, Jesus," Derek whispered, wrapping an arm around me. "Aw, hell, Sara…"

He kissed the top of my head, rocking me as I lost it for just a moment. I was glad Freddie wasn't around to see it.

"Fuck, darlin'. It's not him, it's not him, it's not him." The chant was soothing, and I wondered for a moment if he was saying it for both of us because God, we missed Jack. "I promise. Look at him, Sara."

Steeling myself, I did as he told me, and I saw the infected man for who he truly was. He was older than Jack, certainly not as tall, and he looked nothing like my husband in the face. I tried to overlook the camo, the rotten, decomposed flesh, and the stench of him, but the glint of dog tags caught my eye, showing me a name: *Logan, Andrew.*

Sagging a little, I breathed a heavy sob, taking the bottle of water Derek offered. "For a second…"

"I know. I get it."

I met Derek's gaze, and he smiled sadly, as if he knew what I was about to say. "I need to see Freddie. Like now."

He chuckled. "Then let's get back, yeah?"

"We should hurry back anyway," Josh added. He shifted on his feet as he lifted the bags of wrapped meat. He handed one to Derek to carry. "Looks like they came from camp."

It took about an hour or so before we stepped into the clearing. The sun would set soon, but from what I could tell, everyone was fine.

Carol North and Millie Larson were extremely pleased with the meat we handed them, but it was the little boy on the edge of the lake who I couldn't get to quickly enough. He was a miniature Jack from this distance—in stature, head tilt, and even the way he used his hands. I didn't want to scare him, so I took a seat beside him, reaching over to run my fingers through his hair.

"Hi, Mom," he sang, handing me his fishing pole. He walked to the water, picking up a string that held five fish. "Look!"

"Look at you!" I praised him, holding out my arms. "You're becoming quite the fisherman! Grandpa Hank will be proud!"

He giggled, letting me pull him to my lap. "Ya think?"

"Oh, I know so," I said with a nod and a kiss to his head.

"I still need to learn how to hunt."

This argument was never going to die, especially when everyone in camp was carrying a weapon. Freddie was too much like his father to cower away. I could see it plain as day as I looked at my son.

Sighing heavily, I raked my fingers through his hair again. "I'll make you a deal, Freddie," I told him, handing the pole back.

He took it tentatively but nodded, looking up at me. "What deal?"

"The deal is this…Derek has agreed to teach you, but you'll start small—a hunting rifle, a .22. Not a handgun or shotgun, but a rifle. We think it'll be easier to deal with. *But*…only if you take a few hours every day with Mr. North. You, Janie, and Josh still need school, despite all that's going on. He was a history teacher before he retired, so he's agreed to tutor you guys."

"Aw, *Mom*," he groaned, sounding so much like his dad that tears welled up in my eyes, but I couldn't help but chuckle at the same time.

Kissing his temple, I said, "That's the deal, kiddo. Take it or leave it."

He scowled, gazing down at the ground for a moment, but finally nodded. "Okay, fine. So…when?" he asked excitedly.

Grinning, I ruffled his hair. "Soon. It won't be tonight, but soon. I'll let you know, okay?"

"Okay," he sighed, frowning as he reeled the pole in to check his bait. The worm had definitely seen better days, so he removed it, tossing it into the lake. He set the pole aside, turning to face me. "I wish Dad was here. He'd teach me, not Derek."

Smiling sadly, I nodded. "Me too, baby. And you're probably right."

He studied my face. "It makes you sad to talk about him. Do you think…?"

I kissed his forehead roughly before he could finish that question. "I miss your dad like crazy, Freddie." I swallowed thickly, fighting my panic, my sadness, and my fears. "It makes me sad to talk about him, simply because…he was very far away when things got bad. I don't like to think of him as hurt…or worse. I don't like to think about him worrying about you and me, because you know he'd be losing his mind about us, right?"

Freddie grinned. "Yeah, he'd be like…pulling on his hair and stuff." He mimicked his dad's habit to a T, and even his brow wrinkled like Jack's.

"Exactly. He may not have any hair by now," I said with a laugh, but it died quickly. "I know your dad is strong and smart and brave. I know that your grandparents and Uncle Joel are too. I can only *hope*, Freddie. That's all I've got left. Hope. Faith that your dad is fighting to get to us. When I met him, he was silly and sweet, and he made promises he never should've made, but he kept them. He fought for what was right. He always has. As much as I tease your dad for being stubborn, I know he's a fighter. To think of him any other way…hurts."

I paused for a second, assessing my son, but then I cupped his face. "You're so much like him. You want to help and take care of me, 'cause believe me, I know he told you to watch over me."

Freddie laughed at my raised eyebrow but nodded. "Yeah. He said…he said…to stick close to you, that you were going to be sad while he was gone. He said I was to hug on you a lot so that you'd forget to be sad."

"Okay, well, you're doing an amazing job, buddy," I praised him.

"I want to do more."

"Then give me a hug, pal, 'cause I need it."

Freddie smiled, wrapping his arms around my neck, and I wound mine all the way around his skinny frame. I buried my nose into the space between his shoulder and neck, inhaling deeply. He was sweaty and smelled of dirt and fish, but he was comfort incarnate. He was a living, breathing, adorable reminder of the person we were both missing terribly.

I blew raspberry kisses to his neck before letting him go, and his laugh was light and easy. "C'mon, Freddie, let's get your fish to Millie. Okay? She'll be really happy."

Freddie looked proud as he pulled in his catch for today. I carried his pole, but he toted that string of fish with his head held high.

The venison was being smoked, thanks to Leo's knowledge. Millie was so sweet as she thanked Freddie for the fish. The night fell quickly, but the large fire in the middle of camp kept everyone safe and close, though Derek took the night watch in the tree at the edge of the woods. Discussions of a possible fence were batted around, as were other ideas for keeping us safe. Tina asked about a future garden, but we'd have to come up with some seeds first, and Leo suggested checking out Rocky Point Lodge and its accommodations.

I toyed with Freddie's hair as we all sat around the fire but stiffened when someone took a seat next to me. I let out a long, slow breath before looking over at Brody.

"I know you don't want to hear it, Sara, but we should open up the *in-laws'* cabin. There may be things in there that we need. You're avoiding it, but it's time, you know?"

My eyes narrowed on him at the disdain in his voice at the word in-law. There was a split second where I couldn't decide whether to call him out on it or smack his face to rid it of the pompous smile he wore whenever Jack or his family were mentioned. I didn't do either.

"Fine," I agreed with a single nod. "I'll open it up tomorrow."

"I'll help, Mom," Freddie piped up, eyeing Brody with an interesting expression on his face.

"Ah, like father, like son. Too bad he's..." Brody stopped talking when I shot him a glare, hissing his name.

Tina ruffled Freddie's hair but nudged me from my other side. "Me too. I'll help you."

"Thanks," I whispered, smiling over at her. "We'll do it once the sun is up."

She nodded, patting Janie's leg. "Let's get to the cabin, baby doll," she told her, only to turn to me. "Want me to take Freddie?"

"Yeah." I kissed the top of my son's head. "Buddy, go with Tina and get ready for bed. I'll tuck you in shortly."

Once they walked into my cabin, I rounded on Brody, ignoring the fact that everyone else was still sitting around the fire. "Brody, you will keep your opinions of my husband and his unknown whereabouts to yourself around my son. Am I fucking clear?" I asked him, and when he didn't answer, I leaned closer. "He's seven, you asshole. This shit is hard enough without having him break down about the possibility of losing his dad."

I stood up, fighting not to kick Brody in the face. Just before I turned around, he spoke again.

"I'm not sure it's the kid who's afraid of the breakdown," he said with a derisive chuckle. "Maybe it's you who can't face facts. You're fucking fooling yourself, Sara. That fucker's dead."

The words were like lightning to my heart, shocking and blunt. I could see by Brody's smug face that the mere thought of that made him happy. I shook in order not to punch his face...or shoot him. Both were incredibly appealing, but I wouldn't sink that low. And whether I liked it or not, we needed the extra person, even if he was a selfish asshole.

"Maybe," I finally agreed, shrugging a shoulder. "Though, that still wouldn't change anything. It doesn't erase ten years of being together or eight years of marriage. And believe me, Brody, it doesn't erase the fact that you're still a self-absorbed prick who only thinks of himself. Keep your fucking mouth closed around my son."

I walked away, practically shaking. I walked into my cabin, heading straight into Freddie's room. He was pulling back the covers of his bed. After tucking him in, almost on autopilot, I made my way to my room.

I set the lantern down on the dresser just inside the door, leaning back against it and slipping slowly down to the floor. The sight of that room was killing me, especially after the day's events. The room had seen so much love, so much happiness, that it hurt to see it. It had hardly changed since the first time I'd set foot in it, from the same multicolored quilt to the rough wood furniture. The memories hit me hard as tears ran down my face.

Clear Lake, Oregon
9 Years Prior

"Wow, it's so pretty here," I whispered when Jack parked his truck along the side of a small lake right beside one of four cabins.

His grin was stunning, changing his face from handsome to something just shy of an angel. It was a touch childlike. His entire face smiled—his eyes crinkled, his nose scrunched up, and his head tilted. There were even these bare hints of dimples on either side of his mouth. And God, if he wasn't a beautiful sight for sore eyes. It had been a long seven, almost eight, months.

And I was completely in love with him.

I'd thought that he was hot in high school when I'd first moved to Sandy to live with my dad. Jack had strolled around the school like he'd owned the place with his really pretty girlfriend, who was just as popular. I'd thought he was handsome when he stepped into Shelly's Bar four years later with Derek, both of them unnecessarily coming to my rescue against Brody, though Jack had seen red with my ex. I'd thought he was sweet and caring and so smart with every letter and phone call that had come my way. But seeing him on my father's doorstep after being overseas for so long had sealed my feelings. My heart belonged to him.

We hadn't said the words, but over the course of his tour in Afghanistan, we'd connected in ways I hadn't been expecting. We'd committed to each other, promised to wait, and all but said how we truly felt. When he'd written, asking me to take a weekend with him once he got home, I'd known it was a test. A test of how this thing between us would go.

The cab of his big black truck was quiet, the air charged with everything not said, everything we needed to say, and a chemistry that not only hadn't faded with his tour overseas but had increased exponentially.

Jack's thumb dragged across my knuckles, causing me to snap out of my thoughts. I turned to face him, and his face held a touch of nerves, but the way he was looking at me was so sweet, like I was the light at the end of the tunnel.

He released his seat belt and mine, turning me to face him. Swallowing nervously, he took both my hands in his.

"Tell me what you're thinking, Shortcake, 'cause you've been so quiet on the way here. Nothing has to happen inside that cabin. I just...I wanted to spend time with you at a place that means something to me. I also wanted privacy to talk. *Just talk*, if that's all you want."

His rambling made me smile. I'd only seen the confident senior at Sandy High School, never the silly-sweet thing waiting for my answer. It brought the reality of him, of truly knowing him, slamming home.

He grinned a little, pulling both my hands up to kiss my knuckles. "Where'd that bold girl with the baseball bat go?"

Giggling, I shrugged. "She's here; she's just...really nervous." I let out a deep breath. "I don't wanna mess up, and I'm really happy you're home safe, but I just..." I glanced toward the cabin that was so very perfect in the middle of even more perfect woods. "It's been a long time, and the last..."

"One day, I'm going to beat the shit out of your ex. How much trouble did he really give you while I was away?" he asked me, and the growl in his tone just about made me come undone in the cab of that truck.

I smiled, releasing one of his hands so I could trace the lip Brody had split. There was a tiny, almost invisible scar left, but I had a feeling only I could see it. "Not much...especially after I told my dad what had happened at Shelly's that night, what you and Derek did. You're now my dad's favorite."

Jack laughed, his cheeks reddening just a little. "So that's how I was able to steal you away so easily."

"Mmhmm," I hummed with a nod.

Jack sobered quickly. "There's no messing up here, Shortcake. None. You're what I came home for," he whispered, a wrinkle forming between his brows. "Seeing you...That's more than enough. I wasn't expecting you, Sara, and if being overseas taught me anything, it's that I can't let shit slide. I'm...I really want this. You. Us. This." He shoved his hand into his hair, which was much shorter than the last time I'd seen him, and tugged it with a frustrated sigh. "This isn't... You can't mess up, Sara, because I've already fallen for you. Nothing could fuck that up. Everything you do—"

My lips were on his, probably shocking him, but he caught up so quickly that we both groaned. And it was a rather loud sound inside the truck. His hands slipped into my hair, and I could feel the calloused thumbs rubbing just below my jaw and my ear. Tilting my head, he claimed me with his tongue, tasting and relishing. He slowed us down, his eyes squeezing closed as his forehead fell to mine while we both tried to catch our breath.

"You mean that?" I asked, smiling when he merely nodded against me. "Me too. I thought I was crazy."

He grinned, those long eyelashes of his sweeping up to reveal deep-brown eyes, though the pupils were just about to take over every bit of color. "Then we're both crazy..."

Giggling, I sighed happily. "I really am glad you're home safe," I whispered.

He brushed kisses across my lips, not deepening them. "I'd promised you."

I wanted to tell him it was a promise he shouldn't have made, but he seemed fairly proud of himself.

I huffed a light laugh. "I know you did." Nuzzling his nose with my own, I said, "Take me inside, Jack."

He seemed to steel himself, pushing gently off my forehead, but his smile was sweet when he pulled away and opened his truck door. He reached into the bed and grabbed our bags, slinging them onto his shoulder. When I met him at the front steps of the cabin, he smiled and unlocked it.

"This property is owned by my father's family. The cabins...Three belong to my parents and Derek and me. The fourth one we've considered selling, but right now, it's unoccupied. They're all the same. Three small rooms, a bathroom, and small kitchen and living room. When Derek's parents died—my aunt and uncle—he inherited all of it, though he signed parts of it over when he turned eighteen."

He led me through the place, showing me the different rooms.

"I got this cabin for myself as a graduation present from him," he finally finished, setting the bags down in the main bedroom. He paused, shoving his hands into the front pockets of his jeans—jeans that fit so well that I was about to drool at the sight of him. "You don't have to stay in here. I told you, I don't expect…"

He looked so unsure, so fragile at what I might or might not say, that I couldn't help but blurt out, "I love you."

When his gaze shot up from the wooden floor of the cabin's bedroom to my face, I nodded and smiled, feeling my emotions well up.

"It's the truth," I said softly, shrugging a shoulder. "Somewhere between you asking me if Brody hurt me that night at the bar and your last letter telling me you were coming home, I was just…sure of it. I didn't…I was afraid of what would happen while you were gone, and if you didn't…But you did, and I just want you to know."

Three long strides, and he had me pressed against the wall of the room. One strong arm was braced against the doorframe by my head, and the other trailed a light, fiery touch down the side of my face.

His lips met mine again, consuming me, igniting every inch of my skin from head to toe, and I could see that he'd been holding back, even with all the kissing we'd done the week before he'd shipped out. And now he pressed into me, letting me feel everything. He was warm, with firm, lean muscles and smooth skin, and I could feel his heart pounding in his chest. His biceps bulged beneath my fingers as I tried to hold on, pull him closer, and practically climb him.

"Fuck me, that was…the best thing I've ever heard," he whispered, dragging his lips across my cheek and down my neck. Sweeping his tongue lightly across my skin, he continued softly, "I'm pretty sure it was the baseball bat that won me over, Shortcake."

Giggling, I dropped my head back to the wall behind me with a dull thump. "You know, I'm pretty average at five foot three." Though, I secretly loved that he called me that.

He chuckled, shaking his head, but his hands ran down my sides, only to fully cup my ass. He shifted, gripped, and lifted me up so that I had to wrap my legs around his waist to hold on.

"But I'm six foot two, baby," he argued playfully, grinning when I set my elbows on his strong, broad shoulders. "I need better access," he teased, but the smirk fell quickly when denim brushed against denim in the most delicious of ways. "Jesus…You are so beautiful."

"You're just saying that because you've been stuck in a desert for seven months," I said, blushing at the compliment. I'd been called pretty and hot and cute but never beautiful, and his sincere, handsome face, his unwavering eye contact, told me he really meant it.

"No," he said with a slow shake of his head. "No, it's the truth. It's because I love you too, Sara."

Placing my hands on either side of his face, I kissed him softly, slowly, finally pulling back to smile at him. "Then show me."

He pulled me from the wall and walked me to the bed, settling me down onto the quilt. He loomed over me, his face kind of adorably scrunched up, like he couldn't decide where to start. To say I was nervous would have been an understatement. I'd only ever been with Brody, and we'd been broken up for months prior to Jack walking into the bar that fateful night, so it had been a long time since I'd last had sex. I knew Jack's history too. It had come up during a long, late phone call. Kim had been his first, and there had been one other after her—a girl he'd met at a club in Portland when he and Joel went off base.

However, despite both of our anxiety, we slowly settled into one another like we'd always been together. The more we kissed, the easier the touches came. The more we touched, the more clothing was removed, until there was nothing left between us.

The way Jack touched me, kissed me, made me feel more than I'd ever felt with Brody. It was almost overwhelming, the emotions that came from his mouth, whispering words of beauty, love, and things I couldn't quite hear, but I didn't need to hear them to know what he was feeling. Jack seemed to claim parts of me that he liked most—a swirling tongue around my nipples, a tickling bite to my ribs, and a suckling, never-ending kiss between my legs that had me crying out his name.

When he reached for a condom, I stopped him, pulling him to me. "Just you…and me. I'm on the pill. I want to feel you."

It was a first for him, going bare, and when he sank into me, he froze. "Oh God…you feel…"

I was pretty sure that was the last coherent words we shared. Once he started moving, everything became sensations and swirling emotions, not to mention pure love and lust and want all rolled up into each kiss, thrust, and touch.

Whispered pleas to come—and come together—were barely heard over the slaps of skin meeting skin and groaning kisses. My fingers raked down his back as everything in me pulled him closer when I fell over the edge one more time. Tears ran unchecked out of my eyes and back into my hair when Jack's face buried into my neck as he finally came with a string of curses.

We barely left the bedroom that whole weekend, though I discovered Jack could cook a few things, especially breakfast. We talked about everything, including the possibility of another tour overseas. It made us hold each other close, making love simply to fight the pain of another separation, because now, everything had changed.

A soft knock tapped on the door, bringing me out of the memory, and I stood up from the floor. Tina was on the other side, a worried expression on her face.

"You okay? I heard you crying," she said softly.

I nodded, swiping at my tears, but sat down hard on the edge of the bed. She sat next to me, wrapping an arm around my shoulders.

"It's okay to freak out, you know," she whispered like it was a secret. "You wouldn't be human if you didn't. I get staying strong for Freddie, but…" She sighed deeply, shaking her head. "Sara, you'll make yourself sick holding all this in."

Nodding, I sniffled. "I know. I just…I miss him so much, and Freddie needs him. I *hate* not knowing anything. I hate it. I just…I want him back, Tina. I need him back, safe and sound. I'd give anything…"

Tina simply nodded, wrapping me in a hug. "God, I can't imagine, sweetie. At least I had closure."

She held me until the tears stopped, though they probably could have gone on and on. She finally brought me a cool, wet cloth to wipe my face.

"Get some sleep. We'll tackle that cabin in the morning. And if Brody tries to bug you, I'll shoot him."

Grinning, I sniffled and nodded. "He has a tendency to bring that out in everyone, so don't worry. You're not alone." I stood up from the bed but looked at it. The memory of our first time together was way too fresh in my mind. "I can't sleep in here. I'm going to cuddle with my boy tonight."

"I can't say I blame you. Poor Janie has gotten sick of me doing the same." Tina grinned but hugged me one more time. "See you in the morning."

The pounding of hammer to nail on the outside of Rich and Dottie's cabin was making my headache worse. I'd cried even more the night before after curling myself around Freddie, which left me feeling empty, with scratchy eyes and a pounding head. Freddie hadn't seemed to mind the intrusion.

Derek was slowly cutting off the natural light coming in, but Tina and I had brought a few candles and two lanterns to help us out. The damn cabin was like a time machine. Everything looked exactly the same, completely untouched from the last time I'd set foot in it. There was a fine layer of dust, but otherwise, it was pristine.

Janie and Freddie had offered to come along, and they were currently scoping out the bedrooms and bathroom for anything we could use. The kitchen had a few things—some charcoal, lighter fluid, and a few cooking utensils.

"Hey, Mom," Janie piped up from the living room. "What's this?"

I glanced up when Tina snorted into a soft laugh.

"Janie, girl…you really make me feel old sometimes. You know that?" she countered, rolling her eyes my way as she walked to the shelf with the old wind-up record player.

Laughing at them, I shook my head as I searched a few more cabinets.

"It's a record player," Tina went on to explain. "And a really old one at that." I heard her fiddling with it just before soft music filled the room. "Maybe this will make you appreciate some changes, baby doll. Without power, there are no MP3s or CDs."

"How does it…?" Freddie asked, and I heard the record scratch through the needle.

"Careful, buddy. You'll ruin it," I chided gently with a smile as I watched him pull his hand back. I looked back to Tina. "We'll have to remember that's in here."

"No doubt," she replied with a laugh. "Mrs. North is great and all, but she sings when she…really, really shouldn't."

Grinning, I got back to work. We found another grill, some books that Martin might need to help tutor the kids, and a few hunting supplies in the closet. We'd have to take inventory of ammunition soon. Bullets wouldn't last forever. I also found another bow-and-arrow set.

"Hey, D?" I called out the door.

"Yes, ma'am?" he grunted and then slammed in another nail or two before he stepped into the doorway, brushing off his hands.

"Here," I said, holding the quiver of arrows out for him.

"Ah, excellent. I forgot Uncle Rich had these." He smiled crookedly, looking them and the bow over. "Definitely could use these."

Janie, who was normally so shy she barely spoke, squeaked from the hall and ran into the living room like hell itself was on her tail. "Spider!" she wailed, running through, only to trip over the rug at the end of the room.

"Careful, sweetie," I told her, bending down to help her up, but I froze at the sight of a wooden trap door. "No," I whispered, glancing over my shoulder. "Derek, is this a basement?"

"Hmm?" he hummed, looking up from his newly acquired toy, only to smile. "Nah. Knowing Aunt Dottie? That's probably a bunker…a bomb shelter. The cabin I sold to your dad had one too, but it flooded out."

"Huh," I sighed, looking to Janie, whose face was sweet and curious. She was an adorable girl, with light-brown hair cut into a short bob, hazel eyes, and a face that reminded me of Tinkerbell—like a pretty little elf. "Shall we?" I asked her in a whisper, and she nodded vehemently with a grin on her face.

"Me too! Me too!" Freddie said, dropping to his knees beside us.

"Okay, you two roll back the rug," I instructed, standing up out of the way. I squatted down again and hooked my finger into the pull of the trapdoor, lifting it.

The smell was damp and earthy. The air was cool, almost cold, as it whooshed out from beneath the cabin. Freddie handed me a lantern, and when I shined it down into the basement, I saw a staircase leading down below.

Looking between the kids, I said, "Let me go first, and then you guys can come down. Okay?"

The two nodded, wide-eyed and about to shake out of their skin with curiosity. I envied their ability to see adventure at every turn. To them, the whole new world was an adventure, despite the ugly parts they'd seen already. So their sweet faces made me smile. I hoped to hell they kept that outlook.

The air was stale, cool, and damp down below, but my mouth fell open as to what was inside: everything Dottie needed in some sort of medical emergency. First-aid supplies lined the shelf—gauze, tape, surgical equipment, even a suture kit. There was even a cot down there. Along the other wall were other supplies—water, charcoal, and a few canned goods. All of it could be put to use.

Derek descended the steps, his eyes wide. "Well, holy shit," he drawled, gazing slowly around. "Now ain't this helpful?" He grinned at me when I laughed.

"No kidding," I said softly, nodding a little. "Well, we'll make use of this stuff, for sure. And this hidden bunker-basement thing... This is perfect for storage."

He spun on me. "And hiding," he added, his eyes flickering up to the two kids peering down at us. "Fuck, Sare...This will keep them and the older folks safe should a pack come through here."

"Pack...or not-so-friendly survivors," I added slowly.

Derek thought in silence for a moment, finally nodding. "Okay, good to know. Let's leave the medical supplies down here, get a count on the food and water, and we'll tell the others about this place. We'll set up some sort of emergency plan. This cabin will be a safe zone."

Nodding and waving the kids down, I got to work going through the supplies on the shelf. I tried not to think about Jack or his parents, though knowing Rich and Dottie like I did, they'd have been perfectly fine with what we were doing. I shut out my hurting heart that they, along with Jack and Joel, were not here to see it...or even give permission. I hoped I'd be able to ask for forgiveness one day, but even that seemed like too much to ask.

But...like I'd told my son, I could still hope.

CHAPTER 5
Where: Florida-Alabama state line
When: 2.5 months after Hurricane Beatrice
JACK

JACK

Florida-Alabama State Line
2.5 Months after Hurricane Beatrice

"Ladies and gentlemen, we are just about out of Florida," Joel muttered, pulling the Hummer into a parking lot next to a few abandoned cars. "Please keep all hands inside the vehicle until it comes to a complete stop," he rambled on, but he probably meant that shit.

"Thank fuck," I grumbled, giving the parking lot we were in an assessing gaze as I got out, Sasha right behind me. "That took way longer than it damn well should have."

I pulled my gun from my back to my front, checking the silencer before slipping into the roadside motel's office. We'd learned by trial and error once we'd pulled out of Dexter AFB. Noise drew the zeaks in faster than anything, which meant gunfire was a last resort. However, to save time, avoid up-close contact, and clear our way quickly, guns were the better option. Joel had been really vigilant about the ammo and guns we'd taken from the base, and silencers had been among them—for both handguns and rifles. Though, his crazy ass had found a Marine's dress/ceremony sword on base and had sharpened it enough he could probably shave with the damn thing. Most of one Hummer was taken up with ammo and camping equipment, while the other carried food, clothes, and medical supplies. But tonight, we'd wanted a bed and running water.

I found keys to two separate yet adjoining rooms hanging on a pegboard, smirking Joel's way. "At least we don't need power for these. Those keycard locks don't do us any fucking good if we have to break in to use them."

"Just pray the fucking water's runnin'," he countered as he poked around the office. "Cold or not…I don't care."

"No shit," I sighed, looking down at Sasha, who usually stuck to me like glue. "We're clear, girl?"

She wriggled in response, happy as a clam as she panted heavily. Her demeanor when things were clear was easy and light, but if she sensed zeaks, she was tense, rigid, and fierce. Bringing her along had been a damn good idea, though Joel and I were attached to her, simply because she was the first good thing we'd found in Florida…and the last. She'd proved herself not only helpful as hell but a walking, growling alarm against zeaks and survivors with bad intentions.

Dad was standing guard along the sidewalk in front of the row of motel rooms. Mom was still inside the Hummer they'd been driving the last two weeks. My dad wanted one more vehicle, but not until we'd made it out of Florida, maybe the South altogether. He was hoping for a decent RV but would probably settle for a pickup truck, something with which he could pull a camper.

I tossed a key his way, and he caught it one-handed. "Lucky thirteen, Dad," I told him with a grin.

"Lucky indeed," he replied as we walked to twelve first. "We'll sweep both rooms and then open the door between. Okay?"

"Sir," Joel said with a single nod, slipping the key into the room he and I would share for the next few hours.

We used flashlights and the Hummer's headlights to let us see inside. It was two beds, a dresser, and a beat-up TV, all representative of an old motel. The room looked clean, not that we'd care, and I stepped through to the bathroom, calling clear.

When we'd done the same to my parents' room and propped open the door between them, we unloaded enough supplies and clothes for the night.

I gazed around again. We were just outside the edge of Pensacola, not far from crossing over into Alabama. We'd passed between Blackwater River State Forest and Eglin AFB earlier in the day. We hadn't even stopped. It had been a cesspool of zeaks wandering in swarms. Hell, the whole state had been that way. We were hoping that, once we were out of the dear, sweet Sunshine State, which had been ground zero for this virus, things would get better. We weren't holding our breaths.

We'd traveled up through central Florida, having to avoid most major highways—75 had been sporadic with open roads and I-4 had been a fucking morgue, but we'd occasionally had to switch over to 41. The back roads had been easier. We'd seen more attacks than we could count and tried to help a few people along the way who were simply trying to stay alive and hunker down. A few of the bigger cities had been destroyed—some in part to Hurricane Beatrice, and some looked like they'd waged war. Parts of Orlando had been on fire as we'd driven through. Our guess was that survivors fighting back had gotten out of hand, though we could tell that martial law had been implemented in some places and had fallen. Occasionally the sound of explosions would reach us all the way to where we'd camped that night. To see Disney World in flames had been a strange and surreal experience.

Just before we'd reached I-10 to turn west, we'd driven through farm country—horses, specifically. Fields burned, horses attacked and eaten, and several farmers guarded their property with weapons that rivaled ours. We'd been allowed to camp one night but no more. Unfortunately, it was then we'd fought the hardest. The swarm that had moved through that night was the biggest any of us had ever seen, and we'd tried to save every member of that family on the farm, but we'd barely gotten our own asses out of there intact. It was there we'd seen just how quickly the infection was spreading.

"Son, you want me to take first watch?" Mom asked, and I smiled over at her, shaking my head.

"No, go ahead and take a break," I told her, leaning into her kiss to my cheek.

She may have been my mother and a damn good doctor, but she was just as much a trained officer as the rest of us. She could handle guns and tough situations with a calm assertion that would probably shock her lady friends back in Sandy.

That thought made my chest ache with homesickness. I was homesick for my wife, my son, our house...all of it. I tried not to dwell on just how bad things had turned and what Sandy could look like now.

"You okay, Jack?" she asked, placing a hand on the side of my face and making me look her way, though she didn't believe my nod whatsoever. "Try again, sport."

I grinned briefly but looked down before back at her. "I was thinking about Ocala. They…that was…They were turning in less than a minute. I'm not even sure it took thirty seconds."

"Mmm," she hummed, nodding a little. "Yeah, the virus has changed, adapted. You did everything you could to save that boy."

Frowning, I sighed wearily. "He was protecting his grandfather, which worked, but in running out to the barn, he signed his own death warrant. I tried to stop him."

"I know. His family knew too."

"If they're changing that fast…" I started but looked over when my dad and Joel joined us.

"If I'm estimating correctly, then I'd be willing to bet most of the world is gone," Dad stated, slapping my shoulder. "Go. *I'm* taking the first watch. I want all of you rested when we leave tomorrow. We've got to drive around Pensacola, not to mention try to get around Mobile. Once we're in Alabama, we can turn north a bit, but the large cities are too dangerous, not to mention the roads are deadlocked…Um, no pun intended," he said with a snort, rolling his eyes.

"Well, I'm gonna guess we'll need to start thinking about food somewhere around Mississippi or Arkansas, if we're turning northwest," Joel added. "We can hunt in some of the woods along the way, but we'll need some things by then, I think. And then there's gas. I'll check these cars in the morning." He pointed to the few around us.

"I agree." I nodded, removing the rifle from my shoulder. "Give me a few hours, and I'll relieve you."

"Sure, son," Dad said with a weary smile, and he turned to my mother. "You too. Go on inside. I've got this."

"Smack the windows if you need us," Joel ordered, pointing to the two side-by-side windows.

Dad nodded and then faced the parking lot. We had no choice but to watch out for ourselves this way. Some survivors didn't always approach with the best of intentions, and swarms could sneak up on us, especially at night or in the rain. Damn, if the rain didn't make them worse, even more disgusting than they already were.

Sasha was curled up in the doorway between the rooms, and Joel went about pouring her some food and water.

"You take the first shower, Jacky. Let the water run a bit before you get in," he said, scrunching up his nose. "You never know how long it's been in those pipes."

I nodded, grabbing my gear and a battery-operated lantern. I turned on the water in the shower, leaning in to the mirror. I rubbed the beard that had grown over the last two weeks of travel, smirking at myself at just how much my Sara would've hated it. She preferred smooth skin and to be able to see my face. Groaning at how badly it was going to sting shaving with cold water, I turned the tap on anyway and pulled out soap and a razor.

Once my face was smooth, I stepped inside the shower, hissing at the cold water, but proceeded to make quick work of washing. Dirt, grime, sweat, blood…It all washed down the drain in a muddy color. Small scratches stung, old bruises were yellowing, and my sore muscles tensed, but by the time I stepped back out, I felt a thousand times better—almost normal, relaxed.

I pulled on clean cargo pants, leaving my shirt off for the night. When I stepped back out into the room, Joel was putting together something for us to eat.

"It ain't a steak dinner, but it'll have to do," he said, pushing a can of beef stew my way. He'd gotten really good at using cans of Sterno—one of the things we'd found on base—to heat shit up in a hurry without building a full-blown fire, which could attract the zeaks out of nowhere.

"I'll take it. Thanks," I sighed, falling down on the edge of the bed and pushing myself up to the headboard.

Sasha hopped up there with me, laying her head on my thigh as I finished the whole can.

"You could use a bath too, big girl," I told her, and her sleepy amber eyes rolled up to my face before falling closed again. I ran a hand over her head for a few minutes, grateful for the quiet night.

I had to have dozed off at some point, because I snapped awake at the low, rumbling growl Sasha was emitting. Her face was fierce, her lips twitching, and her ears perked up. Glancing at the other bed, I saw Joel sit up.

"What is it?" I whispered, and he shook his head, stepping up to the window that we'd left open just to hear my dad.

It was then that we heard a sharp tap on our window. We jumped into action, pulling on T-shirts and boots, strapping on weapons, and opening the door.

The sun was just peeking over the trees in the east to a cloudy day, but it gave us a much better view of our surroundings, allowing us to see what had been cloaked in darkness the night before. Across the way was a rather large strip mall, but it was the dark-green van tearing out of the parking lot that had my dad—and Sasha—on alert. The dog was bristled, with her head low and her growl continuing nonstop. She stepped forward but stayed between Joel and me.

"I heard gunshots coming from that Wal-Mart," Dad said softly, jerking his chin across the way.

I rubbed my face to wake up a little more, glancing over when my mother stepped out of her room fully dressed and armed, which was damned good timing, as the van swerved out of the parking lot of the mall and into our motel one.

The side door slid open with a bang, allowing the sound of curses, arguing, and yelling out into the quiet morning. A tall red-haired girl was ejected from the van, a backpack tossed at her feet.

"Tucker, stop! You can't do this! We have to go back for my sister!" She sobbed, snatching up her bag, but before she could reach for the van, the tires squealed, the door slammed closed, and the driver flipped her off as he turned out onto the street.

The girl collapsed to her knees, and sobs met my ears. It was my mother who moved first. She shouldered her weapon and approached the girl carefully.

"Aw, fuck me," I sighed, following behind her.

We didn't know the girl, and there was no telling what her problem was, but I couldn't let my mother go to her alone, which proved a good thing when the girl suddenly lashed out.

"Don't fucking touch me! I have to…You don't…" she rambled through tears and curses and snot, but when she shoved my mother, Joel and I reacted instantly. He went to Mom, and I dodged a slap or two before securing the girl's arms behind her back.

She was strong as hell and fought me tenaciously, but I held her arms tight. My eyes narrowed in on a bruise or two along her face and arms. My hope was that she got them fighting zeaks, not the asshole who'd just dumped her off and left her for dead.

"Calm down!" I snarled in her ear. "We're not gonna hurt you."

"Let me go, let me go, let me go," she chanted, going silent when Joel knelt in front of her.

"He can hold you all damn day, princess, or…you can settle the fuck down," he warned her.

"My sister!" she cried, looking across the street to Wal-Mart. "He…he…The motherfucker just left her!"

My mother stepped away, giving the store a long gaze, but my father had binoculars. "Zeaks," he stated grimly. "A shit-ton of them, or at least the movement I see inside makes me think there are too many."

"She's only thirteen!" She finally sagged, glancing at me over her shoulder. "Please, *please* let me go."

"Can you stay calm?" I asked her, and she nodded.

I released my hold on her, and she squirmed away, scrambling to her feet. She picked up her bag, rummaging around in it until she came out with what looked like a damn steak knife. When she started across the street, my mother stopped her again.

"You can't go in there, sweetheart," she told her, shaking her head. "It's a death sentence."

"I can't leave her. She's all I have left."

I knew the second Joel's shoulders sagged briefly, only to straighten back up, that we were going in.

Gripping my hair, I sighed. "This is…really gonna suck," I muttered but turned toward the Hummers. "Fine! Dad, lock up the rooms." I dove into the Hummer Joel and I were sharing and grabbed a few clips, two .45s, and a couple of knives.

Joel loaded up on his own ammo and weapons, and I turned to the girl. "What's your name?"

"R-Ruby," she sniffled.

"Okay, Ruby. I'm Jack, and that's Joel, and my parents, Rich and Dottie," I introduced as we all walked quickly across the street to the mall parking lot. I took the steak knife out of her hand and threw it several yards. "This…" I held up a military-grade knife that was about five inches longer than the crap she'd had. "This will serve you better."

She took it with a nod.

"Next…Can you shoot a gun?"

"I'm…I *have*, but…I'm not very good."

"You don't have to be good; just slow them down enough so they can't get you. A bullet to the leg puts them to the ground. A bullet to the head stops them completely. Chest shots are bullshit. Got me?"

Ruby nodded, taking the .45 I was handing her.

"Safety, chamber a round, and you're good to go," I instructed, turning to the rest of them. "We do this together."

"Ruby, where was your sister?" Mom asked her.

"B-Bathroom. Back far right corner, but…Tucker wouldn't wait…"

The piercing scream we heard made my skin break out into goose bumps and my brow into a cold sweat. That was the sound of pure terror. A *kid* in terror.

"Once we're inside, split up," I told them. "Ruby, you stay with Joel up the middle. Mom, Dad…take the far left just in case she tried to run. I'll go up the right to the back. What's your sister's name?"

"Ava."

I nodded, leading them all through the busted doors of the store. The stench was what hit me first, decay and rot and blood. But the growling, snarling, and shuffling simply pissed me off.

"Attention Wal-Mart shoppers, the store is about to fucking close," Joel muttered, making me grin in spite of the circumstances.

I stepped quickly inside, the sound of crunching glass under my boots gaining me unwanted attention, and Sasha bounded over it with ease, the click of her nails and her growl gaining even more attention. Three zeaks wandered out from the customer-service desk and two from the registers, and I aimed, taking them out, only to move to the right of the store and up the aisle.

Gunfire sounded all over the store, along with Sasha's barks, but I focused my attention to the back of the building. I passed what used to be the frozen-food section, but it had thawed and smelled of sour milk and rotten food. I jumped over spilled shelves, ransacked clothing racks, and took out four more zeaks before I reached the back of the store.

"C'mon, kid…Where are you?" I muttered to myself, eyeing the long aisle before focusing on the push doors that led to bathrooms and stock. Another scream sounded from that back room, crawling up my spine, and I kicked open the doors. "Ava?"

"Here!"

It was much darker back there. I couldn't see a damn thing, so I shouldered my rifle, pulling out my flashlight and .45. I heard the bastards fumbling around toward the far corner. Shining the light that way, I sighed in relief that the girl was holding her own, but it wouldn't last long. They'd cornered her on top of the shelves, and the poor thing was holding on to the metal rafter in order not to slip and fall.

A greenish-colored hand with missing digits shot out from the shelf beside me, grabbing my arm, but I shrugged it off, spinning to pop off a round. That caught the attention of every zeak pushing on the shelf Ava was barely clinging to. They all turned my way, almost in unison. Teeth snapped, hands reached, but I started shooting. Exploding heads and the sickening wet splatter that went with each bullet echoed around me until I barely even heard it. When I finally cleared the aisle, I checked up and down, finally looking up at Ava.

"Okay, kiddo, come down," I told her, waving my hand.

"Where's Ruby?" she asked, letting go of the metal bar above her, but the shelving unit was weakened by the zeak pushing on it.

"She's here. She asked us to help get you outta here. Whoa, careful…"

The girl reached for the rafter again, but it gave way. The roof opened up, spilling down water and filth, not to mention Ava herself. Rushing forward, I caught her just before her head smacked to the concrete or metal could fall on her.

"You okay?" I panted, looking up at the sky through the now opened roof.

"Yeah…"

"No bites? Nothing?" I asked but set her on her feet when she shook her head no.

Sasha bounded down the aisle toward us, her hackles up, her teeth bared, glowing bright white in the dark storage room. Ava cowered behind me.

"She won't hurt you," I soothed, and I saw that Sasha wasn't barking at the girl but at the opening in the roof.

"Ah, shit," I said, pushing the girl behind me, because I could hear the shuffling, dragging footsteps just before two, three…four zeaks fell down from above. "How in the blue fuck…" I turned to Ava. "Stay right here, okay? Right behind me." When she nodded, I traded my .45 for my rifle.

I felt her hand grip the back of my T-shirt as I noted two more falling from above, smiling when one's head shattered on the concrete floor, the sound not unlike dropping a melon to the ground. The few that remained intact after their plunge started our way.

"Sasha, stay," I commanded, and the dog stood her ground. I didn't need her to corral them; the tight space would work against her anyway.

One more fell from the roof, and I took her out, finally seeing most of those from the roof were dressed the same. They'd been employees simply trying to get away.

The door swung open, and Joel, Ruby, and my parents all came in, but Ava burst into tears again.

"Ruby!" she wailed, rushing to her sister, and I could see the resemblance.

Ava was thin, almost lanky, with the same red hair, only lighter. It was obvious that the younger one would grow to be tall and pretty like the older sibling. They were tears and hugs, apologies and smiles. It was damn good to see.

"You okay?" Dad asked, and I nodded, wiping my face on my shirt sleeve.

Ava stepped to me, tugging my shirt again, and I gazed down into big hazel eyes. "Thank you…" she said, pausing a bit.

"Jack," I said with a smile and a ruffle of her hair. "This is my dad, Rich. That big lug over there is Joel. And my mother, Dottie, is the one over there perusing the shelves."

Ava smiled and nodded, waving.

"Oh, now you're shy?" I chuckled but looked to Mom. "If we're stocking up, there's no better place than this," I told her. "We'll need oil for the trucks and any food or water you can find."

"I'd like to check the pharmacy, too," Dad added.

"Fine, fine. But I want back on the road soon. We've got some rain rolling in," I warned them, starting for the doors back into the store.

"You're leaving us?" Ava asked, ignoring her sister's hissed warning, because there was a panic that I could see starting to build in the kid.

I looked up to see Joel's gaze on Ruby, and then I looked to my parents. Again, my mother stepped forward.

"You're welcome to come with us for however long you wish."

"Where are you headed?"

"Oregon," I answered firmly.

Ruby looked from me, to the rest of us, and finally to her pleading sister's face.

"Please, Ruby? I don't wanna ride with Tucker no more. He's a jerk. He was mean," Ava blurted out, making her sister flinch, but she finally nodded in acquiescence.

"Yeah, well…Tucker is long gone," Joel drawled, rolling his eyes to lighten things, but his face was livid. "C'mon, you'll need clothes and shit. And maybe one of these cars out here, which reminds me…Gas, Jack. We'll need to stock up from this parking lot, siphon what we can."

"Then let's get this shit done. We're looking at a few hours of work," I told them, walking through the doors and into the store.

I shook my head at where we were. Freddie loved his trips with me to Wal-Mart. Somehow, he'd end up with some new damn game or toy or whatever every time we'd go, which Sara always gave me shit about but with barely any oomph behind it.

"Jack! Wait up," Ava called, and I looked down at her when she caught up to me. "I can help. I can carry stuff."

Grinning, I sighed because she was sweet and hyper and an almost painful reminder of my son, who was similar. I eyed her like I did Freddie, with a raised eyebrow and a pursed mouth, like I had to think about it. Her hazel eyes gazed worriedly up at me, and I snorted.

"Okay, okay. So…go grab a bag or box or something. We're gonna need it."

She nodded, racing away.

Sasha sat in front of me, tilting her head.

"Don't judge me, big girl," I told her. "You were just as bad. Now, let's grab you some dog shampoo. You stink. I don't want to be trapped with your smelly ass in the truck all the way to Mississippi."

Clarksdale, Mississippi
2 Months & 3 Weeks after Hurricane Beatrice

The water tower of Clarksdale shone like a beacon in the setting sun. The damn thing was painted gold, which made it even more noticeable. But the town was dead. Literally. There wasn't a sign of life whatsoever as I led our small caravan through the main street.

I continued through town, passing a few beat-up diners, a hardware store, and an old theater that looked like it had fallen into disrepair way before the virus was set loose. The edge of the small town had a motel—the Riverside Motel—and I pulled in, gazing over at Sasha.

"Well?" I asked her, smirking when she glared out the windshield with her ears perked up, then the passenger side window, finally letting out a soft "*boof*."

"If you say so, big girl."

I slipped down from the Hummer, letting Sasha out behind me, and then joined everyone else in the parking lot. The motel overlooked endless fields. The cotton plants were dead, simply withering away. Beyond that was just tall green grass, with trees in the distance.

Joel was surveying everything around us through binoculars—each way down the empty street, the fields, and finally the farm on the farthest side of the open fields. My parents walked to the motel office, most likely looking for keys.

"I've got two zeaks wandering just on the edge of those trees, but we're too far away to attract them," he said, pulling the binoculars away. "We should be clear for now."

My gaze landed on Ruby and Ava, both of whom were looking at the motel with fear…and a little disdain. It wasn't the Ritz, for sure, so I couldn't blame them.

The two had been with us since that morning at Wal-Mart. We'd left Florida that same day. Joel had managed to find a halfway decent RV. It wasn't big, but the inside had been clean, and there was a bed above the van-style cab as well as a foldout sofa. It worked for the two of them, not to mention it made my dad happy to have it. It was extra storage and shelter should we need it, and Joel drove it most of the time.

I had to give Ruby credit. She was tougher than she looked. At first glance, she came across as a bit weak and closed off, but she was far from it. She held her own, and she'd made damn good use of the knife and gun I'd given her as we'd driven across Mississippi. We'd avoided Pensacola and Mobile just fine, but trying to go around Jackson had been touchy. There had been pileups on just about every highway, which almost trapped us with a swarm of zeaks. They'd taken us by surprise when we'd stopped to siphon gas.

However, we were about to enter into Arkansas, and we were hoping to stay just far enough away from Little Rock and Memphis, Tennessee, to avoid trouble. We wanted to drive evenly between them. So far, we were continuing on in a northwestern direction. I was hoping to keep that shit up. Aside from Jackson, things had eased up once we'd left Florida. Though, that made sense, considering it was the first hit with not only the virus but the hurricane as well.

"This place smells funny," Ava said, her nose wrinkled.

"*Boof*," Sasha piped up softly, starting to wander around sniffing everything.

"She agrees with you," I said with a chuckle, glancing over my shoulder when I heard footsteps.

"No keys." Dad shrugged, pointing to the line of doors. "We'll have to bust them open."

Sasha made it to the first door and stiffened, her growl turning into a single bark.

"What you wanna bet there are no keys because every room is full," Joel surmised grimly.

"Damn it," I grumbled, walking to the door and pressing an ear to it. Sasha's bark had stirred up something inside. The telltale moans and scratches on the door proved it. After checking the next few doors, my head fell back in defeat. "I am in no mood to clear this shit out, and even if we did, there's no telling what conditions the rooms are in."

"Eeew!" Ava scowled, shaking her head.

Joel sighed because we were just dead on our feet. We needed a day's rest, or at least one good night's sleep. He lifted the binoculars again, gazing across to the farm.

"Well, we could check out that farm," he suggested. "I mean, worst case, the barn's probably clean. Hell, farms that size have equipment, which means fuel, so maybe we'll get lucky."

"So…farm?" Dad asked, putting it to a vote.

"Yeah, sure." I nodded, scratching Sasha's ear.

When everyone was in agreement, he led us back out onto the street. The farm's driveway was dirt that had grown over just a little, but the tire ruts were pretty set in. In fact, it looked like no one had been in or out of the place for days, possibly weeks. As we neared the home, I noted a silo, the typical red barn, and exactly what Joel had been looking for: gas. Two large tanks sat just outside the barn between two yellow tractors—one marked diesel and the other regular.

However, the closer we got to the house, the more zeaks I could see. They were wandering through the fields, some stumbling out from the trees. If I'd had to guess, I would've said they were the field workers, employees of the farm. I saw some in jeans, some in overalls, a few in coveralls. And they all started to shift toward us when they caught our movement.

Sasha barked lightly at them from the window as we parked under some shade trees. The dog made me smile. She was the hardest worker of all of us.

"Nah, no herding, big girl. We'll take them out long-distance, yeah?" I ruffled the top of her head before reaching into the back for my rifle with the silencer. Sniper had never been my job, but I'd gotten good at it since I'd woken up on the base in Florida.

Using the hood of the Hummer to steady the gun, I aimed, adjusted the sight, and quietly took out the handful of zeaks in the field. Behind me, I heard someone do the same for the other side of the property.

Trading the rifle for my .45, I let Sasha out of the truck, only to gaze up at the house in front of us, where I saw movement on the second floor.

"We'll have to sweep the house," I told Joel, pointing from my eyes to the curtain that was still fluttering. "You and Dad take the downstairs. Ruby and I will go upstairs. Mom can stay with Ava, catching any stragglers coming out of those trees."

"Ten-four," Joel sang, pulling on a baseball cap backward. "Old MacDonald had a farm…E-I-E-I-Ohhh…" His warbling made Ava giggle, which I was pretty sure was his intention because we'd all grown attached to her, but I was damn sure he was even more attached to Ava's older sister. And if I was reading Ruby correctly, the feelings were mutual.

Before Joel could start singing "The Farmer in the Dell," I smacked his shoulder to shut him up as we stepped up onto the porch. He pulled open the screen door slowly, wincing at the creaking it did, only to prop it open with his leg. He let out a quick breath when he reached for the doorknob of the front door. I nodded once to indicate I was ready.

He slowly turned the knob, pushing the door open. It didn't make a sound, except for the soft thump when it touched the wall. I rushed in to the right, with Ruby behind me. Joel took the left, followed closely by my dad.

The house smelled stale, unused. But it also smelled sick, as in an illness. The scent reminded me of visits to my grandmother's house before she'd died. I'd been just a kid, but that smell was almost identical.

Boots fell heavily to the wooden floor as my dad and Joel cleared each room of the first floor. When they circled back, shaking their heads, I nodded to Ruby to move toward the staircase. It was then that we heard it—heavy breathing, dragging footsteps, and finally the growl from the top of the stairs. The zeak was in little-girl pajamas, though she'd probably been a teen when she'd turned. Dark hair was a tangled mass on her head, her neck had been torn open, and her left arm hung limply at her side. The stench of her filled the tight space of the staircase, but Ruby didn't even blink. She raised her gun and fired, the bullet meeting its mark right between the eyes.

The zeak fell, and I pulled Ruby to the side to let it tumble to the first floor.

"Where there's one, there's possibly more," I told her, leading us up to the landing. There were three doors to the right and two to the left, though the end of the hall was clearly a bathroom. A couple of the doors were closed, while the rest were open. It was one of the closed ones that suddenly slammed open.

I raised my weapon at the figure that stepped out into the hallway.

"Don't shoot!" she cried, holding up her hands.

"Jesus, she's alive," Ruby gasped, frowning at the girl at the end of the hallway. "Damn, girl, you just about got killed!"

Grinning at Ruby's temper, I started toward the obviously frightened girl. Though, she wasn't quite a girl. She was probably in her early twenties but was petite, with long, chocolate-colored hair pulled back into a ponytail.

"Fuck, have you been trapped in there?" I asked her, but before the girl could take two steps toward me, a gnarled, twisted gray hand shot out of the closest dark room, grabbing her by that long-ass ponytail.

Ruby and I jumped into action at the same time. She pulled her knife, and I aimed blindly into the dark, popping off three rounds at the same time Ruby's knife came down swiftly. I couldn't be sure if she was aiming for the hand itself or the hair, but she caught the latter, and the ponytail fell to the floor still gripped in that greenish-gray hand as the zeak dropped from my shots.

The girl fell forward on her knees, scrambling quickly away, but I kicked the door to the room open, still hearing the low, hissing growl. One more bullet shut the zeak up.

I let out a deep breath, turning to the sobbing girl on the floor. "That it? Any more in here?"

She shook her head, her hands going to her head, but she gazed up at me. "No, just my mom and my sister."

"That's not your family anymore," Ruby stated almost harshly.

"I know," she said, sniffling and nodding at the same time. "They turned yesterday morning. They'd tried to get some firewood but got caught by surprise in the barn. I should've…I'd been asleep. They'd both been bitten."

The guilt was written all over her face as she looked up at me. There wasn't much to say. It was a shitty new era. Everyone was losing everyone. That thought made my eyes close, had me pushing my fears and worry down deep. To panic now about my family—my wife and son—wouldn't get me anywhere.

Ruby moved me out of the way, kneeling in front of the girl. "I'm Ruby. That's Jack."

"Lexie. Lexie Russell." She tried to smile, but she was still in a touch of shock.

"Sorry about the hair, Lexie," Ruby stated, smacking me when I snorted.

Lexie cracked a small smile, pulling the band out of it. It fell around her face just below her jaw. "It'll grow back, I guess."

"Listen, we were merely looking for a place to camp for the night," I started, but Lexie stood in front of me, already nodding.

"No, I should thank you, so…make yourselves at home," she said, starting for the stairs, but she stopped and faced us again. "But… when you go?" she started, and I nodded for her to continue. "Please, *please…*" She glanced between us. "Please, take me with you. I gotta get out of here. You can have all the food and supplies my dad stored up before he…you know. Just…take me with you."

I looked down the stairs to see Joel and my parents watching us, most likely on alert from all the gunshots. My dad shrugged, my mother smiled, and Joel nodded.

Turning back to Lexie, I nodded. "Okay, but be ready to roll out when the sun comes up."

She sagged in relief and nodded. "No problem. C'mon. I'll get you guys something to eat."

Lexie rushed down the stairs, and Ruby chuckled next to me. "Not exactly Rambo, but she's plenty stocked up."

I sighed, smirking over at her. "There's safety in numbers, I guess. Besides, I couldn't stay here either…not with…" I waved toward what had once been Lexie's mother. "Let's clean these up for her, yeah?"

Ruby's face was calm as she nodded, but she reached for my left hand. She tapped my wedding band. "Is this the reason we're heading to Oregon?" she asked. "I've wanted to ask, but…"

I turned my ring once, twice, three times. "Yes," I whispered, looking down at the glinting gold. "I have to…I promised her and my boy, and even if…I *need to know*," I urged, wrinkling my nose. "She's smart, and I hope I gave her fair warning, but…"

Ruby smiled, patting my shoulder before reaching for the dead woman. "Then I hope we make it. You and Joel…even your parents…you saved my sister, so I owe you. I'll do my best to help you."

Smiling gratefully, I helped her lift the body. "Thanks, Ruby."

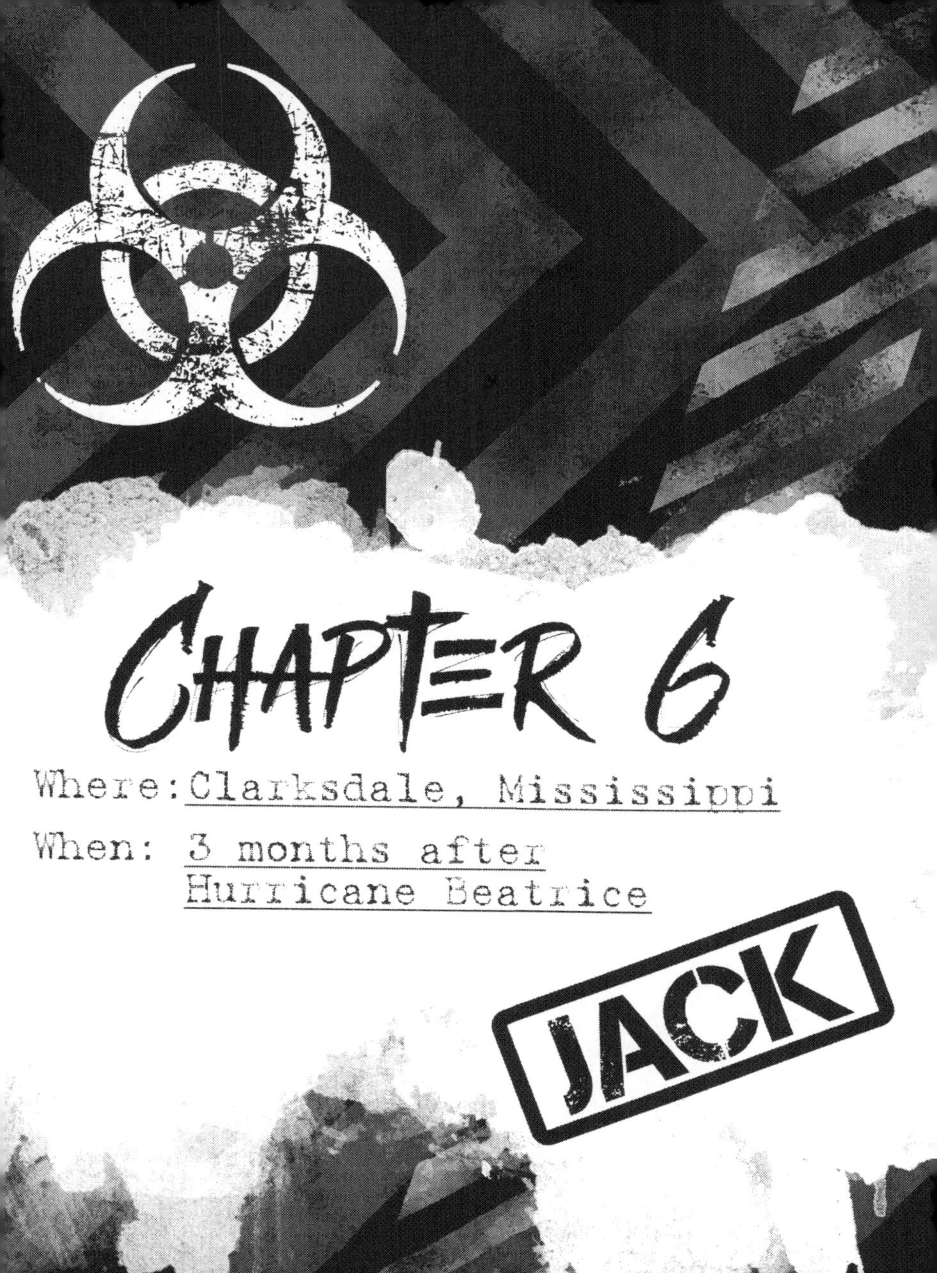

CHAPTER 6

Where: Clarksdale, Mississippi

When: 3 months after Hurricane Beatrice

JACK

JACK

Clarksdale, Mississippi
3 Months after Hurricane Beatrice

"Fuck me, I miss Google," Joel groaned, joining me at the picnic table as he eyed the roadmap I had spread out with hatred and disdain. "And GPS…and oh, hell…McDonald's…"

Snorting, I nodded. "And electricity and phones and refrigeration and…"

"Okay, asshole. I get it. I'm whining."

"Yes. Yes, you are," I agreed without looking up from the route I was trying to plan, though I did shoot a wink to Ava when she giggled.

"I miss microwave popcorn," she piped up, and I grinned her way.

"You can still have popcorn, you know," I told her, and she looked at me like I had three heads. "I'll show you. The next store we stop for supplies, I'll get you popcorn. My son actually likes it better from the stove. I taught him how to make it on the last camping trip we went on."

"No butter," Joel said with a pout.

"Would you shut the hell up?" I snapped almost playfully, rolling my eyes. "I got this. You'll have popcorn. Trust me. It may take a few days, but I'll get it done."

"Sweet," he sang, sharing a fist bump with Ava.

I shook my head, but it was actually nice to have a small moment of normal. Everyone had taken a few days at Lexie's farmhouse to rest. She'd had more than enough supplies, and the area was relatively safe, so we'd opted to stay an extra couple of nights. In all honesty, it was nice to have a roof over our heads, beds or couches to sleep on, and real showers, not to mention Lexie's family were farm owners, which meant they grew, canned, and stocked plenty of their own food. And most of it was already loaded in Ruby's RV.

We'd emptied the regular gas tank on the side of the barn and taken some of the diesel, simply as a lighter fluid. It wouldn't work in the lamps or any of the vehicles, but it did help set dead zeaks on fire, which was how we'd disposed of Lexie's mother and sister.

However, with every night there, my urge to get back on the road made me anxious. It felt wrong to be comfortable when I had no idea about Sara or my son. My eyes studied the map again, but my knee started to bounce. The shit I'd seen since I'd woken up on the base made my imagination, my fears, skyrocket into something I couldn't control. I couldn't shake the thoughts that even if we made it to Clear Lake, they wouldn't be there. Or if they were there, they were no longer…

Crack.

The pencil in my hand snapped in two, and I glared at it for a moment.

"Jack?" Joel called softly. "You okay?"

"Yeah, I just…We need to leave tomorrow. We've stalled long enough." I tossed down the pieces, standing up from the table. "I've marked a route, and I think we'll have enough supplies to get us well into Oklahoma, maybe even Kansas. I'm gonna go check the traps Dad and I put down yesterday."

"Mmm, bunny stew," he hummed, grinning up at me, but it didn't reach his eyes. "Do what you do, Jacky."

"Can I come?" Ava asked.

I nodded, looking to Sasha, who was instantly on her feet. "No, big girl. Stay and watch the house." She plopped down on her haunches, narrowing her eyes at me, but I needed her to guard the ones left behind.

Just as Ava and I passed by the porch, my dad called my name. In his hand was something that made me smirk, reminded me of old times.

"You hoping to give that to Derek?" I asked, smirking at his grin.

"He was always better with this thing than the rest of us," he stated with a nod. "It's Lexie's father's compound bow. Thought maybe you'd want it. The arrows are reusable, at least. We can probably find more along the way."

My eyebrows raised up high because he had a point. "Not to mention silent," I added, taking the weapon from him and turning it over in my hands.

"And silent," my dad echoed, smiling at Ava. "Where're you two headed?"

"Checking traps." She looked rather proud to be going.

"Ah, yes. I'll come with you."

Once he'd grabbed his gun, we stepped out of the yard and into the woods. The trees near the home weren't all that old, but as we stepped farther inside, the canopy above us thickened, almost blocking out the sun. Cicadas droned on and on as the soft, warm breeze rustled through the leaves, and off in the distance, a dog barked, which had me pausing to make sure it wasn't Sasha, although Joel knew to fire his gun should he need us.

When the woods stayed quiet, I kept going, but Ava started chattering, much to my father's amusement.

"Who's Derek?"

"My cousin, but he came to live with us when he was seventeen and I was twelve. He's more like my brother."

"Was he in the Army too?"

"No, he's…was in construction, but he was built for the outdoors—hunting, fishing, camping."

"Where is…Where was…"

Chuckling a little, I helped her out. "He lives in Oregon. Where we're from."

"And that's where we're going?"

"Yes."

"Is he with your wife and son?" she asked, and I flinched. "I'm sorry…"

"Don't be," I muttered, glancing over at my father, who was watching me carefully. I took a deep breath, letting it out slowly. "If *anyone* on this planet can survive this whole thing, it's Derek. And

I'm not sure I trust anyone more to take care of my family. Maybe my father-in-law."

We were quiet for the next few yards, and two out of the three traps had caught rabbits. However, the third trap had caught something we hadn't expected—a zeak.

"Aw, hell," I sighed, pushing Ava back. "Don't go near it."

The zeak was skinny, pulling and pulling at a trap that was attached to the tree next to it. The flesh was literally stripping from his calf. The smell of decay was overwhelming as he saw us and lunged again and again. His death was obvious, with his throat torn open and his jaw hanging slack, but still, he kept reaching for us.

"Not bright, are they?" my dad asked, looking up at me.

Shaking my head, I brought up the compound bow. I took in the empty, feral, lifeless thing. The eyes were muddy, with a hazy glaze over the color, and its skin looked splotchy and sallow, though at some point it could have been olive tone. Lastly, I saw his clothes—coveralls, blue ones. My guess was auto mechanic. But the name on the chest was a slap to the face that, at one point, he'd been someone, a person. He'd been a man with friends, family, responsibilities.

Tom.

Poor Tom had gotten up to go to work one morning. He'd left his family, maybe even kissed his wife and kids good-bye for the day. And then everything went to hell.

"Sorry, Tom," I muttered, setting the arrow loose. It hit the middle of his forehead with a dull thunk. He fell to the forest floor in a heap, and I reached down to pull the arrow free. Holding it up, I looked to Dad. "Good idea."

He nodded but then studied me for a moment. If he thought to say something, he let it go. Finally, he spoke up. "Well, Lexie has potatoes and onions. We should be able to make something with these." He held up our two rabbits.

"Good." I spun on my heel, heading back to the house, and I stayed quiet the whole way back, grateful that we didn't run into any more zeaks along the way.

My mother and Ruby were manning the fire when we walked up, but Ruby's fierce gaze landed on her sister.

"What the hell, Ava? You scared me to death. You don't go anywhere without telling me!"

"I was with Rich and Jack," she argued, pointing to Joel. "Joel knew! I'm not stupid, Ruby! I'm not just gonna run off."

Ruby's gaze landed on me, but I raised my hands. "My bad. Shoulda told you."

"You're damn right."

"Hey!" I snapped. "Relax. We're all on the same side here. She's safe with me, us…all of us."

Ruby sighed, her eyes closing. "I know. I *know!*" She rubbed her face roughly. "Sorry…I just…"

"Panicked. Yeah, I get that. If it had been my kid, I'd have lost my shit too," I told her, leaning the compound bow against the picnic table. "At least you can *see* that she's okay, right?"

"Jack, I'm…" Ruby started, grimacing a little.

"Don't. Just…don't." I walked away, stepping up onto the porch and into the house. It was time to get ready to pull out in the morning, so aside from a change of clothes, I packed up my gear in the room I'd been sleeping in the last two nights.

"You okay?" I heard behind me, and I turned to see Lexie standing in the doorway. I could see that my mother had trimmed her hair up into something not so choppy. Nodding, I turned back to my duffel. "Fine. We're pulling out in the morning, so you might want to get ready. We'll lock this place up as best we can, so you can…"

"I'm ready. I've been ready for like two years," she said with a humorless laugh. "I doubt I'll ever come back here. I didn't exactly fit in with the farm life, ya know?"

Smirking, I nodded again, zipping the bag up and dropping it to the floor.

"I overheard…outside," she said softly, her gaze shifting around to everywhere but me. "You have a kid?"

"Yeah, a son. Freddie."

"Married?" she asked, and my eyes narrowed in on the light blush that bloomed on her cheeks as her gaze fell to my left hand.

"Yes. We've been married for eight years, together two before that. My son turned seven just before all this…" I waved a hand around, but she nodded in understanding.

"What's her name?"

"Sara."

She smiled, though it didn't last long. "Pretty."

I snorted a little. "Yes, she is."

"Do you think…"

"I try very hard *not* to think about what they're going through, Lexie." My voice was firm, almost blunt, but I meant it. It was the blatant fucking truth. "When I *think*, I let my guard down. When I *think*, my imagination shows me a world that I honestly don't want to live in. I'm thirty-three, but I have no desire to start over should something happen to them, especially with the way shit is now."

"That's a sad outlook."

"But it's *my* outlook."

"Did you know? Like the second you saw her?"

Laughing a little at the question that seemed to come from nowhere, I shook my head. "No. We were in school the first time I saw her. It was well after I'd left school and joined the Army that I saw her again. *Then* I knew."

"Why the two years?"

Frowning, I shrugged. "I did a tour overseas. Afghanistan. We were married before I was sent back over. That time, Iraq."

"You were lucky to have come home twice," she stated.

"I was. I'd promised her. And I promised her this time, too. I plan on keeping that promise."

Lexie's face fell a little, and I chose to ignore it. I could see where the line of questioning had been going. I could see it in her body language, hear it in her tone, and feel it in the way she looked at me.

Sara used to tease me all the fucking time about breaking hearts around the world, which I always said was bullshit. Hell, we'd had that conversation the night I asked her to marry me, which had been spur of the moment and slightly panicked but perfect all the same. She used to laugh at me when I couldn't see the women she'd point out, the ones she claimed were "eye-fucking" me, but I saw it. I'd always seen it. It just didn't matter. It hadn't mattered since the day she'd poured me that first beer in Shelly's Bar.

Rubbing my face roughly with my hands, I sighed wearily. God, I just fucking missed my girl. I missed her laugh, her sweet kisses, her arms around me. I missed Sunday mornings when she'd make pancakes for Freddie and me. I missed nights when all three of us were cuddled on the couch, wrapped up in a blanket as we watched whatever cartoon Freddie was obsessed with that week. I missed messy bathrooms, stepping on toys, and hugs when I'd leave for base. I missed tucking my son in at night and making love to my wife when he'd finally crash. I'd give anything to hear her yell about muddy boots or dishes left in the sink or hear Freddie whine when he didn't want broccoli.

"I need some air," I finally said to her, breezing by her in the hallway and rumbling down the stairs.

As pretty as Lexie was and as nice as she seemed to be, I only had eyes for one girl, and I wasn't the type of guy to exploit shit. Again, I was reminded of the night I'd begged Sara to be my wife.

I found my mother sitting at the picnic table. The map was folded, and she was cleaning a few guns. Sitting across from her and cracking my knuckles, I reached to my waistband and pulled out my .45 to do the same, simply to have something to do.

"You have a problem," she stated quietly out of the damn blue, but when I looked at her, her gaze was locked on Lexie, who was coming out of the house.

"No, I really don't."

Mom laughed lightly. "You're so like your father. Blind and stubborn."

"Oh, I know what's up, but I don't consider it a problem."

Mom smirked, shot me a wink, but stayed quiet. We were a lot alike. She knew when silence was better than talking shit out.

As we stayed busy, I gave myself a few minutes to just…think, to remember. My heart ached to revel in my family, but it hurt at the same time. But for just a moment, I wanted to relive the good stuff.

Sandy, Oregon
8 Years Prior

My heart was in my throat as I ran up the steps of Hank Stokes's home. I knocked with one hand and gripped my hair in the other. I grimaced at the fact that I hadn't even changed out of my T-shirt and cargos when I'd left Fort Warner. We'd been running drills all day until we'd been called to a meeting. Though, it was still damn early in the morning.

The door swung open to reveal Sara's dad, who'd given his daughter just about all his features—dark-red hair, deep-blue eyes, and a calm confidence.

"Hank, sir," I greeted with a smile.

"Jack! It's good to see you, son," he said, nodding once and reaching for my hand. "You're early, I think. You may send our girl into a frenzy."

Grinning, I nodded. "Sorry. I was relieved ahead of schedule."

He patted my shoulder, his mouth curling into a smirk. "And you ran like the wind. I understand. How're your parents?"

"Good, sir. They're both still at the naval hospital."

"Tell them I said hello, would'ja?" he asked, but we both looked up when light steps rushed down the stairs.

"Jack!" Sara squealed, beaming like the sunniest of days. "You're early!"

She was off the bottom step and into my arms before either of us really could think, which caused Hank to chuckle and mutter to himself about being wrong. He was a good man, firm and quiet but kind. When I'd finally spoken to him of Brody Matthews, he'd thanked me and told me he'd threatened the boy's life...and freedom. Apparently he'd almost had Matthews arrested by his good friend, Chief Robbins. On what charges, I had no idea. Maybe drunk in public. He'd told me that the only thing that stopped him was Brody's dad—Leo had promised to handle the situation. It had worked for the most part, but occasionally we'd run into the bastard in a store or the diner or someplace in town, and he'd act like an asshole all over again. Mostly verbal, but I was pretty sure he remembered me putting him on his ass. I'd do it again, if needed.

"I've been given a few days leave," I told her, setting her on her feet as I swallowed back my panic. "I needed to talk to you, Shortcake."

She smiled and nodded, taking my hand. "C'mon into the kitchen. There's coffee. Want some, Dad?" she asked him, and I smiled at the way she took care of him, even when he acted like he didn't want her to fuss.

"Oh, I'm good, baby girl." He picked his mug up off the table and took a sip before handing her the cup. "I've got to head into the fire station anyway. You two have a good day."

"Sir." I nodded once, shaking his hand again.

Sara tugged my other hand, letting go once we were in the kitchen. She rinsed out her dad's cup to pour coffee for herself, asking, "Want some?"

"Please."

I sat down at the kitchen table, cracking my knuckles nervously and thanking her when she handed me a mug. Once she sat across from me, I just looked at her. Jesus, she was beautiful. Even dressed casually at home in shorts and a T-shirt—though, it was my Army T-shirt—she was just gorgeous. The morning sun beamed in through the kitchen window, showing off reddish highlights beautifully. Her skin was creamy, smooth, free of makeup, but Sara didn't need makeup. It was those dark-blue eyes I took in last. They were sweet, sharp, and still a touch sleepy, but she looked at me with love and trust and just…everything.

"I love you," I blurted out, smiling when she laughed lightly. "I do."

"Love you too, baby." She got up from her chair and sat cross-ways in my lap, kissing my lips softly. "Now, you look upset about something. Wanna tell me about it?"

Abandoning my coffee, I chose to wrap my arms around her, kissing her shoulder, then her cheek. It was so damn easy with her. It had been since the beginning. Even going overseas had been tolerable, simply because her words, her voice, her beautiful pictures had come with me. They'd been the beacon of light at the end of a long, scary tunnel. That thought made me sigh. I inhaled the scent of her, closing my eyes at how fucking awful this could go.

"Jack, you're scaring me," she whispered.

"I'm scaring me too," I mumbled against her cheek, only to pull back and cup her face. "I have…I got new orders this morning."

My heart broke at the color that drained from her sweet face.

"Where?" she barely uttered aloud.

"Iraq."

The word hung in the room like a fog for a moment, and I watched as she steeled herself, saw her determination to get through it settle over her. She nodded as her eyes lifted from my dog tags that she was playing with up to my face.

"How long?"

"Probably like last time. Six or seven months," I answered her as honestly as I could.

She let out a long breath, swallowing nervously, but she smiled and cupped my face. "Okay, we'll get through it like last time. When do you leave?"

I smiled at her bravery. I wasn't buying a bit of it, but she was my amazing girl giving it her best shot. "Next week."

"Are you on leave until then? Like last time? You know, to get your stuff in order?"

"Mmhmm," I hummed, finally pulling her to me and hugging her tight.

I closed my eyes at the feelings that washed over me. She was it for me. She was home and happiness and comfort all rolled up into one beautiful, petite, blue-eyed package. At twenty-four, almost twenty-five, I knew what I wanted. Her. That was it. Suddenly, the thought of leaving her was unbearable. And the thought of leaving her and not coming back was fucking torture. I wanted to take care of her, love her for the rest of my life. I knew it as well as I knew my own damn name.

"Marry me," I blurted out, smiling when she gasped and pulled back to look at me. "Marry me. Marry me before I leave so I can take care of you, even when I'm gone. You…You're almost finished with school, but you could take more classes if you wanted, or take your time finding the job you want. You could stay here safe with Hank and only work for Shelly when you want to, but you…Fuck, Sara, you're it for me. Marry me, and I'll come back and really take care of you."

Her face was incredulous but ridiculously adorable. "You want to marry me *before* you leave?"

"Yes! I know…I know it sounds insane, but I mean it, Shortcake. You're all I want." I shrugged, not knowing what else to say. "I did this all wrong, I know. I don't even have a ring, but I didn't exactly plan this shit."

Her giggle was like music. "Okay…yes!"

My eyes widened, and my heart stopped, only to sputter into racing beats. "Yeah?"

"Yes," she said firmly, nodding that beautiful head of hers.

Suddenly, I felt guilty, and I held her face in my hands as I kissed her until we both needed air. "I can't…I can't give you the big wedding, but we can…I mean, when I come home…" I kissed her again. "I *will* come home to you."

"You can't make that promise, and I don't need a big wedding, Jack. I just want you to be safe over there, okay?"

Smiling, I nodded. "With you…as my *wife*…I can do anything."

She squeaked, grinning and shifting on my lap until she was straddling me. "I like that."

I began to laugh as my head fell back, but it all turned into a hum when her warm lips pressed to my throat in a smiling kiss. "Me too, Shortcake…"

We lost ourselves for a second, right there in her dad's kitchen. Long, deep, claiming kisses left me wanting her with a fire in my belly and a pressure in my cargos, which she shamelessly rubbed against. My hands searched out skin and ticklish places that usually made her moan sexily, and I wasn't disappointed. The sounds she emitted were amazing and more of a turn-on for me than skimpy lingerie. Before shit really got out of hand, I pulled back, sweeping my lips over hers softly, smiling when her forehead thumped to mine.

"We should just…do this. Courthouse…like now."

Her laugh made me smile. "I agree, but I want my dad there… and your parents. And don't you want Joel and Derek there?"

Wrinkling my nose, I nodded. "I do, but I don't want to waste this week, baby. I want to go to the cabin once we're married."

She smiled. "Yeah, definitely."

That smile was easy and sexy and all mine, making my hands skim down her back and into her shorts as I cupped her ass. Fuck me, she had a sweet ass—in and out of whatever she was wearing.

"But for now…"

"But for now, you're gonna take me up to my room, Mr. Chambers," she commanded, laughing when I stood up from the table.

I kept her in my arms as she wrapped her legs around my waist. "Hank will kill me."

"He's at the station. Just love me, Jack."

I was stupidly happy that she wanted to marry me. My laugh and teasing couldn't be contained, even with my approaching tour of duty overseas. If I had Sara, I'd do anything to get back to her.

We made love more than once in her bed. The first time was silly and playful, with tickles and grins, teasing about hearts breaking everywhere, but the second time was intense, with a realization of what was ahead—a huge step for us and my leaving. When we came together, it was eye to eye, at the same time, and with emotions swirling. I didn't want her to cry, but she wasn't the only one who felt the pull, the fear, and I held her until we were both calmer and could talk details.

We wanted the courthouse and a few days at the cabin at Clear Lake. We wanted a few days of just us. When we finally came up for air, we called Hank and my family. They were surprised at the rush of it but happy for us nonetheless. However, in order to have all of them there, we had to forgo a real, true honeymoon. Instead, we spent our first night as husband and wife at a hotel just outside of Portland, barely leaving the bed.

I came out of that memory with a gasp when someone handed me a bowl. Reality blurred back into clarity, and I took the rabbit stew with a small smile at Ruby, only to stare at my meal.

My vow to Sara before I'd left was that I'd give her the honeymoon we both had truly wanted when I came home, and it would be a graduation present for her at the same time. Those four days had been the best of my fucking life. As I gazed around at the people around me, at the reality of my situation, I shook my head, wishing for a time machine. I'd go back to that second honeymoon at Clear Lake and never come up for air.

I took a big bite of stew, which was damn good, smirking a little. It wasn't long after I'd come home from Iraq that Sara had gotten pregnant with Freddie.

Someone nudged my elbow, and I glanced over to see Ruby watching me. She squeezed my arm. "I'm sorry, Jack. About before. I can't…I can't imagine what you're going through. When my parents died, they left Ava in my care, so…I get a little overprotective."

I huffed a laugh, shaking my head. "No worries. You sound like Sara. She's the same way. She'd wrap our son in bubble wrap if she could."

Ruby chuckled. "Oh, I can't wait to meet her."

Smiling, I took several more bites before standing up from the table. "I hope you get the chance."

Dodge City, Kansas
3 Months & 2 Weeks after Hurricane Beatrice

"It's best to go in on foot from here," I said, shutting off the engine of the old car we'd taken off the highway. I gazed around the rail yard that skirted the edge of the city. All seemed to be clear, but zeaks could be anywhere.

We needed supplies—food, water, and maybe ammo, though the latter wasn't too bad. Joel had gotten really damn good at using that Marine sword of his, and I tended to use the compound bow when we needed to stay silent. The other two with us, however, were better with guns than more up-close weapons.

"Ruby, you and Joel look for clothes, oil for the cars, and anything in the hardware stores that we may need. Lexie and I will scope out food," I told them, getting out of the cab and reaching for my weapons in the bed of the truck. "Water may have to wait until we get into Colorado, but I'll see what we can find."

Personally, I didn't want to split us up, but we needed to get into the city and out as quickly as possible. I also knew that Joel wouldn't want Ruby out of his sight, simply because they were growing closer and closer with every mile we traveled. And that left me with Lexie.

The former farm girl may have been a tiny thing—shorter than my Sara by at least a couple of inches—but she could handle a gun and could move pretty damn fast when needed.

Unfortunately, being with Lexie also meant brushing off starry-eyed stares and flirty smiles. Ruby found it annoying, Joel thought it was hilarious, and my mother's theory was that it was hero worship, considering I'd saved her life at her house. Personally, I had no patience for it, but we had to work together, no matter what her misguided feelings were, because my parents were needed back at our camp to watch over Ava. Sasha was with them. She was needed there more than with us, though I had become dependent on her help… and company, if I were being honest with myself. So Lexie it was.

We walked together, stepping over train tracks, and I caught sight of a small building.

"Here," I stated to all of them, pointing to the shed-sized building. "Two hours, we'll meet right back here. No staying out in the open." I glanced up at the sky that was growing more and more purplish-gray by the minute. "And we picked a fucked-up time to come into a town, that's for damn sure."

As if to prove my point, thunder rolled long and low, and the temperature dropped with the breeze that blew through the train yard. Once that rain started to fall, any and all zeaks would be even deadlier than they usually were.

We left the more industrial side of the city behind, getting closer and closer to town. The problem with cities any bigger than the little shit towns we'd been driving through was the population. More people meant more zeaks. More people also meant assholes protecting the meager shit they had left. On the flip side of that, bigger cities also meant better opportunities for supplies, with chain stores and restaurants. Dodge City wasn't a metropolis, but it was a grid-like layout of houses upon houses, spread out over flat land. I could see a few of the infected wandering in and around doors and parking lots, but luckily, they were too far away to notice us.

It had been a long, hard road since we'd left Lexie's farm. It had taken two full weeks to get through Arkansas and around Tulsa, though we'd been able to hunt for food a few times. We still had some of the canned goods that Lexie had brought with her, but we needed more. There were seven of us now, so the food went quicker.

"Oh." I turned to Lexie. "We need dog food."

She smiled and nodded, but her eyes were on our surroundings.

A major road loomed closer, and Joel caught sight of it. "What'cha think old Wyatt Earp would think of his shit?" he asked, pointing to the Wyatt Earp Boulevard road sign and then the crawling fucker under a bus bench.

"Which one?" Lexie asked softly. "If you're talking Kurt Russell's version in *Tombstone*, he'd probably kick ass and take names. If it's Kevin Costner's, then…we'd be fucked."

Ruby snorted into a chuckle. "Only if we get Val Kilmer's Doc Holiday."

"No shit." I nodded, smiling in spite of the smell around us. The stench of zeaks was growing stronger, as was the feel of impending rain. It made me fucking nervous, which proved valid the very second we stepped around the corner.

I'd never seen so many fucking zeaks all in one place. They crowded the streets, sidewalks, and storefronts. It looked like a crowd waiting for a parade. The four of us froze midstep, not one of us saying a word. Just as the front few caught sight of us, big fat raindrops splattered to the concrete in front of us.

"Oh, fucking hell," Joel barely breathed aloud, giving me a side-glance. "We're gonna move in five seconds, and we're going in the back doors of these stores. No splitting up."

We all nodded, and the sky opened up like buckets of water being dumped out. The sound of pouring rain was overshadowed by the snarls and growls the zeaks let loose. Our scent and the sight of us sent them into a collective stampede.

"Now!" I snapped, turning the first corner and aiming for the closest building. The back door was unlocked, so we rushed inside, slamming it closed behind us, just in time to feel the zeaks pounding from the other side.

Lexie reached by me, turning several deadbolt locks closed. "That will stall them for a moment."

Nodding, I pulled the compound bow around to my front. I'd had it strapped across my back, but we didn't know what was inside the building. Giving the place an assessing glance, it seemed we'd stumbled into a restaurant.

"Perfect," I sighed, jerking my chin as I held out bags. "This'll take longer, but we'll stick together. Take whatever food you can find."

We found a few really large cans of vegetables, a few sacks of rice, and several boxes of instant mashed potatoes. All would be put to use. Joel hoisted the bag to his shoulder, approaching the swinging door from the kitchen to the dining room. He nudged it open slowly, peeking through the crack. He held up a hand, showing four fingers as he looked to me and pulled his sword out at the same time.

We silently told the girls to stay put and then pushed our way into the dining room. The zeaks moved as one, already showing the increased strength and hearing the rain seemed to give them. Three men and one woman—the latter barely able to walk due to the broken ankle she was sporting. It was twisted and gnarled, and she limped my way, so I lifted the compound bow, taking her out. The other three reached for Joel as I reloaded another arrow. He swung the sword in a wide arc, taking two, and I finished off the last one. My arrow lodged in his skull, essentially nailing him to the wall. Blood, black as pitch, decorated the wallpaper in a splash.

The large windows facing the street showed the rain coming down in almost sideways sheets, but it also showed a swarm of zeaks pounding on the glass.

"That glass ain't gonna hold. Ladies, we gotta move!" I ordered, taking back my arrows and pointing to the hallway off to the side.

Joel pushed through a doorway, taking out a lingering zeak and aiming for the emergency exit. The sign warning about an alarm was ignored as he barreled through it. An old bell-type, battery-powered alarm started to ring, which was a blessing and a curse. It drew more zeaks in, giving us a chance to cross to the next building, but a few saw us, following us right to the door.

Lexie and Ruby had no choice but to aim and fire, the gunfire louder than any alarm. Once we were inside, we barricaded the door with a desk, stepping slowly through a hallway and into the front of a store. It seemed to be a small gift shop, but we grabbed a few shirts, some lighters, and I stowed a bag of candy for Ava in my bag.

I walked to the windows, nodding that the zeaks still seemed drawn to the ringing bell next door, when my eyes landed on a building across the street.

"Joel," I called softly, waving him forward. "What are the chances that anything's left?"

He studied the police outpost, not to mention the hunting store next to it that was sealed up tight with roll-down metal doors. He wiped his sweat- and rain-covered face on the sleeve of his shirt, sighing wearily. "I don't know. If shit went to hell this quickly, we may find a few things."

Nodding, I gauged the odds of making it across the street, through the crowd of zeaks still wandering the main strip, and getting inside safely. Going in the front was out, simply because we couldn't break into the metal security doors, so the alleyway next to it was our only shot. My eyes landed on our saving grace: fire escape.

I spun in front of them. "Listen, we're gonna move and move fucking fast. We're not going in the front. You aim straight for the alley and up those stairs. Take out only the zeaks in your way, only those that pose an immediate threat. There's no stopping all of them. Got me?"

The girls nodded, and Joel watched the street as he slowly and silently turned the lock on the front door of the gift shop.

He shot a glance back. "I'll go first. Jack, take our six. On three... Three, two, one..." He yanked open the door, sword at the ready as he took out three zeaks before he even stepped off the sidewalk. Lexie was next, and she was so damn fast and small that she was able to duck and weave through a few, only shooting twice. Ruby was next, and she cleared her way with four shots, and I followed right behind her, opting for my .45 instead of my compound bow, simply because I couldn't afford to leave arrows behind.

The metal steps of the fire escape squeaked and rattled under protest of our weight, but they held until we reached the rooftop.

The sound of a shotgun being engaged caused all of us to snap to attention. Ruby's .45, along with my own and Lexie's rifle, all aimed on instinct, cocked and at the ready. One gun versus three, not to mention a really large man with a long sword raised to remove the hands that held the gun, meant the odds were in our favor.

The shotgun lowered, and my adrenaline calmed just enough that I could see its owner for what he really was.

"Jesus Christ, he's just a kid," I breathed, lowering my weapon just a little, though the girls didn't budge.

"Fuck, dude, you almost got your head chopped off," Joel snapped, shaking his head, though I noticed he didn't lower the sword.

The boy couldn't have been more than eighteen, if he was a day. He had dark hair and blueish-green eyes that were wide with fear. He was just as soaked as the rest of us as we stood out in that pouring rain. But his eyes fell to Joel's chest and then mine.

"Military? Are there more of you?"

I glanced down, seeing my dog tags through my wet T-shirt, but shook my head. "There is no more military, kid. Trust me," I told him, watching what little hope he'd built up fade away like smoke in the wind. "Are you alone?"

He shifted, his eyes glancing around.

"Dude, dude, dude...We're not here to fuck with you," Joel soothed, finally dropping the sword to his side. "We just needed some supplies before we..." He rolled his eyes my way, wearing a smirk. "Before we got the hell out of Dodge."

The kid snorted, and the girls merely looked at Joel with wry, blank stares.

"Really?" I asked, narrowing my eyes on him. "You've been waiting to use that since we decided to come here, haven't you?"

Joel grinned, shrugging a shoulder.

"For fuck's sake..." I sighed, shaking my head and turning back to the boy. "We're not here to hurt anyone..."

"There's no one to hurt," he countered, wearing a dark expression. "I mean, there's a group of people using the zoo as a safe place, due to the fences and shit, but..." He shook his head. "They're pretty fucked up. I saw some women get assaulted, they've hoarded most of the booze, and they're armed to the fucking teeth. I couldn't stay there. You go near there, and they'll take everything you've got." He pointed to the rooftop before wiping away the rain from his face. "I offered to come here for more ammo a few days ago, but I didn't go back. Let them think I got turned or something."

Ruby's face softened, and she looked to me before asking, "What's your name?"

"Raymond Quincy, but everyone calls me Quinn."

"'Kay, Quinn," Ruby greeted, telling the kid our names. "Is there anything left downstairs?"

He nodded, waving us on. "Yeah, and you can have it. The less those assholes have, the better. I'm not sure what's worse: the dead or the idiots in the damn zoo." He led us through the roof door and down into the store. "There's nothing in the police station. I busted a vending machine in order to eat the last few days. The hunting store...That's a different story. There's plenty of shit in here."

Stepping into the room was an ammo fucking dream, and I huffed a laugh to myself as I gazed around. "How in the fuck did this go untouched?"

Quinn smiled, pointing to the windows. "Those roll-down doors, man. The owner closed this place up tighter than a frog's pussy... and that's water tight." He grinned at the girls' laughter but went on. "Anyway, he was like one of the first people to get..."

"Outta Dodge...See? That shit works here," Joel added, glancing up from the glass case.

"And already old," Lexie sang, shaking her head.

"Whatever," Quinn said with a chuckle. "That street out there was a clusterfuck when everything truly went crazy, which happened to be at rush hour on a Friday afternoon. Most of these stores are untouched because those dead assholes tend to crowd the street… like you so obviously found out. And you'll have a bitch of a time getting back the way you came."

"I know," I muttered, taking as many boxes of bullets I could get.

We raided the place, and Quinn stayed quiet, content to watch us. I was able to grab not only a bag of loose popcorn and oil that I'd promised Ava but a couple of bags of dog food. We took everything, from canteens to more arrows for the compound bow. Knives, guns, and flares also made it into bags. Even the girls were able to stock up on toilet paper and the feminine shit they needed, which caused Joel to run away and me to roll my eyes at his idiocy. We'd have a bitch of a time carrying it, but we needed all of it.

"How many of you are there?" he asked once we'd set the bags down.

"Seven total," Joel answered, turning a small propane tank over in his hands, only to reach for a bottle of kerosene on the shelf. He turned to me. "We could use these…" He pointed to the shelf of insulated bottles and then a rack of shirts. "Bombs. Small ones. Toss them at the zeaks to clear the way."

"I've got something that'll help you," Quinn told us, waving us toward a back storage room, only…that wasn't the case when he opened the door. "These bad boys could get you out."

Stepping inside the door, I grinned at the small showroom of ATVs—four-wheelers, three-wheelers, and small trailers that could be pulled by the former. Fuel would have been my next question, but Quinn yanked up a tarp.

"Oh my fucking hell…" I turned to Joel. "Fuel up the two four-wheelers, only take one trailer for all our shit, including those gas cans. Then we need to put together a few bombs to use out in the street. Let's go."

We all broke to get to work, but Quinn's voice brought us up short.

"You'll need someone to guide you out of here." When we only stared at him, his true age came through—a nervous, scared kid. "My…family is gone. I…I don't want to go back to the zoo…and I'm…I can hunt and fish. I'll pull my weight, I swear. But…just don't…"

"Whoa…slow down, kid," Joel said, smirking my way. "What'cha think, Jacky?"

I sighed, running a hand through my still-damp hair. "It's another mouth to feed but another gun too."

The human being, the *father* in me knew I couldn't leave the kid behind, and the soldier knew that the more numbers we had, the safer we'd be, but we'd be taking responsibility for this kid. I also knew that his being a local meant he could skirt us around the zeak swarm outside.

"You got any shit to bring?" I asked him, and he nodded fervently. "Go get it. Move your ass because I want those doors up and open in two minutes. We're gonna haul ass out of here." Before he could leave the room, I stopped him. "And Quinn, you'll listen to us when we tell you something. I won't be responsible for you getting yourself killed. Got me?"

He swallowed nervously but nodded again. "Yeah, yeah…got it."

Once he was out of the room, Ruby mumbled, "Can't leave him." She shrugged, helping Lexie pour kerosene into bottles and stuff soaked rags into the tops. "Wouldn't be right."

"You mean like how we didn't leave you behind," I teased her, ducking the empty bottle she tossed my way as Joel and I attached a small trailer to the back of the four-wheeler.

"Why, yes, jackass. That's exactly what I meant."

Lexie chuckled, then sobered. "It's a new world now. You'd think we'd be better than what he's describing at that zoo, but…apparently, this has still split us. Good humans versus bad humans."

"I guess that makes us the good guys," I grunted as I filled the trailer with all our bags and supplies.

No one said anything, but Quinn reappeared with a backpack and a guitar case, not to mention a garbage bag full of shit he'd pulled from the vending machine he'd mentioned earlier. He tossed it all in the trailer, getting in on top.

"I'll light those," he said, pointing to the bottles. "You just drive and turn when I tell you."

"All right," I agreed, straddling the seat and starting it up.

Ruby started the other one, and Lexie climbed in with Quinn. Both readied themselves with a bottle. Joel stepped to the garage door, reaching down to lift it up. We were lucky that the back alley was empty, and as soon as Joel straddled the seat behind Ruby, we pulled out.

We were clear until we needed to cross Wyatt Earp Boulevard. Quinn called out right and left, guiding us through the back streets, but that main drag was a walking, stalking nightmare. Hundreds of zeaks turned on us, feral and wild as the rain soaked us to the bone.

"Light 'em up!" I called over my shoulder, and two bottles flew over my head, smashing into the street. It caused a temporary wall of fire that blocked the zeaks' way, not to mention that it set several on fire. "Fucking perfect," I murmured to myself as I watched the kerosene essentially stick to them and create a chain reaction of fire.

Quinn called more directions out, and I could finally breathe again when the rail yard loomed closer.

Turning to Ruby, I yelled, "Fuck the car. Leave it. We'll stay on these back to camp. It's only a few miles anyway."

She nodded, grinning my way. "Race you."

With a laugh, I let her take the lead. I had too much weight holding me back, with the trailer and an extra passenger, though Joel probably weighed what Quinn and Lexie did combined…and then some. We skirted the edge of the highway in order to avoid the traffic jams, and I could see Ruby's RV in the distance as the rain started to let up. We'd taken refuge in the parking lot of a rundown roadside diner. It didn't have shit in it, but it was shelter for a bit. Hopefully it had kept my parents, Ava, and Sasha safe while we'd been gone. When all of the above stepped out the doors, I sighed a breath of relief, mentally calculating just how much farther we had to go—four or five more states, several hundred miles…and who knew what we'd run into along the way. At the rate we were going, we were looking at another month on the road…at least.

The only thing I knew for sure was that I wasn't stopping until I got to Clear Lake. The end of the damn world, the endless zeaks, and the long drive…none of it was worrying me as much as finding my family.

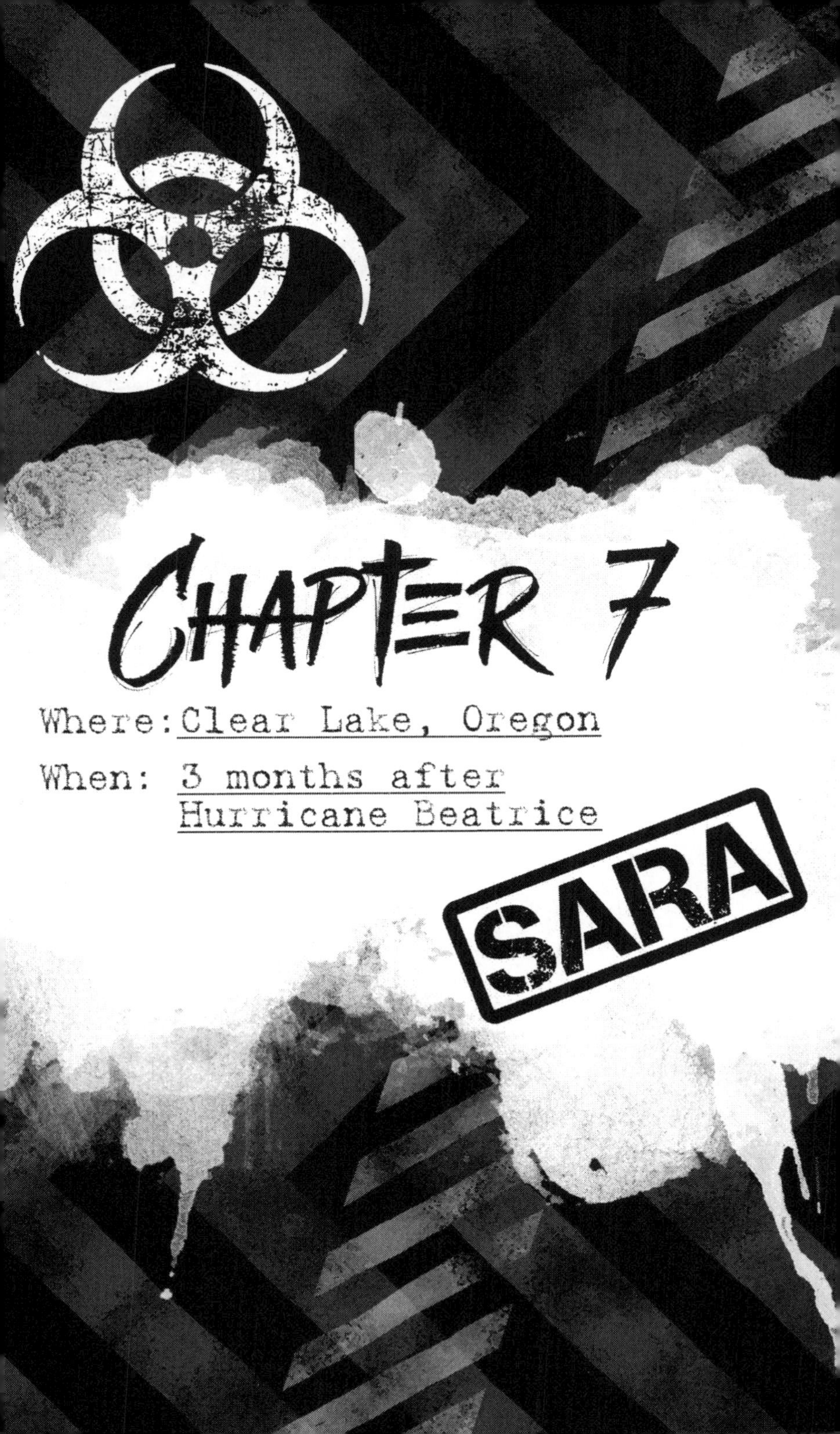
CHAPTER 7
Where: Clear Lake, Oregon
When: 3 months after Hurricane Beatrice
SARA

SARA

Clear Lake, Oregon
3 Months & 3 Weeks after Hurricane Beatrice

"That's what I'm talkin' 'bout!" Derek praised, and I glanced up from the fish I was cleaning to watch him across the small lake with Freddie, who was beaming proudly. "Do it again," he told him, helping him steady the small-caliber rifle.

My boy followed every one of Derek's instructions, from how to stand and aim, to the final shot. They were shooting at tin cans and bottles Derek had set up on the wooden posts of the partially built fence he was working on when he could find the supplies. The pop of the gun rattled around the lake, as did the sound of glass breaking. Again, Freddie reminded me so much of Jack, with the fierce look of determination on his face, to the proud, crooked smile he gave Derek when he'd done well, to the cracking of his knuckles as he prepared for another shot—he was his father made over.

The noise was dangerous but necessary. Derek had put off teaching them until they drove him crazy. At least the rifles were only .22s, so the sound wasn't too bad. Plus, Derek wasn't taking chances, keeping his compound bow within reach.

I smiled again when Freddie stepped back to allow Janie a turn at it, which made the woman next to me groan.

Chuckling, I glanced over at Tina. "You can say no."

"Hell no, I can't," she sighed, rolling her eyes at my laugh. "First of all, she's determined to learn. Second, as much as I hate to say this… she *needs* to know." She took a deep breath and let it out. "God, I hate it, but the world has changed." Her nose wrinkled. "Her father would never have allowed it, but he's not here, and I want her to be strong, able to defend herself. Jerry had some antiquated ideas about women. It had started to become an issue between us. I wanted more for Janie than what I'd done."

Frowning over at her, I said, "There's absolutely nothing wrong with being a wife and mother. Not everyone works."

She snorted and nodded, finishing the fish in front of her before looking my way again. "No, there's not, and I'm very glad I got all that time with Janie, but there were times…"

I nodded in understanding. "Times when you wanted more?" I asked, and she nodded. "Jack never cared. He was a pretty big cheerleader when I was in college. In fact, he urged me to take more classes, if that's what I wanted. He always told me that even though he was too stubborn to go, it didn't mean he couldn't support me."

Tina grinned. "Stubborn?"

"On some things, yeah. As long as we were safe, happy, and healthy, Jack was content. If those things were threatened, then he'd break his neck to simply…*fix* it." My eyes fell on Brody walking across the camp. "And don't even get me started on his feelings concerning Brody."

Tina laughed lightly. "Well, Jack and I would get along just fine, then."

I snorted into a giggle that I couldn't stop, leaning into her. "Jesus, please don't judge me on my past boyfriend."

"Never!" she called out in hysterics.

Still laughing lightly, we went back to work. Leo had taken the kids fishing that morning, so there were plenty to clean, which meant everyone would eat well tonight.

Carol joined us, setting a bowl down. "Look what I found!" she claimed cheerfully. "Cornmeal. I mixed in some spices, so it should taste good once we bread these guys."

We worked together, chatting about nothing in particular. Freddie's and Janie's laughter made us smile. Derek's patience seemed endless, but I was pretty sure that ran in their family. Jack's parents, Rich and Dottie, had always been calm and easygoing, and so was Jack. None of them seemed to panic in the heat of the moment.

My dad's cabin door opened, and Leo rolled out in his wheelchair, with Brody pushing him. Josh followed close behind, and they all made their way to the table.

I smiled over at Leo once he situated himself at the table, leaning into his kiss to my cheek and ignoring his son.

"Sara," Brody said, and I looked up at him. "Josh and I are going to check the traps we put out yesterday. If we've caught anything, we'll need to get it in so those infected bastards don't get it. Plus, we caught sight of a few cabins on the ridge, so we're going to scope those out."

"You're not taking Josh," Millie called out from the lake. "He's got schoolwork to do before Martin's next session. The world may have gone crazy, but he still needs math."

Josh looked like he was about to argue, but Martin stepped up with a smile. He reminded me so much of Rich. He was mellow and smart, determined to keep some sort of civility in the camp. He was always talking about books he'd read, his favorite eras in history, and possible solutions for how things had changed.

"I'll go with you, Brody," he offered, shouldering his shotgun. "Besides, Josh seriously needs to work on his algebra."

Josh grumbled under his breath but sat down on the other side of Carol, who said, "I don't know, Martin. It's getting late in the day..."

"We'll be fine, sweetheart."

"Well, I want you back before dark. I'm not kidding, mister," she told him, and he agreed before kissing her cheek.

"Are you *sure* you should go now? You'll be leaving us down two people," I pointed out.

"It'll be fine," Brody assured, pointing toward Derek. "Besides, Grizzly Adams is teaching the offspring how to shoot. Soon, he'll be killing these dead bastards like the rest of us. Won't *Daddy* be proud?"

I bit my tongue, but Leo didn't.

"Brody, if I could walk, I'd punt your ass into that lake over yonder. You truly need to let the past go, which means Freddie and Derek. Sarah's right; you're leaving us weak should a pack come through."

"We could go first thing in the morning, Brody," Martin offered.

"An hour...two at most, 'kay?" Brody countered, shaking his head. "We'll be back before dark. I don't want to lose anything in those traps, and I'm hoping to find ammo in some of these old hunting cabins.

What we really need to do is head down to Klamath Lake, but we don't have the numbers for that. This, I trust, you guys can handle."

His sarcasm was sharp, but he had a point. We needed ammo, and we couldn't afford to lose any future meals.

"Just…go, Brody." I sighed, waving him away, and looked to Martin. "Be careful."

"Will do, Sara," he agreed, and then he turned to follow Brody around the lake.

They stopped to speak to Derek, whose face was not happy about the new turn of events, but he nodded before shaking his head and going back to Janie and Freddie.

"My apologies, Sara, for my son," Leo said softly.

I tsked, rolling my eyes. "You should stop doing that, Leo. It feels like you've been apologizing for him his whole life. He's said it too, though now I'm not sure he meant it. He's hated me a long time."

Leo laughed. "Hated you? Oh, no, sweet girl. He doesn't hate you. He's been kicking himself for well over ten years. He's pissed off at himself."

Grimacing, I shook my head, though it was amusing to see everyone interested in where this conversation was going. "We'd have been miserable, Leo. Brody had problems being faithful."

"No, he had problems staying sober."

"Bullshit!" I snapped, glaring his way. "I've been drunk, Leo. I've been damn drunk while my husband was overseas, and not *one time* did cheating enter my mind. So don't blame the alcohol; blame the man. Blame the man who laughed when I caught him with Jessica Parham in the office of the garage, the one who practically stalked me at Shelly's Bar. He sent his friends in to watch me. And the only reason I met Jack was because your son showed up fall-down drunk when his buddies called him. They'd told him I was hitting on a guy at the bar. Which I was," I said with a grin to Tina. "Jack was too much to resist. Brody showed up, acting like an ass, and Jack put him on the floor."

Tina laughed, putting her hands together. "Dear Lord," she prayed dramatically, looking up to the sky above. "Please, *please* let me see that event unfold again someday."

In her own way, Tina was also praying for Jack's safe return, but damn, she was funny. She'd quickly become one of the best friends I'd ever had. She was smart, calm, but knew how to lighten things up, and while she'd told me her marriage to Jerry wasn't perfect, she was one hell of a mom.

I turned back to Leo, my amusement fading. "You're my dad's friend, and I love and respect that, but your son is a different story. He does and says whatever he wants, no matter who it hurts. Alcohol or not, he has no one to blame but himself for the way his life turned out. Even now, with all this shit going on."

At the mention of my dad, an ancient sadness, laced with worry, etched over Leo's face. It was an unspoken thing between us. My dad had promised us he'd follow us to Clear Lake, but the longer time went on, the more we were convinced he wasn't coming, and that only made my worry for Jack spark into a raging inferno. To speak of "what if" was too hard for any one of us when it came to family we had left out there in the world.

I locked eyes with Leo, who merely said, "Your dad's tough."

Nodding, I said nothing and went back to work. Once the fish were cleaned, breaded, and ready to fry, I cleaned my hands off in the lake on the way over to see Derek and the kids. I grinned at my son when he immediately started to ramble.

"Mom! Did'joo see? I took out three bottles and a can!" he gushed, rushing to me, and Derek snatched the rifle out of his hands on the way by.

"I saw, buddy," I said, cupping his face until it squished. I kissed his forehead and then pooched lips, finally letting go. "You are a sharpshooter there, partner." Smirking, I tilted my head at him. "Smile, Freddie." When he did, I chuckled. "Well, looky there. Is that…a *loose tooth?*"

He nodded, wiggling it with his tongue. "Yuth," he said, his tongue causing him to lisp.

My heart ached at the steps my son was taking without Jack here to see it. He'd already lost the front top and bottom teeth, which Jack had seen, but now more were loose. He was growing by leaps and bounds every day, and he was changing and learning and doing things I wanted to share with his father. And it was killing me.

"Oh, ho!" Derek sang, coming to stand with me. "Looks like the Tooth Fairy will be visiting soon." I could tell as soon as he said it, he regretted it. Not only was money a long-lost thing, but the Tooth Fairy would've been Jack and me, and that wasn't possible either.

"I bet the Tooth Fairy's a zombie," Janie muttered, frowning down at her hands. "And Santa too."

I met Derek's gaze, and he mouthed, *Sorry.*

Shaking my head, I let out a deep breath. "Oh, guys…Hey, I know a secret. I know that Santa and the Tooth Fairy are protected by magic, so they're safe. Don't you worry."

The kids looked at me like they didn't quite believe me but as if they *really* wanted to. I was just about to tell them they needed to get cleaned up for dinner, but movement caught my eye just behind Derek.

Glancing up, my heart stopped, but I pulled out my gun. "Derek," I whispered, jerking my chin.

He reacted instantly, pushing Janie and Freddie toward me and rushing to the fence post, where his compound bow stood propped up. A dozen or so infected stepped from the edge of the trees, and Derek ran back to us. He handed the kids the rifles they'd been using.

"Get them to Rich's cabin. Now, Sara!" he ordered, pushing us until we started to run.

As we made our way around the side of the small lake, with the pack of dead following us, screams and gunshots rang out by the cabins.

The pack was enormous, and it was coming in from the north and east sides of the lake clearing, which meant they were migrating in from Portland and most likely OR-26. I saw several stumble around from behind all the cabins, weaving their way toward Leo, Carol, Josh, and Tina. Josh was already firing away, doing his best to keep the circle from closing in on them. Leo had his shotgun, trying to move his wheelchair at the same time. If someone didn't help him, he'd be a sitting duck.

"We're leading more their way," I told Derek, panting in fear and exertion.

"We don't have a choice. Move," he said, finally spinning to check behind us. He aimed his compound bow and released an arrow. I didn't need to look to know he'd hit his target. He then opted for the handgun strapped to his thigh. "Sara, get them in that cabin and down below. You can aim through the windows once they're safe. And take Leo with you!"

I left Derek as he stopped to take a stand on the group on our tail, urging the kids up the embankment toward the table where we'd all been sitting. Josh was standing on top of the table; he dropped his rifle and began using a pistol. Two of the infected reached for the kids, and I pointed, aimed, and took them both out, not bothering to slow down.

Rich's cabin was between mine and Derek's, with mine being on the end. Carol was struggling with Leo's chair, the grass hindering her. He was aiming all around them, telling her to leave him, but she wouldn't. The wheel lodged in a muddy hole, almost launching Carol over Leo, and he spilled out of the chair. Four dead bastards moved in on them, and no amount of yelling or running would get me there quickly enough, though I aimed and fired anyway. I nailed two of them, one in the head and the other in the neck, which barely slowed it down. The other two fell on Leo and Carol.

The sound of snarls, ripping flesh, and screams from Carol and Leo sent chills up my spine. I couldn't stop to help them, and I knew the second they were bitten that they were done.

"Josh! Tina!" I called, finally reaching the steps of Rich's cabin. Wrapping my arms around both kids, I lifted them to the porch. "You two, inside. Now!" I yelled, glancing back for Derek, but he seemed to be holding his own as he fought the small pack around him.

Josh grabbed Tina's arm once he'd cleared a path to the cabin, pulling her with him, but his weapons were empty. She ran toward us and used a long knife to avoid a few, though her eyes widened when she looked my way.

Both kids screamed, a sound I'd never wanted to hear, and even less did I ever want to see my son raise a weapon, but he did. The damn thing had scrambled up the left side of the porch, pushing and crawling our way, and Freddie's hands shook, but he pulled the trigger, catching what used to be a woman in the jaw. It didn't stop her, but it damn well slowed her down. He chambered another round before I could aim at her myself, and then he pulled the trigger again. The woman's head split wide open at the temple, and she collapsed to the wooden porch floor.

Freddie froze, eyes wide and breathing heavy.

"Go, baby. Inside and down below. Take Janie. Go!" I reached for the door and slammed it open, then pushed both kids inside the cabin, only to pull the door closed again.

Tina and I rounded to face the camp. Derek was pulling arrows from the dead, using the butt of his compound bow to smash skulls. Josh was struggling with a few down by the fire and table, using a large hunting knife. Millie was using a rifle off my dad's porch. I leaped off the porch, killing one that was reaching for Josh from behind. I also took out the bastard that was feasting on Carol and the three working on Leo.

Derek finally rushed to us, reloading his compound bow. "I swear to God, Sara. What part of get *inside* didn't you understand?" he snapped, glaring my way before lodging an arrow at an infected ten feet away.

"The kids are safe…but Leo, Carol…" I rasped.

Derek's face was pained, but he nodded. "There're maybe ten left," he panted, and he was covered in blood and chaos.

The remaining infected were quickly taken care of, and I gave the camp one more long gaze before falling to my knees, my head falling forward.

"Sara," Tina called, and I jumped when she placed a hand on my back. "Sweetie, you gotta move away from them. Now."

Confusion must have been written all over my face when I looked up at her, but her eyes were on the ground. My stomach roiled at the sight in front of me. Carol's hands were twitching, her eyes fluttering. Leo was already on the move, his growl such a sharp contrast to the sweet man he'd once been that a sob ripped from me. His inability to walk followed him over, so he could only drag himself along the grass and through the mud.

Carol rolled over and had started to sit up when an arrow slammed into her temple. It had come from behind Tina and me, but I could only watch Leo. He'd been a man I'd known and loved my whole life, it seemed. He'd taken my side against his son more times than I could count.

My hands shook as I raised my weapon and aimed. Leo snarled, snapped, and continued to crawl my way.

"Sara…"

I heard Tina's voice somewhere behind me, and Derek's joined her, but I knew Leo would hate what he'd become. With a wet sob, I pulled the trigger.

"No!" I heard behind me, knowing Brody's voice anywhere, and just the sound of it sent me over the edge.

I stood up from the muddy ground, my eyes on him as he and Martin rushed to us. I couldn't focus on Martin's cry of heartache; my focus was Brody.

"Was it worth it, Brody?" I asked, sneering at him. "Leaving us short? Was it?"

I knew it was unfair to blame him completely. And from the heavy bags he was toting, the run had been successful. But the entire camp was a war zone. There were bodies everywhere—some still moving. Martin's sobs finally made me break from Brody's face, which was still in shock.

"Martin, you should know...She died trying to save Leo. He told her to leave him, but she wouldn't," I told him softly.

"Did you let them get at him, Sara? Is this some sort of revenge?" Brody suddenly snapped, and Derek moved before I could, the sound of fist meeting flesh echoing across the lake.

Brody's tall frame crumpled, his knees landing heavily in the mud. Bags fell around him as he shook off the hit. Derek grabbed the collar of his T-shirt as Josh and Tina tried to hold him back.

"You stupid son of a bitch!" Derek snarled. "You weren't here, motherfucker! You have no idea. They came in on two sides of us!" He gestured wildly around to where the dead lay everywhere, only to ball up his fist again. "Blame her again. I fucking dare you," he warned Brody. "I told you before you left not to go. I told you we were due, but you didn't fucking listen. You'll listen from now on, asshole, or I'll shoot you myself. Are we clear?"

Brody only nodded, sagging in defeat. Derek loomed over him with no fear and more emotion in his face than I'd ever seen. It reminded me somewhat of Jack's face the night we'd met in Shelly's Bar. It had been Brody then too. Rubbing my face, I could only focus on getting to Freddie.

Giving once last glance at Leo, I stood up, turning to Tina. "We need to burn these bodies. We'll use Jack's truck to make it easier. You know, just drive, load them up...I need to check on my son and Janie," I said, but my tone sounded empty to my own ears.

"Sara?" Derek called tentatively.

Shaking my head, I walked toward Rich's cabin. Before opening the door, I shoved the body of the woman—the one Freddie had shot—off the porch with my foot. Though the gore was left behind, at least my son wouldn't have to look at her again.

I went inside, tapping on the door in the floor. "Guys, it's me."

The lock disengaged, and I saw Janie's sweet face peering up at me.

"Hey, you two okay?"

She nodded, holding her hands out, and I lifted her up and out, but she whispered, "He's…not talking."

"Okay," I whispered back, smiling her way. "It's pretty ugly out there, so if you want to hang out here, I'll understand."

"My mom okay?"

"Oh, yeah, Janie. She's fine, but…"

"I saw Leo and Miss Carol," she sighed, wearing a sad face.

Nodding, I cupped her face, only to slip down to the steps. I found Freddie sitting on the edge of the cot down there, his rifle leaning next to him, but he was staring down at the floor.

"Freddie?" I called, kneeling in front of him. "Buddy, you okay?"

He nodded, but when his eyes met mine, they were haunted, exhausted, and just plain scared. "I…I…"

"C'mere," I whispered, pulling him to my lap. "You didn't do anything wrong, baby. You were very, very brave."

"It…It was coming for us…you…I couldn't…and I was…" he rambled, his thin frame shivering in my arms.

"Freddie, you were protecting yourself…us. I promise, you did perfect," I soothed as he wrapped himself around me.

"I miss Daddy," he suddenly wailed, and tears welled up in my eyes at the pure pain I could hear in him. "I miss Daddy, and I couldn't let it get you, too."

The fact that he was calling him "Daddy" was not lost on me. He hadn't called Jack that since he'd started school, but at the moment, my baby was feeling everything all at once, and that included the absence of his father. He'd seen so much since the beginning—loss of life, grotesque things, and the upheaval of everything he knew.

Without saying anything, I stood up, keeping him in my arms. Holding him with one hand, I picked up his rifle and ascended the steps. Janie was still there when I came up, and she was sweet enough to take the rifle and close the trap door for me. I made my way outside and down the steps.

"Sara?" Derek rushed to me. "He okay? Is he hurt?"

"No, he'll be fine," I told him, smiling sadly, but I couldn't hide my tears. Not this time.

I took Freddie into our cabin, opting for his room. I sat down on his bed, hoping he'd lie down, but he was content on my lap, so I leaned back against the wall.

"I love you, Freddie, and your daddy would be *so proud* of you," I told him honestly, and when he pulled his face from my neck, I smiled a little. "He would be, you know. He always used to tease me that I'd put you in football pads just to go to the grocery store if I could get away with it." I grinned when Freddie sniffled and giggled a little at the same time. "It's true. I never wanted anything to happen to you. You bumped your head once when you were just two, and I about went crazy, drove all the way to Grandpa Rich's so he could look at you.

"Your dad, however, laughed at me. He told me that you were a boy and that I'd better get used to bumps, scrapes, and bruises, that you'd get them every day just because..." I pinched his chin gently between my thumb and forefinger. "What you did...He'd be proud of you because there's absolutely nothing wrong with protecting those people you love, Freddie. Nothing. These are scary, ugly times, and I hate that you're seeing it, but it's the truth, the reality that surrounds us."

"I've...started to...forget what he looks like."

Tears ran unchecked down my face, but I nodded, reaching for his scrapbook. "Here, sweetheart."

I flipped past the news articles, aiming for the things he'd posted in there toward the back. I bypassed ticket stubs and stuff from the zoo in Portland, finally finding the picture I wanted. It was of the three of us, with silly smiles and happy eyes. It had been taken on my phone, but I'd printed it at the kiosk at the drug store. Jack was in his camo, and Freddie absolutely *had* to match him.

"Here, Freddie." I tapped the picture. "This...This is where you came from. Never, ever forget that. Don't you dare forget that we love you so much, that you came from that love."

Freddie reached out and ripped the picture from the scrapbook, holding it in his hands. I let him have a moment, and my eyes drifted to Jack's old dog tags. Freddie had even left the chain attached. For almost a year, Freddie had worn them, wanting to be just like Jack.

"I miss him too, Freddie," I whispered, nodding when my son turned my way. "So...what do we do about that? I'm kinda running on blind, stupid faith here, buddy. I want to believe he's out there coming for us, that he's fighting, but…every day gets harder and harder. I'm just being honest here, kiddo."

Freddie pointed to the poem on the opposite page. "*Be still, sad heart,*" he read, nodding a little. "*Behind the clouds is the sun still shining…*"

Smiling, I kissed his cheek. "Do you have any idea how many times your dad has said that to me?"

He grinned, swiping at his face. "Lots?"

"Tons."

He reached down and pulled the dog tags from the page, tossing away the tape that held it. Straightening the chain, he lifted it over my head.

"He'd want us to keep fighting," he said wisely. "He'd tell us it won't always be so bad."

Staring at my beautiful, smart son, I nodded. "You're right, he would."

"And he promised."

"He did, baby, but…"

"I'm not dumb, Mom. I know what could happen. I just think he'd be mad if we gave up."

Grinning, I broke into a chuckle. "A little bit, yeah." We stared at each other for a moment, and I sighed, running my hands through his hair. "So…we hang on?"

He nodded, folding that picture of us and tucking it into the pocket of his jeans.

"You know those hugs you promised?"

He nodded, falling back into my arms, and I wrapped him up tight but curled up on my side in the bed. I closed my eyes, taking a minute to simply hold my son. The fact that he'd quoted Jack's poem to me brought memories flying to the surface of my mind.

God, I just missed my husband. I missed the silly things he'd say and do just to hear Freddie and me laugh. I missed pancakes on Sunday mornings, messy bathrooms, and cartoon marathons on the couch. I missed being able to let out everything that was stressing me out, only to have him smile at me, lift me in a hug, and kiss me until I forgot what had originally upset me. And as much as everyone was doing their damnedest to keep us safe, it came nowhere near how Jack made me feel.

Freddie's fingers twirled a lock of my hair from my ponytail, and slowly, reality blurred away.

Sandy, Oregon
8.5 Years Prior

"Let me see you," Jack whispered, pulling me into the bedroom of the cabin. He sat on the edge of the bed, situating me to stand between his legs. "I just wanna look at you, Shortcake."

"You've looked enough already," I teased him, squealing when his long fingers dug into my sides, tickling without mercy. "Jack! Stop!" I begged in a fit of giggles, trying to get away, but he merely tossed me on the bed and pinned me with his body.

His smile was glorious and a sight for sore eyes. He'd barely been home long enough to drive to my house, much less come straight to the cabin. Our long-awaited honeymoon was officially here, not to mention he was home safe from his last tour and I'd just finished my last class.

My breathing was heavy, but his gaze made my heart race faster. It raked all over my face, as if he was memorizing it. Finally, he looked to my left hand.

"You got it sized okay?" he asked softly, kissing the ring from the palm side.

"Yeah, like a week after you left," I said with a nod, looking at his ring next to it as he threaded our fingers together.

The rings matched and had been bought the day of our quick wedding. They weren't fancy, nor were they all that expensive in the great big scheme of things, but they meant everything to us. We'd picked them out together, though Jack had promised me diamonds later. I didn't care. Just having something that said we belonged to each other meant the world to me. The simple bands matched his emotional and spur-of-the-moment proposal and the quick courthouse wedding with just our family in attendance. I loved it all, everything about it.

"What's making you smile so pretty, Sara?" he asked me in a sing-song voice as he bent to my neck to press kisses to my skin. It was soft and sexy and soothing all at once.

"You're home safe. I'm done with college. We can…truly start… just us."

He grinned and nodded at my throat, not even bothering to pull away. With every kiss, he spoke softly against flesh, making me want him with each push of breath along my neck. "*Be still, sad heart*," he quoted, lips dragging and tongue tasting. "*Behind the clouds is the sun still shining*." Pushing himself up a little, he gazed down at me. "I told you, Shortcake, the bad times, the hard times don't last forever. They may seem like it, but the rain stops eventually."

I cupped his handsome face. "I love you."

His smile said it back without the words. "I want everything with you, Sara," he said instead. "All of it. The house, the kids…the dog."

Laughing, I nodded. He'd said it before, in letters while he was gone and on the rare phone calls he'd been able to make while in Iraq. Now that we were married, he had no shame in stating it over and over.

"Me too. Dog?"

He chuckled sexily, kissing my lips, the tip of my nose, and forehead. "Maybe. Just…keep an open mind, Shortcake." He kissed my lips again. "I've put in for a more permanent position at the base, baby, so if you want that house you told me about—the one in your dad's neighborhood—then we'll talk about it, okay?"

"No more overseas?" I asked him, my mouth hanging open.

"I can't promise that, but the likelihood is slimmer now, Sara. You know there's always a possibility, but since we've gone over twice…" He shrugged, grimacing I was guessing because he couldn't promise me something.

"I'll take what I can get."

He laughed, his head falling to my chest. "God, I'd give you anything, Sara. I owe Derek my life for stopping for that beer…"

Giggling, I pressed my head into the pillow behind me. "Maybe we owe Brody for acting like an ass…"

"Don't remind me," he growled low, skimming his nose along my cheek. "I could've killed that fucker that night for daring to touch you when you'd said no. Besides, he'd interrupted me asking you out…"

"Moot point, Jack," I said haughtily, wiggling my fingers at him before raking them through his hair. "Wife."

"Fuck, that sounds so sexy," he purred, his eyes darkening to almost black. "Which brings us around to the real point…why we're here…in this bed…for four whole fucking days…"

"What point?" I teased, biting my lip and laughing lightly, but he chose that moment to grind into me, so my laugh broke off into a long moan. "Oh my God, I've missed you."

His kiss was searing and almost harsh but filled with love and need. It was claiming and all-consuming, showing me that he'd missed me, too. It seemed we couldn't get close enough or naked enough to be able to truly feel. But when he finally slipped inside me, I finally felt safe, finally felt at home.

"Freddie? Sara?" I heard through the foggy curtain of sleep. When I cracked an eye open, it was dark in Freddie's room, but Derek knelt beside the bed with a lantern. "I brought you guys some dinner," he said, and Freddie shifted from my arms.

"Gosh, Freddie," I said through a wide yawn. "We kinda crashed out, huh?"

He nodded, rubbing his face, but sat up to face Derek, who was handing him a plate.

"We were lucky that Carol had covered the fish," he said softly, grimacing a little.

"What time is it?" I asked but then gasped. "Oh, I was gonna help with cleanup…"

"Don't sweat it," he said, handing me a plate as well, and he reached out to brush my hair from my face in a gesture that was too familiar, so I pulled away a little. "It's done. And we um…We buried Carol and Leo in that open spot on the bank."

My eyes were already scratchy from crying earlier with Freddie, so the tears simply burned my eyes, but I nodded, poking at the fish with my fork. Derek's rough hand covered mine, urging me to eat, a calloused thumb rubbing across my knuckles. When I looked to his face, his gaze was locked on to the dog tags Freddie had put on me, which were still around my neck. He quickly pulled away and rubbed his face, but his expression was unreadable when he met my gaze with a smile that didn't quite reach his eyes.

"How's Brody handling it?"

"The black eye I gave him or Leo?"

"Yeah, sure…"

"You gave Brody a black eye?" Freddie gasped through a mouthful of food.

"Chew!" Derek chuckled but looked to me. "He helped with cleanup and then with the graves, but he's been holed up in your dad's cabin ever since."

Nodding, I ate without saying much, and I didn't want to see what was happening with Derek. I loved him as family, like a big brother, but I could see where things could become muddy. We'd grown closer, for sure, but I ignored the new looks, the easy touches, and the overprotectiveness that Derek hadn't always had. My heart, my mind, my soul was still with Jack—wherever that may be—and I knew that would never change. I didn't think I'd ever feel like I could see another man the way I felt about Jack, and I hoped Derek wouldn't push that.

I finished my food, kissing Freddie's head. "You better now, buddy?" I asked him, and he nodded.

Derek watched us closely, taking our plates, but he nudged my son. "I heard what you did, Freddie. Taking out the infected to protect your mom and Janie? Dude, that's some big-time brave stuff. You okay?"

Freddie looked to me but smiled back at Derek. "Yeah, I'm okay. I did everything you told me to," he said proudly.

Derek grinned. "Thatta boy!" he praised, ruffling his hair.

We both laughed at Freddie when he ran his fingers through it trying to fix it. He rolled his eyes at us but cracked his knuckles. He was Jack's clone in that moment, and I loved him with a sickness. I knew Derek saw it too, because he sighed deeply.

"C'mon, you two," he said, standing up. "We're gonna need to sort some stuff out after today's events."

The front door of the cabin slammed open, and Tina rushed to Freddie's doorway. "Aw, hell, guys…We got headlights coming up the road. We need you out here."

"Shit," Derek hissed, setting the plates down on the nightstand.

We ran out of the cabin to meet up with Josh, Martin, and Janie at the table and fire. The pit was burning low inside the high wall Derek and Martin had built around it.

Josh handed me my gun, which was fully loaded, as Derek snatched up his compound bow. We were all on edge as headlights bounced in from the long drive. Brody was still absent, but I didn't expect him anytime soon.

"Freddie, I want you and Janie inside Grandpa Rich's cabin. You wait until I come get you. This is different than a pack, buddy, so don't argue. Okay?" I asked him, and he didn't argue, but he did take his rifle with him anyway.

Once the door closed behind the kids, Derek stood next to me. "We'll stand our ground, Sara. Just like the ones from the trip up here, we won't back down or give up what we've been able to salvage. Got me?"

We had about a minute or two before the vehicles would reach the camp, but we jumped when a slam echoed behind us. My eyes narrowed on Brody, who was swaying on the front porch of my dad's cabin.

"Jesus, is he drunk?" I asked, my eyes falling to his hand where a half-empty bottle of liquor sloshed. "Where the hell…"

"Fuck me to tears," Derek hissed under his breath. "You know, the bastard could've shared."

Snorting, I smacked at him, but I knew what drunk Brody could be like. If he was an asshole stone-cold sober, he was even worse when he'd been drinking.

"Oh, look!" Brody sang with a laugh. "We've got company!"

"I've got him," Martin stated, keeping his shotgun draped across his shoulder as he walked to Brody.

"Can't we just…shoot him?" Tina muttered.

"Tempting, but no," I sighed, shaking my head and facing the road again. "Hopefully Martin can stuff him in a closet until this is over."

Two pickup trucks and two large RVs pulled into the lake's clearing. Tina, Josh, Derek, and I all stood with weapons at the ready. I could still hear Martin trying to persuade Brody to go inside or give up the bottle, but I was pretty sure neither would be happening.

The door to the pickup opened and slammed, but I couldn't see beyond the bright headlights, just the silhouette of a tall form.

Derek engaged the shotgun in his hand. "Hold it right there, asshole. That's far enough. What'choo want?"

The legs stopped in midstride, but I heard footsteps behind me, and suddenly Brody had me spun around, his grip hard on my arm.

"Brody, you need to let go," I hissed at him. "If you can't tell, we've got a bit of a situation here."

"I gotta know, Sara...Did you? Did you let them at my dad on purpose?" he yelled. He got right in my face and screamed, "*Did you let them kill my dad?"* He was whiskey and anger and grief.

"Brody, let go of me," I growled, finally bringing my knee to his groin, hard and fast.

He doubled over, groaning and cursing me, but when he looked back at me, there was nothing but pure hate. The bottle in his hand smashed against the trunk of the tree next to him, but before anyone could react, he was pressed against the same tree, his neck in a firm grip.

"Brody Matthews, I won't shoot you, but I can damn well tie you up to this tree to rot. Am I clear, son?"

My mouth fell open at the familiar voice and even the familiar threat. "D-Daddy?" I barely breathed aloud. "Dad?"

He turned to face me, and he looked exhausted and like he'd aged ten years, but he was the first true glimmer of hope I'd had in what seemed like forever.

"Jesus, Hank," Derek gasped.

"Yeah, sorry it took so long," Dad said, dropping Brody to the ground, where he stayed in a heap.

"It doesn't matter," I sobbed, finally letting my guard down.

"Aw, baby girl, I'm sorry," he said, and I found myself in the best of hugs. "Baby, where's...where's Freddie?"

"He's okay, he's okay," I chanted, nodding to Tina that it was okay to let the kids out of Rich's cabin.

My dad gazed around, signaling to someone behind me, but focused back on me. "Any...Um, Jack?" he asked, but I shook my head no.

"Not yet."

"Okay," he sighed, rubbing his face. "What's that fool babbling about?"

"We were attacked today. Huge pack came through. We lost Leo and Carol North while Brody and Martin were off—at Brody's insistence—getting food from the traps."

"Aw, hell," he groaned, pulling me into a hug again. "I'm sorry, Sare. I tried to come sooner, but things got out of hand back at home. A pack came through, and somehow they got inside the nursing home. There was that and finding fuel to get here. I brought who was left."

He kissed the top of my head but turned me around. There were faces I recognized, but some I didn't. All of them looked road-weary. If I had to guess, I would've said there were ten or twelve.

"We emptied Sandy of supplies and made our way here. Took about a week, but...Those with the RVs will stay in those. Some will have to bunk up until we can figure out other arrangements, but...I couldn't leave them, Sara."

"No, no," I said, shaking my head. "Of course not. The more, the safer...I mean, we were struggling as it was."

Dad nodded but looked down when Freddie sneaked up on us.

"Oh God, Freddie!" He scooped my son up into his arms, and my tears started all over again.

"Grandpa Hank...Have I got lots to tell *you!*"

If anything could break the emotional moment, it was that.

"Buddy, let me get these people safe and settled, and then I'm all yours," Dad promised, and I could tell his smile was wavering. There were emotions there that he'd never allow to surface, but I'd have been willing to bet he hadn't known exactly *what* he'd find once he'd arrived at Clear Lake.

"Good, then you can stay with us!" Freddie commanded, and I actually agreed with him, nodding up at my dad.

"Please," was all I added.

He kissed my forehead. "You got it, kiddos."

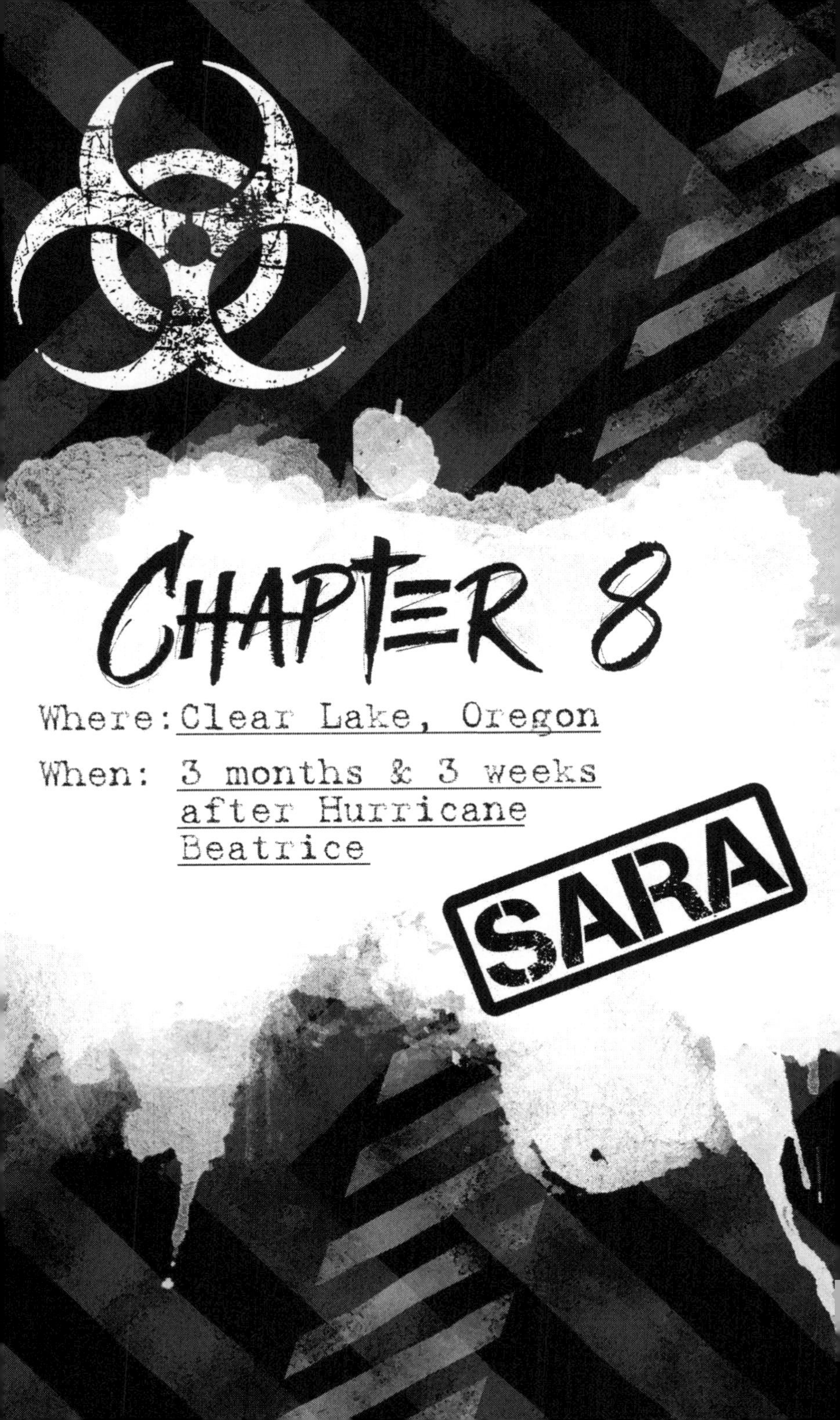

CHAPTER 8

Where: Clear Lake, Oregon

When: 3 months & 3 weeks after Hurricane Beatrice

SARA

SARA

Clear Lake, Oregon
3 Months & 3 Weeks after Hurricane Beatrice

Dreams were blurry swirls, then vivid colors and faces. My heart ached yet carried hope. I shifted, trying to grasp hold of reality and reaching for Freddie at the same time, only to come up empty.

Sighing, I sat up, rubbing the sleep from my eyes. It didn't take long to get dressed, considering I rarely undressed completely at night. It helped when emergencies popped up in the middle of the night. And my gun was never farther than arm's reach.

Stepping out onto the cabin's porch was surreal. There were new faces and now two large RVs parked along the side of the lake. I knew I needed to meet everyone, since the night before had been chaos. Between the pack of zombies that had come through, the loss of Leo and Carol, Brody's drunken behavior, and my dad's arrival, everyone was just about to collapse under the weight of it all.

As promised, though, Dad had told the people who'd come with him to settle in, keep watch, and that all introductions would be made the next morning. He'd then sat with Freddie for what seemed like hours, giving us both his undivided attention. Only when Freddie was yawning every other word did Dad finally urge us to bed, opting for the sofa in my cabin for himself.

Glancing down at the wildflowers by the porch, I sighed and picked two small bouquets. Before I joined anyone for breakfast or started anything for the day, I needed to pay my respects.

I found two makeshift crosses up on the hill overlooking the lake. Derek had picked a good spot to put them, with plenty of shade and sun throughout the day, pretty flowers on either side, and a stunning view of the entire camp. Kneeling between the two mounds of newly turned soil, I set the bouquets up against the crosses.

"You shouldn't wander off alone," I heard behind me, which made me smile, reach behind my back to my waistband, and set my gun beside me on the ground.

"I'm never alone, Dad," I said softly, turning when he sat beside me. "It's impossible here."

He was in jeans and a navy-blue Sandy Fire Department T-shirt that had been worn thin. Around his waist was a police gun belt, along with a knife strapped to his thigh. I noted plenty of changes—scars along his arms, a new one slicing through his left eyebrow, and he was due a shave, but his small smile was still the most comforting thing on his face, not to mention the warm concern glaring back at me from eyes that matched my own.

Now that I could truly see him, I saw weariness and worry. "What the hell happened back in Sandy, Dad?"

"You want to hear that now? Or meet everyone? I suppose Derek needs to hear it too," he surmised, rubbing his face.

"Yeah, I guess you're right," I muttered, looking back at the graves.

"You need a minute?"

I nodded a little, feeling a kiss to the side of my head. "We fought...Leo and I. Just before," I blurted out in a whisper, but Dad kissed my head again.

"About?"

I snorted, rolling my eyes up to his. "What do you *think?* Brody, of course. He's been such a ray of sunshine this whole time, Dad; you have no idea." My sarcasm was sharp, making him smirk, but I turned back to the cross. "I told Leo to stop apologizing for his son, especially since his son left us down two people. And then...they came in...*so many.* There had to be fifty of them. From there...and there," I explained, pointing to the two sides of the lake from which the pack had emerged out of the woods.

"I tried really hard to get to them, to Leo and Carol, but they surrounded us. And Leo's chair got stuck..." I was rambling, tears filling my eyes. "Dad, they *turned*. I had to put a bullet in your friend!" I hissed, my hands balling up into fists. "I *knew* he'd hate what he'd become, and he wasn't Leo anymore...but I put him down like a rabid dog. I've killed so many of these...these...*things* that I barely bat an eye, but that?" I shook my head, swiping at my face. "And then...to watch my son raise a weapon to protect me..."

I found myself pulled to my feet and wrapped in a hug. "Sara, stop. Don't torture yourself. You did everything you could. Don't think that Martin and Derek haven't told me already. That Freddie hasn't told me. They have. You did all you could. Trust me, we're all doing our damnedest to get through."

Nodding, I sniffled, getting myself together and finally looking up at him. "I'm glad you're here."

"Well, getting here was a miracle," he countered, "and it took way longer than I'd imagined."

I took his hand and led him down the hill back toward camp. Several people milled about—some I thought I recognized from Sandy, others were strangers, but one I'd recognize anywhere.

"Travis?" I called, smiling when the man spun around. We'd attended high school together, but he'd been Sandy's youngest police officer. He'd been a good friend in school.

"Sara," he sighed, walking to me and hugging me. "God, you have no idea how happy I am that you and Freddie are okay. For... you know...Grumpy's sake." He jerked a thumb toward my dad.

Grinning at my dad's chuckle, I nodded. "Yeah, well, thanks for sticking with him."

"Bah, no worries." He rolled his eyes probably at how trite that sounded. "Okay, so it was a bitch getting out of there, but...none of us would have made it this far, if not for your dad's calm head. Nick didn't make it, though..." His voice trailed off at the mention of a young firefighter who'd worked with my dad.

"Well, I want to hear about it," Derek piped up from the table.

"Introductions first," Dad insisted, pointing to the group of people who were gathering around us.

There were eight people, aside from Travis. Ivan and Margaret Leary had made it as far as Sandy from Gresham before their car broke down, and they'd lost her sister, Elise, to a pack as they'd tried to find another vehicle. If I were guessing, I'd have pegged them at around early to mid-forties. They were sharing an RV with two girls—sisters—Hannah and Mallory Gold, who were barely out of their teens. They were blonde and fit and quiet.

One gentleman I knew from Shelly's Bar: Moses—or Mose, as he liked to be called. He was a tall African-American, with a big smile and an obsession with football, not to mention a love for cold beer.

"Omigod, Mose!" I gasped, rushing to him and laughing when he lifted me into a big bear hug.

"It's good to see you, Miss Sara," he rumbled in my ear. "Any word on that soldier of yours?" he asked in a whisper, keeping me in his arms. When I shook my head, his face fell. "Damn." He sighed, kissing my cheek. "Hang in there, huh?"

"Shelly?" I asked tentatively when he set me on my feet. When he simply shook his head sadly, I turned my attention back to Dad's people.

The oldest among them was Jonah Winston. He used a cane to steady himself but seemed fairly spry for a man who proudly proclaimed his age as seventy-one. He had a mellow demeanor and an easy smile. He was the owner of the other large RV and had come in from Tillamook, hoping to find his brother in Sandy, but had come up empty. He shared his space with the last two people, who stepped forward. They were a young couple, Jesse and Lucy Camden, and I gaped at the two of them.

"Oh, hell," I murmured, shaking my head at the large, pregnant belly the girl was rubbing. She was seven months along if she was a day.

"Do you see? Why I couldn't leave any of them?" Dad asked, rubbing the back of his neck.

"Yeah, definitely, but…we'll need to prepare for that baby, Dad."

"I know. Believe me, I know. I have EMT training, but Miss Margaret over there is a nurse, so she's our best hope when it comes time for that baby," he sighed, starting to pace by the table. "We'd had a few things stored already, but…" He let out a breath, facing me. "Sandy fell…and hard."

Freddie walked to me, and I pulled him into my lap, kissing his head as we waited for Grandpa Hank to tell us what happened.

"Sara, Derek…when you guys left, I had hoped that someone would come secure that nursing home," he started, looking between us. "No one came. Not a soul. Hell, I don't think there's anyone left, to be honest. At least not in any surrounding cities. The bigger ones, anyway." He pointed to Ivan and Margaret. "Gresham was on fire when they left. With no power and people trying to defend themselves, things simply got out of hand." He sniffed once, seeming to steel himself to continue. "Travis, Nick, and I tried our best to secure that building. We had a few nurses left who were able to care for the sick, dole out what meds were left, that sort of thing. Anyone we saw who was still living, we brought them in, turning the large cafeteria into a camping ground. We were able to shelter about fifty people."

Dad started to pace again. "We had willing young men and women who went out daily, scouring homes, stores, schools, clinics, and abandoned cars for supplies. They did really well. They used a four-person buddy system with a pickup truck. They'd drive door to door, raiding everything they could find, from food, to baby stuff, to medicine and first-aid supplies. They'd even bring any survivors who needed a safe place."

He pointed to Moses. "Mose there…He set up a checkpoint at the home. No bites, no flu-like symptoms, no scratches were allowed inside. And it worked…except someone in that one group had to have gotten cornered while out scouting and then got scared and hid their wounds, because one night we all went to bed, and the next morning, I had a nursing home full of infected killers. They turned—just about all of them—and they trapped us in there for days. And they could turn in less than thirty seconds."

He pointed around the crowd. "Who you see? That's who made it out. We were able to fight through it, using medical equipment and what ammo we had on us. Nick was with us, but he fell trying to help Lucy through a window. We had to leave everything inside because I wanted that building closed and locked up. So we had to start from scratch," he explained, shrugging a shoulder. "We holed up at the station for a few days, but eventually we were going to run out of food and ammunition. We *needed* what we'd stocked up in the nursing home."

"Who went in?" Derek asked, narrowing his eyes a little.

"Me," Dad answered, nodding. "Along with Mose, Travis, and Jesse. We strapped our arms and legs down with magazines and duct tape to prevent bites getting through, we strapped knives to the end of our shotguns and rifles like bayonets, and we wore riot helmets.

It was the only way. We got most of it, though we lost a few things. The crib, baby clothes...They were ruined. Unfortunately, we set most of those dead people free out on the street. We had no choice."

Frowning, I kissed Freddie's head again as he toyed with Jack's dog tags around my neck. "When was this?" I asked Dad.

"About a month ago," he answered, his nose wrinkling. "It took us quite a bit of time to get the cars and RVs together, fueled up, and find enough food to make the trip. We got separated when another bunch came through, but we finally got the hell out of there. I saw the path you took, Sara. You cleared it beautifully, but there were packs of dead on the road. We stopped to hunt and made a couple of side trips into a few small towns to grab what we could."

I couldn't stop staring at him. If my dad—being a firefighter—could make it, if he was standing in front of me, then my hopes and prayers and dreams went out silently that the other half of my family could make it. I so badly needed them to make it that I started to shake, and I hugged Freddie closer. My husband, Joel, Rich, and Dottie were all military trained soldiers. They were so smart, so strong, and so capable that my hope renewed almost to a point that it made me drunk, but I pushed it down. No one, aside from Freddie and me, felt as positive as we did. I saw their pity-filled looks, their disbelief, and their sadness. To voice my hope would make me sound pathetic and crazy, but something deep down told me that my heart would just...*know* if Jack's beautiful spirit was gone, if it no longer existed on this planet.

Derek whistled low, shaking his head. "You are officially a member of the badass club, Henry Stokes," he praised, giving him a mock salute.

Dad laughed, shaking his head. "That's a good thing?"

"That's the best thing," he sighed. "I guess what we need to figure out is this whole living here, campsite thing. Rich's cabin is free, but we've been using the bunker below it for storage and emergency shelter. If you want to add what you've got, we'll have a better idea as to where we stand."

"We can do that," Hannah, the older of the sisters, piped up. "We used to work at the market in Sandy, so...Yeah, kinda got the grocery thing down."

Dad chuckled. "Okay, you two get started on that. Josh, you can show them and give them a hand. Travis, if you could sort the ammo, see what the combined stock comes to..."

"Yeah, Hank. No sweat."

"I have a suggestion," Mose stated, smiling when we turned to him. "I don't want to step on toes or nothin', but this fence…It won't hold, even when you finish it. Not against a large pack like you said came through yesterday. If you want, I've got an easier, better solution."

"Man, I'm all ears," Derek stated, standing up from the table.

"Spikes, crisscrossed each way," Mose said, mimicking an X with his hands. "Those zombies…they don't seem to be able to avoid running into stuff, so it would basically skewer them. We'd need plenty of trees chopped down, but you know, it seems to be the one thing you have in spades. It'll take some time to fence the whole camp, even longer if you include the lake. It won't keep out humans, but it will stop those walking nightmares."

I laughed, simply because we were deep in the woods. Trees were in abundance.

The door to my dad's cabin slammed open, and Brody's hung-over ass stumbled out into the camp. He squinted at the sunlight, and I was happy to see just how hard Derek had hit him, not to mention the slight limp he walked with from my knee to his balls. As he got closer, I could even see a handprint around his neck from my dad the night before.

"Oh, I bet he feels like rainbows and glitter today," Tina drawled wryly.

I had to hide my laugh in Freddie's hair, but my dad heard her, smirking her way before turning to Brody.

"Just the man I needed to see!" he boomed loudly, most likely on purpose to make Brody flinch. My ex groaned when Dad's heavy hand slapped his shoulder. "I've heard some things, Brody," he started slowly, a warning tone to his voice. "I don't like them…these things people are telling me. Your cooperation starts now. I'm sorry about Leo, son, but if you again blame my daughter or anyone else you left behind that day, you'll find yourself tied to a tree until the next pack comes through. You know damn well they didn't allow it on purpose."

Brody narrowed his gaze on me, and Freddie sat up straighter. I smirked when Dad called his name again—especially loud—in his ear.

"Now…you're gonna go back to my cabin, grab everything you were able to procure yesterday, and give it to the young ladies sorting the food. That includes alcohol, son. I'm not joking. Next, you'll be joining Mose and Derek here. We're gonna need some trees cut down. Lots of them. And I have a brand new set of tools in my truck." He slapped his shoulder again.

I moaned, looking to Tina. "You know, my first hangover...Dad did that same thing. Suddenly he needed help mowing the lawn *really* early the next morning."

Tina chuckled. "Cruel but helpful. Look."

Brody stumbled away, muttering under his breath as he trudged back into the cabin.

"Gentlemen, the first foul word he blurts out," Dad told Mose and Derek, "I wanna know about it."

"Yeah, Hank," they both said through highly amused grins.

I set Freddie on his feet, walked to my dad, and kissed his cheek. "Welcome to Clear Lake, Dad. Glad you could make it."

4 Months & 10 Days after Hurricane Beatrice

"What do you think?" Dad asked, tapping the map of Mount Hood National Forest.

Derek and Josh studied where he was pointing. They were trying to figure out the easiest, safest way to hunt. We needed meat. Fishing was fine, though there was a concern that we'd already caused a dip in the amount of fish in the lake. The food stores were holding steady, with plenty of vegetables, dry goods, and soups. There were very few fresh veggies, but Millie had started to work a small garden just to keep us supplied with tomatoes, onions, and potatoes. She was hoping for more, but she was happy with what she'd accomplished. However, canned and fresh meat was scarce, and we needed a real, true hunting trip.

"I think...here...and here," Derek said, dragging his finger from one point to another. "When you came in, was 770 still clear, empty?"

"Yeah," Dad answered, nodding a little. "There were a few straggling dead but not anything you guys couldn't handle. They're just wandering aimlessly."

Derek nodded, looking to Josh. They'd volunteered to go off on the hunt for us. Just the two of them. The thought was scary, but with Derek's Jeep, Josh's quick feet, and both of them being really good shots, they were the best option we had. The Jeep's four-wheel drive alone could get them around and through tight spots and narrow roads. Any more than that, and they'd have to take a truck, which would limit their mobility.

"This will be more than just one day," Josh explained, flinching when his mother tsked. "Mom! We don't have a choice! Martin can't go with that ankle he twisted. Hank's needed here. Mose and Brody are barely making headway with that fence. Who else could go? Who else can track deer?"

Millie sagged in defeat, and I wrapped an arm around her shoulders. I completely understood her fears. Josh was all she had left. He was her son, her baby. My eyes immediately sought out my own son, and I found Freddie laughing and playing by the lake with Janie, Tina, and the two Gold girls. I'd found out Hannah was eighteen, but little Mallory, despite how mature she looked, was only fourteen… and crushing on Josh big-time. Martin was watching over them all, despite his wrapped ankle—a silly accident he'd gotten coming up the slippery bank of the lake. It pissed him off something fierce; he felt useless.

"Millie, I wouldn't send them if I didn't think they couldn't handle it," my dad soothed, and I smirked at the affection I saw there, now wondering if there was a bigger reason he'd asked me to take Millie and Josh with me when we'd left Sandy.

My dad, despite how he probably didn't see it, was a born leader. People instantly looked to him for what to do. I'd seen it the second he stepped onto the campsite. Even Derek had relinquished some of the control, simply because Dad could handle it. It may have been his personality, or even the fact that he'd been the fire station's captain, but it was most likely both, added with his calm, level head.

"What about Jesse?" I asked in a whisper.

"Nah," Derek immediately answered. "I can't risk a *daddy-to-be* out there. It's not cool. Just like you aren't going either." He pointed at me, but I chuckled.

"Not a damn chance," Dad added.

I sighed, shaking my head. "Well, then, I guess it's you two, only because Ivan and Jonah are working on some sort of water thing.

They've rigged a few barrels to catch rain water, and they're working on some sort of pump. We still can't drink it without boiling it, but running water for a shower and washing clothes sounds damn nice."

"No kidding," Millie agreed.

"Here's what you're gonna do," Dad stated firmly. "You'll take exactly twenty-four hours. I want your asses back in this camp same time tomorrow. Not a single argument, and I don't care if you've caught anything by then or not. If you haven't, then we'll set up another trip, but I don't want you gone any longer than that."

Derek looked like he was about to argue, but Josh smacked his shoulder, saying, "Got it. If nothing else, we'll snag some rabbits."

"I don't care if you catch *frogs*, son, just get back here in twenty-four hours," Dad countered.

Derek snorted, shouldering his compound bow. "Yeah, Hank."

Standing up from the table, I zipped up the backpack I'd put together for them—bottles of water, a first-aid kit, some food, and extra ammo. I handed it to Derek, who set it down in the backseat, leaving the passenger side for Josh.

He busied himself, checking the Jeep over, then his weapons. Without looking my way, he spoke softly. "This is one of those times I wish Jack was here. He's good in the woods. He always was, but then…you probably wouldn't let him go."

Snorting, I shrugged, toying with the dog tags I now refused to take off. They comforted me, and they seemed to keep Derek's feelings in check. He'd backed off a little, though I wasn't sure that wasn't due to my dad's presence, not just my husband's name around my neck.

"I don't know, D," I told him, shrugging a little. "I can't say what I'd do if he were here. That's a painful game to play. I want him here so badly, it makes me physically sick to speak of it."

Derek sniffed and nodded. "Even if you knew, had closure…" He trailed off, changing directions. "What if he never shows?"

"What if he does?" I fired back.

There was the pity I'd come to expect from everyone when Jack—or even Rich, Dottie, or Joel—was mentioned.

"Don't," I snapped. "Don't do that. Derek, it took us nearly a week to travel a hundred and fifty miles. It took my dad almost two. How long would it take to come across the country?" When he didn't answer, I went on. "Then, ask yourself this…If Jack had enough knowledge to call me, to prepare me for coming *to this place*, wouldn't you think he'd prepare for the worst where he was? He's never been stupid, Derek Dunn. And neither are his parents, as you could tell from how Dottie stocked that bunker."

Derek grimaced but nodded. "Believe me, I hope like hell you're right, despite…" He finally smiled, and it was the lazy, friendly, half smile that was just Derek. "Look…I love my cousin, my aunt and uncle, and even that big oaf Jack dragged home so long ago. Joel's a loyal-as-hell friend. They're my family. I promised Jack I would watch over you and Freddie…and I intend to keep that promise, Sara, even if I have to fight his ghost to do it."

"Derek," I sighed and groaned at the same time.

"No, I get it," he said through a laugh. "Jesus, Sara, you've forgotten I was there the day he set eyes on you…and you on him. There's nothing like that in the world. Believe me, I wish there was. And now the world is even smaller."

I heard approaching footsteps, and I turned to see Josh and my dad walking toward us. Turning to Derek again, I whispered, "Please, be careful out there."

"Yup," he grunted, pulling himself up into the Jeep and looking past me. "Twenty-four hours, Hank."

"Good," Dad replied. "Watch each other's backs out there. It won't destroy us if you don't find anything the first time. Got me?"

Josh nodded as he got in beside Derek, who cranked up the Jeep. They circled around us, heading down the long driveway, with Brody and Mose closing a makeshift gate behind them.

"You're killing that man, Sara," Dad muttered with amusement.

I rounded on him so fast that he flinched. "I'm doing no such thing."

He sighed, shaking his head. "He's a good man, kiddo. He's done a helluva job with keeping you two safe, with this whole place, really."

"He has. And he's a good *friend*."

Dad smirked, narrowing his eyes on me. "And he's well aware that he'd take second place in your heart for the rest of his life. That's tough for a man to swallow. Hell, he sees where your heart is every time you set eyes on Freddie."

"I can't help that, Dad. I just can't."

"He'd take care of you, you know, if—"

"Really, Dad?" I asked incredulously. "This is coming from the man who never stopped pining over my mother for *how* long? I was… what? Two when she left? So fourteen years, right? Don't even go there with me, Daddy. It's an argument you won't win, especially when you and Mom accused me of being just like you my whole damn life."

He snorted, holding up his hands in surrender. "I'm just looking out for you, Sara. The world has changed…"

"But *I* haven't."

With that, I walked away to relieve Travis on the security watch.

It was a long day and an even longer, quiet night. We were all worried about Derek and Josh. It was a complex set of emotions. We needed the food, but we needed them safe. It was hard for any of us to sit still. Freddie followed my dad around like a lost puppy the next morning. He'd missed his grandfather so much, and the fact that they were attempting to fish together again, just like they used to, made me smile.

I'd promised Millie I'd help wash clothes. It was a long, drawn-out process, doing it by hand, but we'd kind of gotten the hang of it. As I made my way from my cabin, I noted all the changes around camp that had taken place in a little less than a month. They were enormous. Most of us had sorted out a schedule for standing watch—one on the tree stand Brody had built and one on top of Jonah's RV. At my dad's insistence, all of the adults stayed armed at all times. With the fence still incomplete, the occasional pack could still sneak up on us, especially in the rain or at night.

Millie's garden was small but green and healthy. The picnic table now had two large folding tables with it. And the fire pit had been expanded, not to mention my dad had brought a fairly large grill. Ivan and Jonah were still working on our water. Without power, the pumps wouldn't work, so they wanted to find a hand pump—or build one.

Millie was already at work as she poured a bucket of water into an aluminum tub when I found her between Rich's cabin and mine. She smiled sweetly, pointing to the few remaining bottles of laundry soap.

"See what you can get out of those, sweet pea," she told me. "I've already separated everything into easier stacks. We'll do sheets first, then underwear. We'll save the dirtier stuff for last. We may have just enough sunlight to get it all done today."

I let her ramble. It was sweet and soothing. She chattered on and on about nothing in particular, and I loved it. There was no agenda when it came to Millie, and I was able to lose myself in my head for a bit and watch Freddie with my dad at the same time. She was worried about Josh, so I knew she was hoping that time would fly by.

As load after load were wrung out and hung on the lines between the two cabins, I could feel the camp grow more and more anxious. Derek and Josh were due back at any moment, at least we hoped.

When the laundry was done and lunch had come and gone, anxiety kicked up to murmurs of worry, of what steps to take to find them.

"I need you guys to calm down," Dad said firmly at the table. "We'll give them a little while longer."

"Any longer, and you'll lose daylight," Jonah advised. "If you know the area they were going…"

"I do, and I also know Derek well enough that he wouldn't do anything foolish," Dad countered.

"Derek, maybe. Josh is just a kid," Brody stated, rolling his eyes.

"Brody Leonard Matthews, I can still put you over my knee, son," Millie warned him. "I used to do it when you were a child, and I'll do it again."

Brody's tan skin blushed a deep red, especially when there were cheers to see it. He started to get up from the table, but the rumble of a familiar engine caused all of us to stand up.

Mose rushed to the gate, pulling it open enough to let the Jeep through. I had to smile because strapped across the hood was a beautiful, healthy doe. Dad and I met them just as Derek turned off the engine, and instead of the usual laid-back smile, it was somber and serious that greeted us.

"We have a problem, Hank," he stated, shaking his head. "We'd have been back sooner, but…we ran into some people."

Dad grunted, his eyes narrowing. "Survivors?"

"Yeah, and desperate ones." Derek nodded, gesturing to Josh. "Josh here gave up some rabbits, tryin' to help them out."

"How many we talkin'?" Dad asked.

"There were two of them. Just kids, really. They looked pretty ragged. But they spoke like there were more and that they weren't far. I just…wanted to give you a head's up, Hank."

Dad gripped his shoulder. "No, no…You did the right thing. Both of you." He inhaled deeply, letting it out. "We'll just keep watch, stay sharp, but this is a big forest, so hopefully they'll leave us be, yeah?"

"I hope so," Derek agreed.

"In the meantime, let's dress this deer," Dad praised, slapping Josh's shoulder. "Well done, guys."

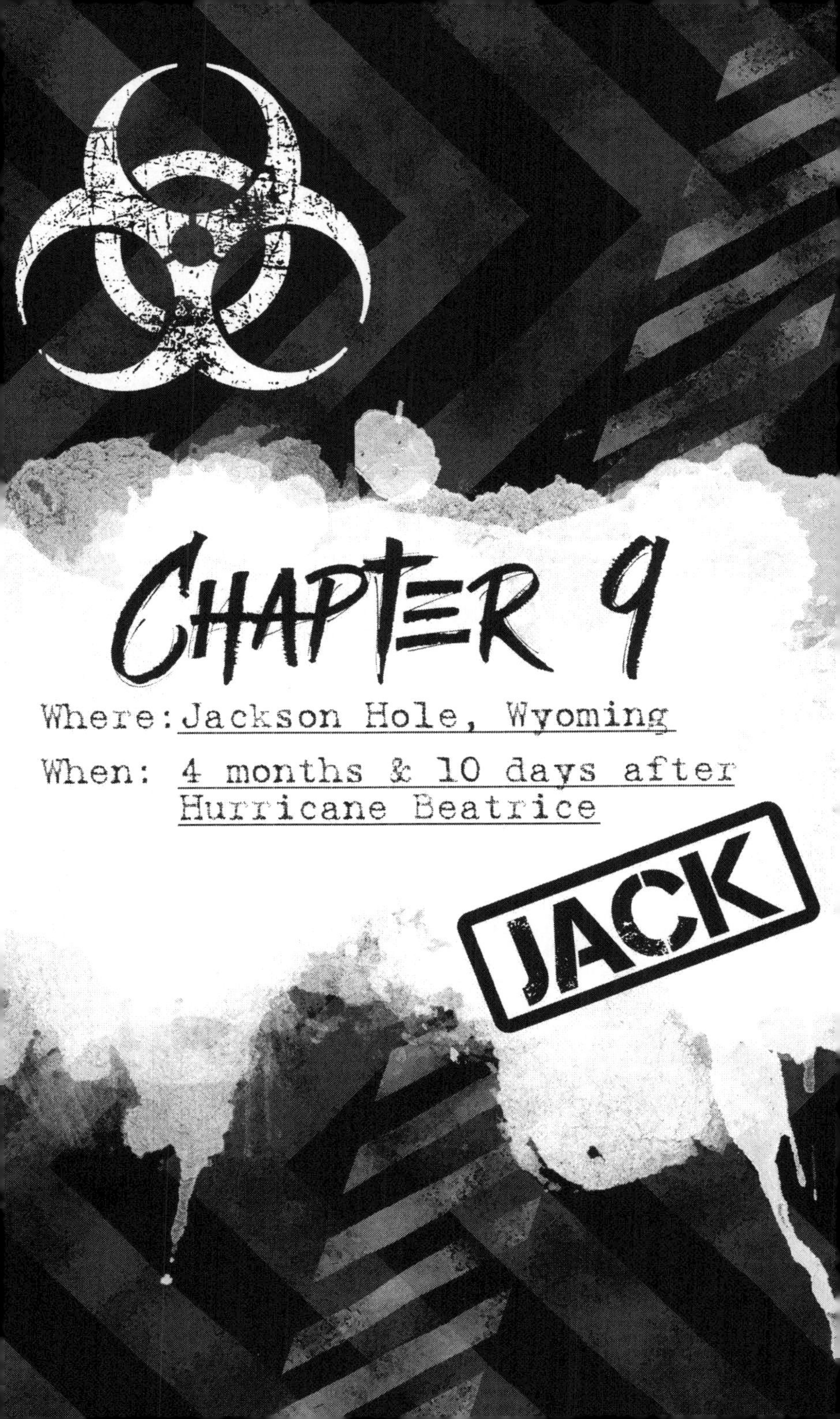
CHAPTER 9
Where: Jackson Hole, Wyoming
When: 4 months & 10 days after Hurricane Beatrice
JACK

JACK

Jackson Hole, Wyoming
4 Months & 10 Days after
Hurricane Beatrice

"What the fuck is that?" Quinn hissed in a whisper as we crouched low in the woods.

"Bison," I answered, aiming the compound bow. "Think of it as a big, hefty cow."

He groaned in appreciation. "Oh my fucking hell…*Steak*."

"Exactly," I sang low, waiting until the big bastard turned just right and it was completely oblivious of us as it grazed along the small clearing.

"We can't carry that shit."

"We're not taking all of it. Just enough to feed us for a couple days," I told him, smiling when the bison finally moved perfectly into my sight. The arrow left the compound bow in a whoosh, landing exactly where I needed it: the head. "I hate to waste it, but we don't have a choice. C'mon, let's get this done," I said louder as I stood, pulling out my knife.

"Did you hunt? You know, *before?*"

"Yeah. More so as a kid, but yeah. My cousin is the big game hunter," I stated with a grunt when my knife went to work on the bison. "After I joined the Army, killing shit—even animals—tends to be not so…exciting anymore. When you've shot people…" I shrugged, looking up at him. "Now, it's just…"

"Survival. Yeah," he said with a nod.

He was a good kid and had proven himself more times than I could count over the last couple of weeks. I'd been off on his age when I'd first set eyes on him but only by a year. He was seventeen. He'd lost his entire family to the virus—mother, father, baby sister. They'd been attacked on the way home from church. All of it made him a bit harder than he should've been, but my mother had already adopted him without shame. Actually, all the women doted on him, and I was pretty sure my buddy, Ava, had a crush, which I teased her about relentlessly. It was the guitar, I was damn certain of it. The kid could play well and even sing a little, and he'd do it at night around the fire. I wasn't sure if it was for all of us or to soothe himself, but he wasn't half bad.

I was still cutting the meat when I heard the telltale grunts, growls, and heavy breathing. "Aw, shit!" I snapped, jerking my chin. "Try to hold them off. I'm almost done. When we leave, they'll fall on this thing quick, fast, and in a hurry, so it'll give us a chance to run. Yeah?"

"Yeah, yeah…on it."

He stood up, pulling out the machete he'd been using the last few days. It was a silent weapon he'd used when we went through the outskirts of Denver. That city had been pure hell, something we should've known when "Welcome to Hell" had been recently spray-painted across the city-limits sign. Joel was sporting the Velcro cast again because we'd gotten into a scuffle with some asshole survivors who'd wanted one of the Hummers, which they'd succeeded in taking—but only after Joel beat the living hell out of one of them. It had been the one my parents had been driving since Florida. Fortunately, most of my mother's research had been in the RV, as well as the meager amount of food we'd been able to salvage along the road, but we'd lost a shit-ton of first-aid supplies and camping equipment.

Joel had sprained his wrist in that fight, and that was why Quinn was hunting with me instead of him.

I wrapped the meat up in newspaper, then in several sheets of plastic, before shoving it into my backpack. Glancing up, I saw Quinn take the heads of two zeaks stumbling from the tree line, though a few more were zoning in on the scent of blood in the air. They could have it.

I whistled sharply. "Let's go, Quinn. Let them have it!"

He backed away several steps, only to turn tail and run my way. The zeaks followed him, but the fresh meat on the ground was irresistible. They fell on the bison in a heap of snapping teeth, fierce growls, and tearing fingers.

We needed to get back to the edge of the small town where we'd left the four-wheeler. Those bastards had come in handy. We still had Ruby's RV, my Hummer with the store of ammo, and now a large pickup truck with a trailer for the two four-wheelers we'd taken in Dodge City. They used less fuel and were perfect for short excursions like this one.

It was downhill back to the street. The layout of Jackson Hole was right in front of us, situated in Jackson Hole Valley. In the winter, the place would've been overflowing with skiers, but it being summer, it was green…and really fucking quiet.

Reaching the four-wheeler, I quickly dumped the backpack into the storage compartment, scanning around us for more zeaks. There were a few here and there, but they were moving slowly enough that we could afford to catch our breaths.

"Okay, check the list. What else we gotta find?" I asked him, straddling the seat.

"Let's see." He reached into the back pocket of his jeans, pulling out a wrinkled piece of paper. "Your mom still needs first-aid stuff, so whatever we can find. Doc wants razors." He huffed a laugh. "Apparently you and he are looking like cavemen."

Snorting, I rubbed the beard on my face. "It's a bitch, for real. My wife would've already cut it off in my sleep."

Quinn smiled, going back to the list, but his face paled. "Um… Lexie and Ruby need…"

I rolled my eyes, starting the engine. "Right, they need pads or tampons or whatever. Got it. You and Joel, I swear."

"It don't squick you out or nothin'?"

Laughing, I shook my head. "Trust me, kid. It's just a part of life. I've bought more boxes than I can count for Sara, so…It's no different than toilet paper or fucking condoms."

"Of which we need both," he said, looking back at the list before hopping on behind me.

"Condoms?" I asked, swerving around two gnarled and decayed zeaks stumbling and reaching for us. Quinn swung the machete left-handed, taking the closest one out.

"Joel and Ruby," he mumbled, making me laugh.

"Okay, okay," I sighed, shaking my head as we left the wooded hill and entered the small town. "Pharmacy, it is."

We rolled down streets devoid of any movement, with cars parked here and there, some with dead inside. Quinn was watching out for stores we could use, but my eyes scanned upper-floor windows, shop doorways, and alleyways. We'd stopped at a lot of places since the very beginning, and I'd seen shit I never wanted to see again, but this place with its lack of chaos was almost creepier than if the streets had been filled with zeaks. It truly was a ghost town; all it was missing was the rolling tumbleweeds.

I came to a slow stop in the center of what looked like the downtown area. A small park that was now overgrown seemed to be the town square. But it was the archway leading into the park that caused me to stop.

"Wow, dude. That's really…"

"Disturbing," I finished for him softly.

I could imagine that at one point, the archway had been a focal point. At about twenty feet tall, it was completely made up of antlers—white, sun-bleached antlers. It looked like a combination of deer, moose, and whatever else, but still, it may have been some sort of art installation. However, the antlers were now being used… like flypaper. Skewered in several random places were zeaks. All told, maybe ten or so, but I couldn't see the other side. Some were still, some saw us and started to writhe, but they were hanging there, unable to move other than flailing arms. I couldn't decide if it was a deterrent or some sort of display of human mental illness.

"Did'joo ever see *Texas Chainsaw Massacre*?"

Chuckling at Quinn, I nodded and pulled away. We drove around the small park to the other side of town. It was there that more movement started to catch my eye—in windows and along the streets.

"There, Jack," Quinn said, tapping my shoulder and pointing to a storefront on the corner.

I pulled up onto the sidewalk, right at the door. It was obvious the place had been abandoned, because there was no sign of raiding or of someone having broken in.

"Perfect," I muttered, taking the key out of the four-wheeler once I turned off the engine. "Quinn, we're gonna go in quick. I need you to watch my back and our ride. I think we're being watched. And fuck that machete...Use your gun."

He nodded fervently, reaching for the door of the pharmacy. A bell chimed at the top, making me flinch at the sharp sound piercing the silence in the streets. I reached up to stop it, freezing long enough to listen inside the store. No shuffles, no growls, no stumbling met my ears, so I let out a breath, and we let the door close behind us.

"You stay at that door," I ordered him. "Eyes and ears open for anything. Got me?"

"Yeah, just...hurry, Jack. Will ya?"

"Trust me, kid, I understand. Now, let me have that list."

I worked quickly, filling the empty duffel I'd brought with the shit we needed. The place was pretty bare, but there were a few things left on the shelves. I reached the feminine products, grabbing what I could find, but the condom section made me chuckle out loud.

"What's so funny?" Quinn hissed in a whisper across the store.

"Apparently safe sex is *not* a priority anymore," I stated through a chuckle. "The shelf is practically untouched."

Quinn snorted into a harsh laugh. "Seriously? Well, I guess an STD isn't the worst thing you can catch nowadays."

"Very true," I muttered, snagging a bunch of boxes just to shut Joel up.

The last section of the store I needed to check was behind the pharmacy counter. I'd already grabbed the basics—alcohol, peroxide, and a couple of packs of bandages—but I knew my parents; they'd want antibiotics and painkillers, just in case. It was all the way in the back, and the sunlight from the front windows didn't exactly reach every corner. Pulling out a flashlight, I clicked it on and stepped around the register.

The shelves were ransacked but still had a few things. I grabbed what I could, freezing when the stench of decay wafted around me. I barely had time to register the smell before the shelf beside me shattered and a blackish-purple hand grabbed my arm.

"Aw, fuck!" I yelped, yanking my arm out of the zeak's grasp, but it pushed against the other side of the shelf, causing it to fall toward me. Boxes, bottles, and pills scattered everywhere when I tried to stop the tall shelf from falling on me.

"Quinn!"

I couldn't fight the zeak and the shelf at the same time. That same twisted, rotten hand reached and grasped at my hand, my arm, anything it could latch on to. The growls and snarls grew louder, as did Quinn's running steps.

"Christ," he hissed, and the pop of his handgun rang loud in the tight space, making my ears ring for just a second, but I collapsed back to the floor, looking up to see the shelf was leaning against the one next to it at an angle.

"Jack, you okay?" he called from the other side.

"Yeah, I think so," I sighed, shaking my head at how close that was to going really fucking badly. "Can you tilt the shelf back?"

He appeared at the end of the aisle, braced his hands on the case, and pushed. It wobbled enough that I could scoot out from behind it.

"How the hell…" I grumbled, knocking pills off me to the floor and wiping the sweat from my brow on the sleeve of my old Army jacket.

"You mean why didn't the zeak come a'runnin' when the bell rang at the door?" he joked, grinning. "Look at him…"

I snatched up my flashlight and shone it on the other side of the shelf. Apparently the pharmacist had been on duty when he was turned. His lab coat was no longer stark white but covered in vile shit and blood. But it was his legs that my eyes sought out.

"Oh." I gripped my hair, only to rub my scruffy jaw.

The zeak's legs were at least six feet away at the back door, but the bastard had dragged itself across the back room, only to practically climb the shelf to get to me.

I cracked my knuckles, shaking my head. "Someone's been at him. As in, they shot those legs off. I'd say shotgun? Maybe?"

"Yeah, well…he still thought you were tasty."

I waved that statement away, shaking off the adrenaline still coursing through me.

"Can we be done now?" Quinn asked. "I'm fucking starving."

"Yeah, kid. C'mon," I sighed, shouldering the now heavy duffel bag. "I think I got everything, and if I didn't…we'll live."

We hurried through the store and burst out the doorway, ignoring the chiming bell this time. I dropped the duffel onto the seat of the four-wheeler, spinning when Quinn cursed, his gun engaging.

"Put that gun down!" I snapped, pushing the barrel of his weapon toward the sidewalk.

Standing in pure eerie silence was a little girl who couldn't have been much older than Freddie. She was filthy, her pink dress covered in smudges of what looked like food and blood. She had light-brown hair and dark-blue eyes that reminded me of my Sara's. Her shoulders were strapped down with what looked to be a heavy backpack. She wasn't a zeak, simply because tears coursed down the little girl's face, clearing her pale skin with those tear tracks.

"Jesus, sweetheart…You just scared us. That's all. You okay?" I asked her, stepping slowly toward her. As I got closer, I could see that she wasn't carrying a backpack but another kid—a baby. The infant was weighing the girl down, but she was holding her own at the moment. Kneeling down in front of her, I asked, "You alone? What's your name?"

"Sabrina, but Mommy calls me Rina."

"Well, I'm Jack. This here's Quinn." I pointed a thumb behind me. "Now, why are you out here alone?"

She hiccupped a sob, shaking her head. "Mom…mommy…She's sick, and I couldn't…And…I can't reach…"

Groaning, I closed my eyes for a second, only to nod slowly and reach out to wipe away her tears. "Okay, shhh…Where's your mommy?"

She simply pointed around the corner, which gave me a look at the baby on her back. He was at least healthy and quiet, chewing happily on his fist, his legs kicking restlessly.

"Hey, big guy," I called, smiling when I received a rather dimply, toothy grin.

"That's my baby brother, Aiden," Sabrina whispered.

"Sweetheart, why don't you let me carry Aiden, and you take me to your mom, okay?" I asked, not really giving her a choice. The chubby little boy was weighing her down quite a bit.

"Jack…should we?" Quinn started but shut up when I stood with Aiden in my arms.

"I can't leave them, Quinn. Not until I know just how sick her mother is," I explained, raising an eyebrow at him. "Bring that bag."

"Ah, shit. Okay," he sighed but nodded as he waved us on.

Sabrina was a fast little thing once free of her brother, darting around the corner.

"Hey, kid, wait up," Quinn called. "You can't know what's around these corners."

"Don't worry. Bob gots the bad guys," she stated firmly before taking a quick right into a doorway.

I heard her footsteps trudge up some stairs, and Quinn and I followed with Aiden now firmly gripping my dog tags. I snorted, thinking Freddie did the same damn thing when he was about Aiden's age.

The building was three stories and old. Each floor we passed, I could hear the scratching, the growling behind each apartment door. Sabrina didn't even bat an eye at any of it, which was both a relief that she wasn't allowing it to scare her and sad that this new world had already hardened the young. I forced that thought out of my head, simply because my son was seeing this new world—I hoped—and I couldn't fathom how he was handling it.

Sabrina stopped in front of a door at the end of the hallway, waiting until we caught up with her. She turned the knob and went in. The apartment was a mess. Clothes and toys were everywhere, not to mention open cans of food. Aiden wriggled in my arms, and I set him down in a toy-filled playpen, ruffling his hair, which was slightly darker than his sister's.

Sabrina, suddenly quiet and shy, stood in the hallway, pointing to a bedroom door. "Mommy's in there."

I glanced over my shoulder to Quinn, who grimaced and slowly wrapped his hand around the handle of the machete in his belt. I did the same to the knife on my thigh, not sure what I'd find inside that bedroom. The door creaked a little when I pushed on it. The room smelled of sickness—the smell that came with medicines used to help someone breathe, the stale, still air of a room that had been closed up.

There was no movement in the room, but the bed wasn't empty. A woman with dark hair lay there sweating and unconscious. Her face was flushed, her brow wrinkled. Her leg was out from under the covers and haphazardly bandaged.

"Her name's Olivia," Sabrina whispered, only to bolt when Aiden started to fuss.

"Olivia?" I called, placing a hand on her brow. "Jesus, she's burning up."

"'Cause she's in shock, I think," Quinn whispered, lifting the bandage on her leg.

"Oh shit…" I reached into my jeans pocket and pulled out the key to the four-wheeler. "You know the way back to camp, Quinn?"

"Yeah, but I'm not leaving you, Jack. Your parents will kick my ass. Your dad, especially. And Joel will pound me!"

I shook my head. "No, you're gonna bring all of them here. Now! I need my parents for this, and tell my mother to bring everything she's got. Go! Lead them straight through town and set up camp in the street downstairs. Go as quickly as you can!" I pressed the keys into his hand, spinning him and shoving him out the door.

He was out of the room and slamming the apartment door before I could tell him again. Walking back into the living room, I saw that Sabrina was keeping her brother occupied. I opened the duffel I'd filled at the pharmacy, grabbing the bottles of alcohol and peroxide, as well as a roll of gauze. Their kitchen was a mess, but I didn't pay it much attention, considering there was no telling how long the little girl had been fending for herself and her brother. Her mother looked like she'd been out of it for some time.

Inside the cabinets, I found a bowl, half a bottle of water, and a few dishcloths. Pouring some water and alcohol into the bowl, I dropped one of the rags in there. I had to get her fever down. My parents could look at the wound on her leg. It didn't look like a zeak bite. If it had, then it would only be a matter of time before she turned…or she would've turned already. No, that looked like a bullet wound or a graze of a bullet. I couldn't be sure, which was why my parents were needed.

As I entered the bedroom again, I heard the four-wheeler's tires squeal on the pavement below as Quinn turned around to head back to camp. It wasn't far, just up in the hills. It would take him less than ten minutes to reach them and several more to move camp. If Quinn was smart, he'd bring at least one of my parents back with him with first-aid supplies. The rest could move the camp.

Reaching into the bowl, I wrung out the cool liquid, setting the rag on her forehead. She flinched, moaned in her sleep, but didn't wake. I wiped her face and wrung out the cloth again, only this time, I left the rag on her forehead. Carefully, gently, I checked where I could see for more wounds. I looked for bites, scratches, any sign that this was something other than shock or the flu or both.

I heard shuffling at the doorway, and I smiled at the little girl. "How long has your mommy been like this? Sick, I mean."

She shrugged. "I dunno. She was all stuffy yesterday and went to the store for sumpin' to stop her coughin'. She came back bleedin'."

I nodded, eyeing that leg again and then the shotgun in the corner of the bedroom. If I was guessing, then I'd say she ran into that zeak that had pushed the pill case on me. She'd most likely been surprised by him. If she fell, pulling the trigger at the same time, she could have accidently grazed herself with buckshot, but at least she'd rid the zeak of his damn legs. It had probably given her enough time to get the hell out of there—with or without the wound.

I wrung out the rag again, putting it back on her forehead. Olivia still didn't wake. I paced from the bedroom window to the living room window. The street was silent, eerie. After my fourth or fifth pass, movement caught my eye from the living room's view of the street.

A giant of a man was pushing a cart down the street. My brow wrinkled at the dead zeak on top of the cart. The white-coat-wearing, legless bastard from the pharmacy, with his legs piled atop his chest.

"Dat's Bob," Sabrina whispered.

"Who is he?"

"The garbage man," she stated, like I should've known such basic information, which made me chuckle at her.

As Bob passed by under the window, I noticed he had made himself some sort of body armor using duct tape and sports equipment—shin pads, shoulder pads, and something around his forearms. He stopped and pulled a baseball bat from the bottom of the cart, and his lips moved like he was talking to himself. He walked without fear, without hesitation, to a zeak slowly stumbling out of an alleyway. One strong swing, and the zeak's head imploded. Bob lifted the body as easily as I'd carried Aiden, dropping him on top of the pharmacy zeak, only to continue on down the street.

"He takes them to the park."

Grimacing at that, I nodded and started to pace again. I lost count of how many laps I did around that tiny-ass apartment, but when I finally heard the four-wheeler's engine on the street below, I rushed back to the living room window. Quinn had brought my mother, who was wearing the backpack with whatever medical supplies she'd been able to salvage.

I ran down the stairs of the building, meeting her at the door, but pointed to Quinn. "Go help everyone else."

"I don't need to, Jack. They're coming," he stated, pointing behind him with a thumb. "I gave them directions."

"Where is she?" Mom asked, and I led both of them back upstairs. As soon as she saw the disarray in the apartment, then the two little ones, her face turned up to mine. "Oh, Jack."

"Yeah, exactly why I sent for you," I muttered as she followed me to the bedroom. "She's burning up. And this looks like a bullet to me, but…I don't know. It's not a bite, for sure."

"No, no…it's not." She checked the woman over. "She's dehydrated, fever. Probably the flu. But shock too, with this wound. I'll need to clean it out, but it might have been too long to stitch it."

"Do what you do," I told her as she pulled on rubber gloves.

"I'll need your help until your father gets here."

Nodding, I followed every instruction. Quinn piped up that everyone was pulling up downstairs as Mom started an IV of saline, asking me to hold it up until she moved a coatrack that had been by the front door so that she could hang it. She removed the haphazard bandage, flinching at the wound, but got to work immediately on checking it, cleaning it, and feeling around in it for any bullets or fragments. The *plink* of metal onto the nightstand proved my theory correct. She'd accidently caught a stray while defending herself—whether by ricochet or just plain fuck-up.

Olivia moaned in pain when Mom cleaned the wound and rewrapped it tight, but my mother glanced over her shoulder when my dad appeared in the doorway.

"We need to get antibiotics in her," she stated.

"I got some at the pharmacy, but they're pills," I told them.

"Check the bag, Rich. If there's not a vial, then we'll crush up the ones Jack has."

The two of them went to work on the poor woman, so I left the room, finding Ruby and Ava with the kids. Ava was playing with Aiden, and Ruby was giving Sabrina's face a wipe down at the same time the poor girl was trying to shove an apple in her face.

"How is she?" Ruby asked.

I shrugged. "She's not awake; that's all I know."

"Joel said to tell you he needs your help setting up downstairs. He's gonna smoke that meat you guys got today. And these two need food."

Nodding, I raked my fingers through my hair and then rubbed the back of my neck. "What if…"

Ruby glanced between the two little ones. "I don't know, Jack." She sighed, but her sad hazel eyes locked on mine. "What *can* we do?"

Shaking my head, I made for the apartment door. "I think this one's on my parents."

It was a long damn night. Olivia stayed unconscious through it all. My parents watched over her in shifts, changing the IVs, monitoring her fever, and checking her pupils. We were down to one last bag of saline, which meant hunting down more, but if she came out of this shit, it would be worth it. Watching the kids with Lexie, Ava, Joel, and Ruby was amusing. We were all worried they'd be orphaned by morning. If that were the case, we didn't know what we'd do.

Aiden got fussy after he'd eaten almost his weight in steak and canned green beans. He'd shoved it into his face by the tiny fistful, but he fought sleep. We were all piled in the living room of the apartment when he started to truly lose his shit.

"Here," I said, holding my hands out for him. "My son was like him at that age. It's teeth and stubbornness."

"Well, I can't imagine where he got that," Lexie taunted, and I rolled my eyes at the chuckles around the room but gathered the little guy up.

"Quinn, play something. Something soft, easy."

The kid smirked, but he'd already been plucking at the guitar anyway. He sat forward, resting the beautiful natural-wood instrument on his knees. His song choice was familiar and almost painful. Smiling in memory of first meeting Sara, of slow dances the night before I had to ship out to Afghanistan, and of long kisses I'd wanted to last forever, I hummed the song against Aiden's head. He picked up my dog tags and gripped them, starting to pull them to his mouth, but I offered him my fingers instead—at least they were clean.

The little guy grumbled a bit more while Quinn sang words of tough times and being there for someone, begging to be a friend or more. Aiden let out a shaky sigh, but his head fell to my shoulder as I paced slowly, rubbing sore gums with my finger.

Fuck me, I missed Freddie and Sara. She'd have been all over this situation, loving and doting on Sabrina and Aiden. She was an amazing mother, which gave me hope, and it made me sad too, simply because we'd talked about another baby. She'd wanted more time with Freddie, and I'd wanted to be out of the Army when we even attempted it. We'd been on the same page, but now I hated that we'd waited. Or maybe I didn't. Life was iffy and short now. Shit had changed, but all I wanted was the chance to even have that talk again. Even if the outcome was no, I'd have killed to just...*talk* to my wife.

"Jack," Lexie whispered, coming to me. "Sweetie, he's out. You can put him down."

I set him down in the playpen, and he grumbled again but stayed out. When I stood up, I could see that Aiden wasn't the only one who'd crashed. Ava was curled up like a cat in an armchair in the corner. Joel had an arm around Ruby, and they were taking up most of the loveseat. My dad was stretched out on the couch, which meant my mother was probably in with Olivia. Quinn set the guitar aside, leaning back against the wall as he stretched his legs out in front of him.

As exhausted as I felt, I was still restless. I reached for my compound bow leaning at the door, saying, "I'm gonna check our shit downstairs. This town isn't empty." Sasha perked up and joined me at the door.

"I'll come with you," Lexie offered, adjusting her .45 to the small of her back.

The night was eerily quiet, and without streetlamps, every star in the sky was visible overhead. It was amazing how much we took for granted, how much useless and constant noise was in our ears all the fucking time, and taking all that away was almost frightening. No planes, cars, or helicopters. No chatter, television, or radio. There weren't any howling cats or barking dogs. And suddenly, I hated the silence, despised it. It made my boots seem loud as I checked the locks on the Hummer, the truck, and the RV, which were all parked along the sidewalk.

I adjusted the compound bow across my back and took a seat on the stoop, bracing my elbows on my knees. Sasha sat between my feet, lying down contentedly. She let out a deep sigh when I raked my fingers through her fur. Lexie sat beside me, almost too close, but I ignored it.

"You must've been a good dad," she said softly, but the noise was shocking in the quiet night.

"Mmm," I hummed with a nod. "I'd like to think so. At least I was based close to home and I wasn't sent anywhere very often. I was able to be there for just about everything." Snorting humorlessly, I added, "In fact, Florida was the first long trip in almost two years. I'd been sent to a few places but never for long. I was *this close* to being out of the Army." I held up my thumb and forefinger close together. "Joel too, really. We were so close to being done. We were gonna go work with my cousin in construction."

"Derek, right?"

"Mmhmm."

Lexie was quiet for a moment but then sighed. "I was supposed to go to college. Two years in a row. I'd almost gotten off that damn farm, but every time I got an opportunity, my dad needed help or my mom asked me to stay with my sister, Haley. And she needed me as a buffer. My parents weren't all that…lovable. They provided for us, but…" She shrugged a shoulder. "They didn't see the need to do anything other than farm."

I looked over at her, and tears welled up in her eyes as she tucked her hair behind her ear.

"I hated them. When the virus went crazy, I said we needed to go, but they didn't listen. They were convinced we could stay, but…"

I wrapped an arm around her, and her tears fell hard.

"I'm so *mad* at them," she hissed through gritted teeth, her fists balling up in her lap as her head fell to my upper arm. "And that makes me feel guilty…"

"It's normal, Lexie. You lost your whole family."

She shook her head, sitting up straight and swiping at her tears, and I pulled my arm back. "I just…I saw you in there with those babies, and…I don't remember my parents ever being that way. And they're not even your kids! I can't imagine you with Freddie…"

Chuckling, I shrugged. "They're the innocents in this. Just because they're strangers, it doesn't mean they don't deserve comfort. They…they need it; babies thrive on it. They're scared…and possibly alone come morning.

"The world is different now," I huffed, shaking my head. "It's raw and ugly, and we've been sent back to…what? The Wild fucking West. We're gun-toting scavengers who simply need to survive, but we don't have to go back to those ways of thinking. Civility shouldn't be lost in all this shit. I don't know. I guess that's wishful thinking," I sighed at the end of my rant.

Lexie leaned closer, her eyes on my face—my eyes, my mouth.

"Don't," I told her, placing a hand on her shoulder and pulling back a little. "I'm not what you're looking for; I can't be what you need, Lexie. I'm married, and all I want is to get home."

"No one needs to know. I'm not asking for—"

"Stop! *I would know.* Me. It can't happen. I'm not that kinda guy, Lexie. I'm sorry."

"What if she's—"

"Don't finish that question. Believe me, I ask myself every fucking day. It's a reality I'd have to face, but if she's not—if Sara and Freddie are waiting for me—then how could I betray them?"

The hurt that crossed her face was painful. Rejection was an ugly fucking thing, but I couldn't help it. I simply wasn't a cheat or a user. I'd never been that way. Even back in high school, when I'd been cocky and confident, I'd been faithful to my girlfriend, Kim. Even when the new, pretty, blue-eyed daughter of the fire department captain moved into town, I noticed but didn't act. I knew men who did, especially overseas where they thought they'd get away with it. They'd have girls or wives back home but fuck around on them on the sly. No, never going to happen.

"It's just not me. I'm sorry, Lexie. Truly. We've become friends, but..." I stood up, and Sasha was instantly on her feet.

"No, no...It's fine. I just thought..."

I could see that it wasn't fine, but she had no choice but to accept it. I waited for her to finish that sentence, but a sound echoed up the quiet street—the scuffling drag, the heavy, hissing breath, and the low growl. My head spun, checking toward the center of town and then the other way. There were three, moving slowly up the street in the dark. I could only see their silhouettes, but I could tell by the way they moved.

"Shit," Lexie grunted, getting up from the steps.

"We can either ignore it and go upstairs, or we can take care of it," I told her, but Sasha was already crouched low, ears perked up and teeth gleaming in the moonlight. "Sasha, stay," I commanded, looking back to Lexie.

"Let's just...get it done. If I ever turn into one of these fuckers, feel free to put me outta my misery, 'kay?" she rambled, standing up from the stoop and pulling out her long knife.

"Duly noted."

We stepped off the curb and into the street, and I raised the compound bow. But as the three zeaks stepped into the moonlight, I saw what was behind them.

"Oh, hell," I whispered. "We've got more than three. I'd say the swarm is…a dozen? But they've seen us now; they'll follow us up to the apartment."

"Well, then, we'll just have to wake the others," she chortled, putting her knife away and pulling out her gun.

Letting the first arrow fly, I lodged it in the closest zeak, and Lexie's gun completely destroyed not only the quiet but the zeak reaching for her. I heard the window upstairs slam up, but I was already working with Sasha.

"Sasha, separate!"

The big dog jumped into action, running full speed at the coming swarm, and they took the bait like always. She ran circles around them, causing them to bump into each other, falter in their steps, and forget about us for a moment, which gave me time to reload another arrow.

Quinn, Dad, and Ruby ran up beside us, raising their guns. They looked shaken but at the ready. Joel stayed in the window of the apartment, using the high advantage with his rifle.

"Sasha, heel!" I called out, taking out a straggler as Joel nailed the one behind it. The click of Sasha's nails on the asphalt grew close, and she plopped her butt down in front of me. "Good girl."

She panted, looking back at me with her tongue lolling out the side of her mouth in a big doggy grin. We all walked around them, finishing off the ones that were still moving, and I took back my arrows.

The sound of rolling wheels startled us, and every last one of us engaged our weapons at the same time. I lowered mine because I'd seen Bob already.

"Rina says his name is Bob," I whispered to my dad. "Calls him the garbage man."

Dad's eyebrows lifted high, and he lowered his weapon to speak to the enormous man, but Bob was in his own world.

"Bob thanks…thanks you…Gotta clean up. Nothing in the street," he rambled to himself. "Bob can do it."

"Oh." Ruby sighed sadly, looking at Bob with pity.

He was still wearing his makeshift duct-tape-and-sports-pad armor, and he picked up the closest body and tossed it on the bottom part of his cart, doing the same with two more, only to turn around and head back toward the park.

"Don't know you," he said, barely looking at us. "Gotta keep clean. Cleanliness is next to godliness."

"He's…" I grimaced, tapping my temple. "Right? I'm thinking that park archway is his doing."

"Probably. And to interrupt him may be…bad," Quinn said, grimacing a little. "My friend had a brother like that. To disrupt their…thing…whatever it is he's doing…Well, Ralphie used to have these wicked panic attacks. I mean, I can try to help the guy, but…" When I nodded, he headed off for the trailer of the pickup, where he'd probably use the four-wheeler to move bodies.

"Least he's a big bastard," I said, shrugging. "I watched him handle a baseball bat better than Jeter, so…"

Ruby snorted, rolling her eyes at me.

"Rich! Jack!" we heard my mother call from the window. "She's awake."

"Go on," Ruby said. "I'll help Quinn, but send Joel down."

Nodding, I jogged with Dad back into the apartment building and up the steps. We found my mother gently trying to calm Olivia down.

"My babies," she rasped, squeezing her eyes closed. "Sabrina… Aiden…"

"Easy, sweetie," Mom soothed her, which made her flinch.

"Who are you?"

"I'm Dr. Dottie Chambers," she replied, checking Olivia's forehead for fever. "Our group was moving through Wyoming, and my son, Jack, found your children outside. I assure you, they're safe."

Olivia's bleary-eyed gaze flitted around the room. "What do you want?"

"Nothing," I told her, rubbing the back of my neck and then cracking my knuckles. "I just…couldn't leave those kids if you were… It wouldn't have been right. I have a kid of my own, so I hope…"

Olivia's face cracked a hint of a smile. "Thank you. I don't know what happened. I went down to the pharmacy to get some cold medicine, but…" Her eyes widened. "There was…Doug, the pharmacist, was in there, but he'd changed already. I tripped when he popped out the back. I..."

"Shh," my mother hushed her gently. "It's quite understandable. I gave you some fluids, antibiotics, and redressed that leg, and I found the buckshot just shy of shattering your shin bone, but..."

"Oh God, what was I thinking?" Olivia sobbed. "I could've left them...They'd have been—"

"But you didn't," I urged, stepping forward. "That's quite the smart girl you have."

Olivia huffed a sniffly laugh. "She's five going on forty."

Grinning, I nodded. "Yeah, my son...He's seven and the same way."

My mother helped Olivia sit up, placing pillows behind her.

"Is he here? Is he..."

I shook my head. "No, I'm...We're trying to make it home."

"Oh." She let out a deep breath. "I'm sorry to have kept you."

My dad stepped forward. "Is there...Are you all alone here?" he asked her.

"Well, there's Bob, but...you can't really speak to him. He's supposed to be on meds but not anymore. And I think there was a couple a few streets over," she replied weakly, licking her lips. "Oh, but Mr. Cutter! He was in the building next door, second floor. We were taking care of each other, but I..."

I looked to my father, who nodded and started for the door. "I'll go check on him." When he looked to me, he added, "I'll take Joel with me."

A racking cough barked out of Olivia, and I grimaced.

"You need your rest, Olivia," Mom told her. "Your kids are fed and safe, and we won't leave until you're okay."

"I can't do that to you guys."

Smirking at her, I shrugged a shoulder. "Then you can come with us. You're almost out of food here, and you'd be safer with more people."

She coughed again, trying to nod, and then when she'd calmed down, she asked more about our group and our travels.

I told her more about where we'd found Ruby and Ava, Lexie, and then Quinn and had just started telling her about Sara and Freddie, but she looked past me when there was a light knock at the open door.

An elderly gentleman stood there, weary and worried. He was wringing an old blue baseball cap in his hands.

"Olivia? We should go with them. The doc here was telling me how they're traveling, together, safer," he stated, walking to the side of her bed. He gently took her hand, patting the top. "I'm not…I can't…" He sighed forlornly. "Sweetheart, we won't make it alone. Me, being too old, and you, with those beautiful babies. Please…"

Olivia's face pained, but she finally nodded in acceptance.

"Get your rest," I told her. "We'll do everything else. Okay?" She smiled, thanking me, and I nodded once, turning to Mr. Cutter. "Jack, sir. Just let us know if you need any help with your things. And we've got some food if you're hungry."

"Much obliged, son. Call me Abe."

I nodded again and shook his hand, sighing that we were set back for a day or so, but I wanted to talk to the rest of the group so that we could use it to our advantage. The town was practically empty, so I wanted to stock up on supplies as much as we could, including restocking some of the first-aid supplies we'd used on Olivia.

My dad smiled when I walked to him. "Give her a day or two."

"No, no…it's fine. We can load up here—rest up too."

He slapped my shoulder and then gave it a squeeze. "It'll most likely be just the four of them. Bob just about killed Quinn with that baseball bat of his, yelling about having to stay and clean up."

"Well, Olivia mentioned a couple on another street. We'll keep an eye out for them."

"Okay, son. Now, why don't you get some rest?" he asked, just as Aiden started to fuss in the other room. "Don't even think about it, Jackson Alan Chambers. I raised you, babysat my grandson, and I'm a certified doctor, so I'm fairly certain I'm fully qualified to rock a cranky toddler."

Grinning, I nodded, giving him a salute. "Yes, sir."

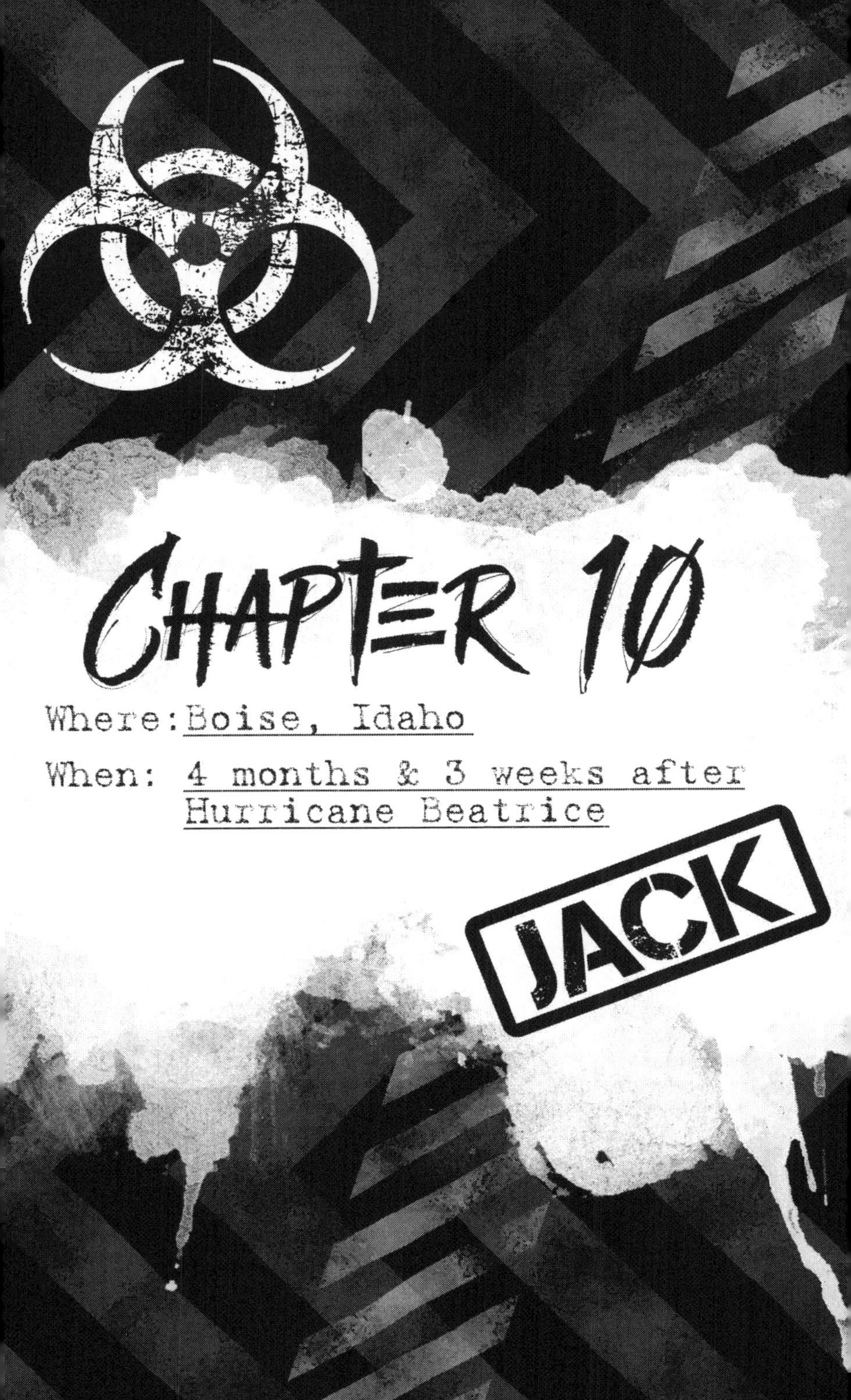

Chapter 10

Where: Boise, Idaho

When: 4 months & 3 weeks after Hurricane Beatrice

JACK

JACK

Boise, Idaho
4 Months & 3 Weeks after
Hurricane Beatrice

"We are *not* stepping foot in Boise," I stated, gazing out from the hillside view. "That's over two hundred thousand fuckers possibly turned, and if they're not turned, they'll be desperate as shit." I cracked my knuckles, only to shove both hands into my hair, gripping roughly as I eyed a few burning sections of the large city spread out before me.

"We need fuel, son," Dad stated the obvious, looking up from the map that was laid out over the tailgate of the pickup truck.

"I know. And we need to work our way over to the 20. I *know!*" I sighed, tearing my gaze away from the city.

I didn't want to go anywhere near it. We were so fucking close to home I could taste it. And with every mile we conquered, the more anxious I became. Boise sat just on the Idaho-Oregon state line, but it was a huge hurdle we needed to jump. We needed fuel, food, and safe passage into Oregon.

Joel tapped the map. "I'm with Jack. That shit is asking for trouble." He pointed toward the skyline. "My vote is that we get over to 20, follow that all the way to 97 North, and then we'll hit 26 all the way home. We'll go right through Deschutes State Forest. We could hunt out there, not to mention there'll be plenty of cars to snag gas from. It just seems safer. There are too many of us to sneak around anymore."

Nodding in agreement, I looked to Dad, who seemed to be mulling it over. My gaze landed on our group, and I shook my head. We'd grown so much since Florida. Hell, we'd almost doubled our size when we'd left Wyoming. Not only had Mr. Cutter—who kept telling everyone to call him Abe—Olivia, Sabrina, and Aiden come with us, but we'd run into the couple Olivia had told us about. Tim and Nikki Watts were in their mid-thirties and had been struggling to find food and ammo up until we'd come across them in Jackson Hole. They pulled their weight just fine, and Tim was pretty good with cars, so he'd been a big help when Ruby's RV gave us trouble in Idaho Falls, just after we'd left Wyoming.

"That doesn't solve the gas problem now," Ruby piped up. "We're all low."

Dad checked his watch, then the sky. "Why don't a group of us scout for fuel and food while everyone else sets up camp for the night? This ridge is safe."

I sniffed, eyeing the group and the vehicles. Aside from my Hummer, we still had Ruby's RV, which housed Olivia and her two kids, as well as Joel, who did most of the driving. Dad still had his pickup truck with the trailer that carried the four-wheelers. Lexie and Quinn rode with him and my mother. And now we had a minivan for Tim and Nikki and extra storage. Abe and Ava rode with Sasha and me most of the time. Every last vehicle was getting low on gas.

"Quinn!" I called.

When he finished attaching the small trailer to one of the four-wheelers, he jogged over.

Tapping the map, I said, "I'm gonna take Joel, Tim, and Nikki with me on a run. We'll go no farther than here. I don't feel comfortable going any closer to that city. I want you up on that RV as a lookout while they set up camp. Take the rifle out of the Hummer. If we're not back in three hours, you and my dad take the other four-wheeler up this road. Got me?"

"Yeah, man. Got it. You sure you don't want me to come?"

I smiled a little. The kid was quick on his feet, for sure, but I needed the strongest of us to lift and carry supplies and gas cans. Joel was perfect, and so was Tim. Nikki didn't like to be separated from him, so I had no choice but to include her.

"Jack," Ruby said, stepping closer. "Let me go. Leave Joel here."

Sniffing, I nodded. "Fine, then we'll take Sasha with us."

At the sound of her name, the dog sat up from where she'd been snoozing hard beneath the shade of a tree. Her bleary, sleepy gaze shot around, and then she was on her feet and trotting to me.

"Naptime's over, big girl." I chuckled, ruffling her fur on the top of her head. "Work time."

"*Boof*," she huffed, shaking all over and plopping down on her butt.

Everyone who was leaving gathered their weapons as the rest started to set up camp. Tim and Nikki climbed into the trailer with Sasha, while Ruby straddled the seat, leaving enough space for me to sit in front of her. Dad clapped my shoulder, telling me to be careful, and my mother handed me a list.

"Jack," Joel called, giving me a few clips of ammo and securing the compound bow to the side of the handlebars. "Take care of her. I'm not kidding."

Smirking, I nodded. "You have my word."

"Three hours," he reiterated, holding up three fingers. "And it'll be me coming with Quinn if your ass isn't back here, so…make it quick, yeah?"

Nodding, I scanned the rest of the group, smiling at Ava when she rushed to her sister with bottles of water. Then she handed one to me.

"Thanks, Half Pint," I told her, chuckling when she rolled her eyes.

"Hurry back," she told the both of us, glancing over her shoulder to Sabrina and then Lexie, who wasn't paying us any attention. "I'm tired of babysitting, and Lexie is no fun," she whispered.

Ruby laughed, tugging Ava's ponytail. "Rina looks up to you, so suck it up. As for…" She grimaced. "She's just…tired, sweetie. Hang in there. We won't be gone long."

"'Kay," she sighed. "Popcorn tonight, Jack? Please?"

I pulled her to me, giving the top of her head a kiss. "Absolutely! Have it all ready to go when I get back."

Her grin and happy jump were my reward. She was a good girl, smart and funny. She'd chatter on and on when she rode in the Hummer, asking a thousand questions. Abe adored her, and he loved even more that she listened to whatever stories he told her.

I straddled the seat and started the four-wheeler, pulling away from camp. I kept on the main road I'd shown Quinn, and it stayed fairly empty for the first mile or so, until we approached some houses. I pulled off to the side, turning off the engine.

"Okay. I think...pairs?" I suggested.

"You want us to hit these houses?" Tim asked.

"Yeah, just...gather whatever you can find, but gas is the priority, so take a tube and can with you. Each. Try not to use gunfire. Quiet is better." Turning to Ruby, I said, "You and I are going to cut through the woods, see if there are any rabbits, or...hell, squirrels or something."

Ruby's nose wrinkled, but she nodded. "Let me guess...It tastes like chicken."

"Couldn't tell you, but at this point, I'd eat just about anything that wasn't a zeak."

Sasha hopped out of the trailer, and she followed us as we split away from the other two. Ruby and I stepped into the woods, immediately engulfed in the shade of the canopy overhead.

"You know damn well Lexie isn't tired," I finally said after a few paces into the trees.

She laughed, watching Sasha scout ahead, only to wait for us to catch up. "She is tired, so that's not a lie, but...Her attitude problem is—"

"Me," I sighed, shaking my head. "Yeah, I know. But there's nothing I can do about that."

Lexie had become quiet after Wyoming, opting to ignore me after I'd stopped her from kissing me. However, the closer we got to Oregon, the surlier she became.

"Aw hell, Jack," Ruby said, coming to a stop and looking over at me. "She's...I'm with your mom on this one. I think she's young and deep, deep into hero worship. You saved her life, removed her from someplace she'd never been happy, and you...well, you're you."

"What the fuck does *that* mean?"

She shoved me with a laugh. "You're not exactly hideous, Jack. And then...you're all about getting back to Sara and Freddie, you've got an amazing way with kids, and I swear, Aiden and Rina are like little magnets to you. That's not exactly a turn-off for a woman. In all honesty, it probably makes it worse."

"Ah, Jesus," I groaned, gripping my hair and starting to move forward again.

Ruby giggled, a light sound coming from her. "There's that too. You have no clue how attractive you are…or can be, really. I'm willing to bet Sara pointed it out all the time."

"Daily," I muttered, smirking at her laugh.

"But the kicker is…we're almost there," she said solemnly. "Seriously. We're a day's drive from your home state, and the closer we get, the closer the possibility is that you'll get your family back. Your *wife*." Ruby looked up at me. "Imagine the guilt. She's crushing on you really hard, and the only thing *you* want is your life back. This whole time, it's all you've strived for. To wish differently is selfish and mean, but she wants you anyway. And she's well aware of it all. That's some tough shit to reconcile."

"Oh."

"She's young and a little immature, if not stunted by those parents of hers, who kept her on that farm without any regard as to what she wanted," Ruby went on to explain. "She's starved for affection, Jack. To her, you're fucking perfect."

Laughing humorlessly, I shook my head. "Hardly."

"Well, right, but take it from someone who knows, yeah?" She grimaced a little. "I thought the same thing once."

"Tucker?"

"Yeah," she sighed, glancing around when a twig snapped somewhere off to our left. "He got me out of a tough bind after the virus went crazy, but he was no knight in shining armor, that's for sure."

Nodding, I gazed around us, my eyes landing on Sasha, who was tense and alert. Another scan of the woods, and I saw what she was eyeballing.

"Zeaks. Two…maybe three. We'll do this quietly."

It was two women and a man. Their stench met our noses before they even caught sight of us. From where I was standing, I aimed the compound bow, taking out the man and reloading the next arrow. Ruby walked swiftly, staying in the trees to keep her distance, but using her knife, she ended the two women. We left them where they fell after grabbing my arrow and then moved on.

A few more yards, and I could see the houses we were behind, but I also saw movement in the bushes. Rabbits. Two of them. I knew one shot would most likely scare one of them away, but one rabbit was better than no rabbit at all. I aimed for the largest one, killing it with one arrow, and Ruby stashed it in the bag across her shoulder.

The two of us stayed pretty quiet the rest of the time. We stepped into the small neighborhood, raiding several houses and killing a handful of zeaks. We were able to siphon almost two large cans of gas from cars parked in garages or broken down in the street. Ruby had even found a partial can stashed by a lawnmower. There were some canned goods and bottled water in one house, a few boxes of cereal in another, and a single jar of peanut butter in the last house.

"I say we head back," I sighed wearily, hoisting the duffel bag up onto my shoulder and adjusting the compound bow to my back before picking up the two cans of gas. Ruby was just as loaded down, but she was able to keep one hand free to hold her knife as she nodded.

We took the woods back just like we came in, hoping to catch another rabbit. However, as the road came into view, voices also got louder, and they weren't Tim's and Nikki's.

"Give up the key, asshole," a rough male voice threatened.

"I don't have the key!" Tim snapped back, and I recognized the sound of fist meeting flesh.

Ruby and I stopped, setting our stuff down behind the trunk of a large tree. I put a finger to my lips, gesturing for her to trade knife for gun, which she did. Carefully and quietly, I led us to the edge of the forest, stopping behind a V-shaped tree trunk. I patted the pocket of my filthy jeans, grimacing at the fact that I had the key.

"Shit," I sighed, watching as three men pointed guns at Tim and Nikki, who were kneeling on the ground, their hands behind their heads.

"Maybe your girl here has the key," one said, stepping to Nikki, who was visibly shaking in the grip of a man nearly three times her size. "Why don't I just check for myself..."

He went to reach for her, and I aimed the compound bow at the tall, thinner man who seemed to be the leader. I heard Sasha's growl too late, though.

"Ah, ah, ah," I heard beside me, the cold metal of a gun pressing into my temple. "Don't do it, motherfucker. I'll blow your brains all over that hot ginger."

My whole body tensed, but I didn't lower the arrow, and my lip twitched in hatred as I glanced over at Ruby to see her pretty fucking pissed as she lowered her .45.

"Move it, asswipe," the man beside me ordered, and I did as he said, stepping out of the woods and back onto the side of the road.

"Well, what have we here?" the skinny fucking leader sang. "Maybe *you* have the key. Drop the gun and the bow."

Smiling, I shrugged, letting the man with the gun to my head strip me of my compound bow, and Ruby handed the .45 over. They were dropped to the ground in front of us. I balled my fists up, making the knuckles crack in the process.

"You'd have to check to find out," I said, but it was a warning. When one man started forward, Sasha's head lowered, her teeth flashed white, sharp, and menacing, and her growl raised the hairs on the back of my neck. "Sasha, heel," I muttered, and she looked at me like I was crazy as hell.

"He also stashed a shit-ton of stuff back in the woods, Ethan."

"Thank you so much for making this easier," Ethan stated in a sarcastic, sing-song manner as he walked to me and put his gun in the middle of my forehead. "Donnie, why don't you go ahead and get that stuff from the woods, hmm?"

Donnie stepped away, and Ethan smiled at Sasha's fierce, low growl. "That dog comes anywhere near me, and I'll put a bullet in her head. Then I'm gonna see what the ginger over there tastes like. However, I think Nate has taken a liking to the other one. Once we're done, I'll leave you for the cannibals."

I glanced over at Ruby as the asshole dared to touch her, and I saw that she'd broken out into a sweat, but it wasn't the threat or even the unwanted touch that made her nervous; it was the other side of the road. The woods had movement—slow, wobbling, growling movement—and lots of it. And if my guess was correct, the swarm was pretty fucking big. However, their timing couldn't have been better, and our captors had no idea.

"Now, hotshot...give up the key."

Grinning evilly, I said, "You'll have to take it from me, fuckwit." I glanced to Sasha. "Sasha, separate."

Sasha's head snapped around, and she bolted across the street and into the woods, her bark loud and sharp as it echoed out of the trees. Ethan was momentarily distracted by her, and I used it to my advantage, bringing my head back and slamming it forward. The sharp blow to his temple hurt him more than me, though I felt my skin split open just above my eyebrow. He'd been unprepared for it, and he doubled over, spewing curse words of every kind. He recovered quickly, reaching for me, but I swung my fist hard at his stomach, only to bring my knee to his face.

Ruby moved faster than I expected, throwing my compound bow to me and grabbing her gun. I used the end of the bow to smash Ethan's head again, but Ruby's gun popped off two rounds, dropping the guy behind Tim.

The guy behind Nikki snatched her up by the hair, pointing his weapon beneath her chin and giving a kick to Tim's face, which sent him sprawling across the asphalt in front of the four-wheeler.

"Let her go!" I snapped, aiming an arrow for his face, but I couldn't get a clear shot. My gaze flickered from him to the zeaks now pouring out of the woods, with Sasha running circles around them. "You gotta move, man!"

"Nate!" I heard behind me, but Donnie, who was loaded down with our shit, wasn't going to make it to his last remaining friend.

"Don't shoot him," I warned Ruby. "You could hit the gas cans and blow us all to hell." I swung around, releasing the arrow and nailing the thieving bastard straight in the chest. Donnie went down, along with the bags and two cans of gas.

"All alone, buddy," Ruby told Nate, shrugging a shoulder. "And you'd better move. Just go."

Nate wavered for a moment, and it was his—and our—undoing. The swarm of zeaks ignored Sasha's barking and teasing, falling on the closest thing: people. Before I could pull my gun out, they were on Tim, Nikki, and the last thief. Screams rang out loud in the darkening woods.

"God damn it!" I snapped, firing round after round at the zeaks coming our way.

Ruby did the same, but there was nothing we could do for Tim or Nikki. Ethan started to come around, and I kicked him just enough that the zeaks fell on him. It stalled them just long enough for Ruby and me to finish them off, including our friends.

I fell to my knees as the silence fell back around us. "Fuck!" I snarled, shaking my head and gripping my hair.

"We gotta go, Jack," Ruby told me, pulling at my arm. "We've drawn more in."

That snapped me out of my anger just long enough to order Sasha to separate again. Ruby and I moved as quickly as we could to load up all that we'd had in the woods and what Donnie had dropped when he fell. The trailer had a few more cans of gas and some bags of food, thanks to Tim and Nikki. I pulled my arrow out of Donnie's chest, wiping it on his shirt before stowing it away.

"Now, Jack!" Ruby yelled, gathering up the weapons our thieves had used against us and tossing them into the trailer.

Rushing to the four-wheeler, I hopped on, starting it up. I called for Sasha, and she gave another loud bark to the zeaks in front of her before dodging the new wave of dead bastards stumbling out of the woods for us. The dog leaped over the bodies and into the trailer as I turned around to head back to camp. Ruby's arms trembled as she held on to me, and I practically pushed the four-wheeler to its limit to get us back.

Camp was set up when we pulled in. A low, glowing fire was situated in the middle of the circle of vehicles. When we pulled up, everyone came to meet us, but Dad's gaze was sharp.

"Where's…"

Shaking my head, I got off the four-wheeler, only to punch the seat. "We lost them!"

"You guys okay?" Joel asked, his gaze falling onto my face. "Jesus, what happened?"

Gentle fingers lifted my chin, and I met the worried eyes of my mother. "You need stitches," she stated, but I merely shook my head and waved it off. "Well then, at least let me clean and butterfly it."

Ruby explained to everyone what had happened, but I stayed quiet as my mother did her thing. She was listening to the conversation behind her as everyone sorted what we'd brought and filled the gas tanks with the fuel. I groaned when it was decided to unload the minivan, salvage whatever gas it had left it in, and drop it from the caravan.

"I'm sure you did your best, sport," Mom whispered.

"I don't know," I muttered back. "I just…" I sighed, flinching when the shit she was using stung like a bitch. "Ow, damn it."

She grinned. "Gut up, Jack. Gut up," she teased me, cupping my face. "I'm…I'm a selfish woman. I'm just glad you're back. Now hold still…"

She finished cleaning my forehead, ignoring my pussy complaining and bandaging it up as best she could. When she was done, she stepped back to eye her work.

"He was gonna kill us," I whispered, shaking my head. "And he threatened Ruby with…terrible things."

"Then you did the right thing by fighting back. I'm sorry we lost people in the process, but I'm sure you did what you could. I know you, Jack. I'm sure you fought like a lion."

"I just want to get on the road…first thing. It seems like everything is against us the closer we get."

Mom leaned forward, pressing her lips to my forehead. "*Be still, sad heart…*" she whispered the poem against my skin, smiling when I snorted and nodded. "*Into each life some rain must fall.* We'll make it, Jack. In fact, I fear for anyone who tries to stop you. Of all of us, you have the most to fight for, okay?"

My heart hurt, but I nodded. "I miss her, Mom. I miss them both *so fucking much.*"

"I know you do, sweetheart. Your father and I miss them, too. We'll be in Oregon by midday tomorrow. There's light at the end of the tunnel. Promise me you'll keep sight of that. Okay?"

I swallowed thickly but nodded again. "Yes, ma'am."

Sandy, Oregon
Just Shy of 5 Months after Hurricane Beatrice

I'd never seen anything like it. I'd been in wars and seen what felt like every fucking state from the East Coast to the West Coast since the world fell to this virus. I wasn't sure if it was simply because Sandy had always represented safety and home or if the small town really was hit this badly.

We drove slowly through town. A few zeaks perked up at the sound of us, but I hardly paid them any attention. I took in Shelly's Bar, which was a burned-out hollow shell. The police and fire stations didn't look too badly hit, but the front door to the police station stood wide open. A zeak in a Sandy PD shirt stumbled out the door, and I shook my head at who it was. Nick. He'd been a friend for years. A few blocks down was the nursing home, and scattered about the front doors, side windows, and the parking lot were several dead bodies.

I finally couldn't take this slow fucking pace any longer. I practically floored it to the next street, the tires of the Hummer squealing when I took the corner too quickly.

"Son, calm down. You told her to get out, right?" Abe asked, putting a hand on my shoulder as I turned again. "You gave her warning?"

I barely checked to see if everyone was following me as I could only nod in answer.

My heart broke at the sight of my neighborhood. I passed by Hank's house—the house Sara had lived in when I'd met her. His windows were boarded up, the wood on the front door splintered a little but not open, and his truck was still in the driveway. I didn't stop.

I held my breath until the little two-story house came into view. My heart hurt at the sight of Sara's car in the driveway, but my truck was absent. I pulled in behind the little blue car, unable to move for just a moment.

"Is that her car, Jack?" Ava asked softly.

"Yeah, but my truck is gone," I barely uttered aloud.

"Maybe she took that," Abe surmised with hope in his voice.

I heard the caravan come to a stop on the street, car doors slamming closed. Dad appeared at my door.

"C'mon, Jack. We'll check inside. I'll go with you," he stated, stepping back from the window so I could open the door.

Joel was already up on the porch, looking to me for the go-ahead to open the door. I hesitated, gazing around the yard that had obviously seen some shit. There were boards covering every downstairs window. Sara's flowers were squashed, though they were trying to come back. The grass was overgrown. The porch chairs were shattered and covered in dark stains.

If anything kicked my ass into gear, it was those blood stains. I ran across the yard, leaping up onto the porch. Joel stepped out of the way, but his gun was in his hand, and my father armed himself as well.

My home was unrecognizable, not because it was destroyed, but Sara rarely let shit clutter up. And this was more than clutter. This was moving in a fucking hurry. There were empty boxes and bags tossed to the side, clothes and toys piled up on the sofa, and the cabinets in the kitchen were open and empty.

"Clear the room, Joel," Dad said softly.

I took my stairs two or three at a time, coming up to the second floor with my heart in my throat. Freddie's room was empty, his dresser drawers hanging open and ransacked, and his bed looked like he'd just gotten up from a night's sleep. His TV, gaming system, and toy box were all there, untouched. Melted candles were on the windowsill, and I could see that he'd pulled out every backpack and duffel bag he owned; only the too-small ones were left behind in front of the closet.

Pushing away from the door, I found Dad standing in the doorway of the room I shared with my wife. I locked gazes with him.

"It's clear, son," he stated, which made me hopeful. "She did what you told her."

Nodding, I swallowed nervously, stepping into the room that had seen so many smiles, laughs, and tears. It looked pretty much the same as Freddie's room, with open, empty drawers and abandoned suitcases and bags. Sara had packed in a hurry. The closet still had clothes, mainly mine and her dressier shit.

"Jack," Dad called, and I turned to see him by our dresser, pointing to a picture folded in half and standing upright.

My name was written on the outside in Sara's pretty handwriting.

The picture had been taken the last time we'd gone to Clear Lake with just the three of us, which had been a few years back. Freddie was little, with his baby teeth and chubby cheeks. He'd shot up several inches since then, thinning out quite a bit. Sara used to tell him he'd be long and lean like me.

Written on the bottom of the picture was a note to me.

> *Come to us. We went where you said to go.*
> *Love you,*
> *Shortcake*

She'd dated it, and I realized that she'd survived in this house for two months after the hurricane and that the virus had probably hit hard by the time she'd written it. She'd left just about the time we were getting ready to leave Dexter AFB. And that meant…my wife and son had been alive inside this house.

I sat down on the edge of our bed, unable to take my eyes off the picture of the two most important people in my life. The picture started to blur due to my tears, and my breathing picked up. It had taken me almost five months through hell to get here, and just knowing they'd made it out of this place like I'd begged her to made my whole body practically sag with relief.

I spun my gaze around the room again, tucking that picture inside the back pocket of my jeans for safekeeping. Smiling, I let out a small breath. Gone were our photo albums, as was my handgun—the nightstand drawer I kept locked to prevent Freddie from getting into it was wide open…and empty.

"She got out," I whispered to Dad, who nodded once and smiled a little.

"Thatta girl," he praised her softly, gripping my shoulder. "She's smart and strong, Jack. She would've had Hank and Derek protecting her and Freddie."

Nodding, I didn't say anything as I simply gazed around the room again.

I walked to the closet, pulling out some of my clothes and tossing them onto the bed, though my head snapped up when I heard Sasha's bark.

Dad walked to the window. "Zeaks. A few coming down the street. You finish in here, son. We got this."

I grabbed my older Army duffel as he ran downstairs, and I shoved clothes into it. I needed cleaner, newer shit anyway, so it might as well be my own stuff. Jeans, cargos, T-shirts…It all went in haphazardly.

I sat down hard on the edge of the bed for just a moment. I needed to calm the fuck down, or I'd lose my shit in front of God and everyone. To see my house, my *home*, looking this way made my heart hurt. Sara had wanted this house so badly. She loved that it was close to her dad, that she could keep a watch over him, even when he didn't think he needed it. She loved the fairytale look of soft-yellow paint and white shutters. To see it looking like it sat in a war zone was heartbreaking…for *her*. It must've killed her to nail up the boards, to leave the place we loved so much.

"Oh, Shortcake," I sighed, shaking my head. I thought back to the day we met here to talk to the Realtor.

Sandy, Oregon
7.5 Years Prior

I pulled into the driveway behind Sara's car, smiling at my girl as she waited on the front porch. I honestly didn't think I could be any more in love with her, but watching her hand rub the just-starting-to-show bump made me stupidly crazy about her.

We hadn't intended to start trying so soon after my return from Iraq, but I couldn't find a fucking thing wrong with a single bit of it. While I was gone, she'd stayed with her father but had slowly gotten us a tiny apartment just across town, and we'd moved in about a week after we'd come home from our real honeymoon. When she'd written to me about this house going up for sale, I was willing to take a look. Now…we needed it. We needed a nursery and a backyard and swings and anything the kid could ever want.

Getting out of the car, I smiled down at her. "Sorry I'm late. I got held up a little."

"You're here," she said, kissing my lips. "You're safe. That's all I care about. Late is fine, as long as you arrive."

My hand immediately found her tummy and rubbed in greeting, and I smiled down at her. "And how's Shortcake Jr. today?"

She giggled. "Starving. So when we're done here, you're in charge of feeding us."

"Yes, ma'am." I smirked at her, but I saw her face. "Oh, baby, you want it."

"I do. So much!" she squealed in happiness, grabbing my hand. "Come look and meet Mr. Grear."

I didn't need to see the house, except to maybe check that the fucker wasn't hideous. If the house made her smile like that, then I was in. I'd survived two tours overseas with her full support and love, so if she wanted it, then I'd bust my ass to make it happen. Though I didn't need to, since I'd stashed away for a rainy day…or this.

Mr. Grear was the Realtor Shelly had suggested to Sara, and even Hank knew he was trustworthy. He showed us everything about the house. And most of it had been renovated recently, so there wasn't much to do but decide and sign. The family had moved to Portland due to a job transfer, but it was obvious that they'd loved and cared for the place.

When he gave us a minute to talk, I lifted my girl to the kitchen counter so I could look her in the eye.

"Talk to me, Shortcake," I told her, cupping her face with one hand and smoothing her hair back with the other. "What'cha think? You're the numbers girl."

Grinning, she laughed a little, looking down at her hands and then back to my eyes. I wanted to kiss her silly over the hopeful yet tentative expression on her face.

"It's a lot to put down…"

"I have the down payment, baby," I countered immediately.

"I can still work. Shelly's paying me to keep her books, the Turners asked if I could sort out the bookkeeping at the store, and I could do some of it from my home computer."

"Which needs replacing," I added, chuckling when she snorted. "Okay, one thing at a time. Got it." I kissed her softly. "You want to work, that's your call, baby. You wanna stay home with Shortcake Jr., then…"

"Or Little Jack," she argued with a laugh, because she wasn't far enough along to know just yet.

"Or…Little Jack," I agreed for the moment with a smile I couldn't fight. "Then stay home or work from home…I don't care. But Sara, we can make it work; you just have to tell me."

Her sweet face scrunched up adorably. "I want it. Jack, I want it. It's so perfect. It's exactly what we want…and I think that first bedroom would be the perfect nursery, but maybe we should have Derek look at it just to make sure it's—"

"I've already talked to him, Sara. He did some of the work here, so he already knew about it. He says it's a good house. New roof, new wiring, new plumbing."

Those big, beautiful blue eyes met mine, gazing up from beneath long, dark eyelashes, and I chuckled. "Okay, okay…Let's go tell him we want it."

Her little dance on top of that counter was probably the most adorable, graceless, childish thing ever, and I stepped between her legs and pulled her mouth to mine with a gentle tug on the back of her neck. I kissed my girl hard and deep, loving the moan that I could elicit from her. Even better were the legs that wrapped around my thighs to bring me in closer and the grip she had on the back of my Army cargos, making me grind into her. Pregnant Sara was a needy Sara, and I usually couldn't stop myself, though this time I had to try.

"Baby," I mumbled against her lips. "Aw fuck…Sara…"

"Sorry," she panted, pushing back.

"Jesus," I groaned, my forehead falling to her shoulder. "Never, ever be sorry for that, but as much as I intend to desecrate this entire house, I'd rather do it when it's ours. And not when an old man is pacing on the front porch."

Her giggle was silent at first, buried in my neck, and it made me smile. It shook us both, but it was sweet music when it erupted even louder when she pulled away.

I cupped her face, kissing her roughly before wrapping my arms all the way around her to set her back with her feet on the kitchen floor.

"The entire house, Jack?" she asked, still chuckling.

"Every fucking inch, Sara Chambers," I growled in her ear, spinning her around so we could go talk to the Realtor. "No surface will be safe. Trust me, Shortcake."

Her back met my chest as she groaned a little, and I kissed her cheek before opening the front door.

"Well, kids?" Mr. Grear greeted us again, smiling our way.

I wrapped an arm around Sara from behind, pulling her to me. "Let's make an offer..."

I came up out of the memory when footsteps thundered down the hallway. Joel smiled a little when he stepped into the bedroom.

"I bet Sara was *pissed* when she had to nail shit to the outside of her house," he sang, shaking his head again.

Laughing in spite of it all, I nodded. "No shit. I wonder whose ass she tore up."

"Hank's."

We nodded in agreement, but he glanced around the room. Ruby appeared at the door, looking a bit worried.

"She made it out of here," I told her, pulling out the picture with the note.

"Oh, God, she did." Ruby gasped softly, and she smiled when she met my gaze. "She's beautiful, Jack. And Jesus, is Freddie a clone?"

"She is," I stated solemnly with a nod. "And you'd think he was, but he's like her in many ways."

She handed the picture back but cupped my face. "Your dad went to check Hank's house, but he wants to camp at your parents' place for the night. It's as safe a place as any, says he's got roll-down shutters. He said to ask you if you needed a bit of time..."

I nodded, standing up in front of her. "We'll head over there together. He's right; their place is better. Besides, it feels wrong… without them here." Joel and Ruby nodded in understanding as I picked up the bag of clothes I'd just packed. "We can sleep indoors tonight," I told them, leading them back downstairs.

"Doc says it's about a hundred and fifty miles to the cabins," Joel piped up, "but we'll have to navigate 26 some more to get there."

Grimacing, I nodded. "Yeah, normally it would've taken about three hours or so, but…We'll need to be prepared to rough it a few nights."

"Then I'm glad we stocked up on gas along the way," he sighed, nodding a little. He stepped outside onto the porch with me, gripping my shoulder. "Jack, we'll head out ASAP. As soon as we get some rest and some food in us, we'll be on the road. We're almost there, so just hang in there. We've made it this far, so nothing can stop us now."

"I know," I sighed, stepping back onto the driveway. "We can hunt at my parents' place. Maybe snag a deer. That'll be enough meat that you could smoke it to save it."

"That's what I was hoping you'd say," he replied, rubbing his hands together.

My dad had everyone gathered on my front lawn, but I gave him a nod, so he turned to face them.

"Okay, everyone. We're going just a bit farther. We'll get some rest, hunt a little, and then we'll be back on the road again. We'll do our best to scavenge what we can here, but I doubt we'll find much. Load 'em up."

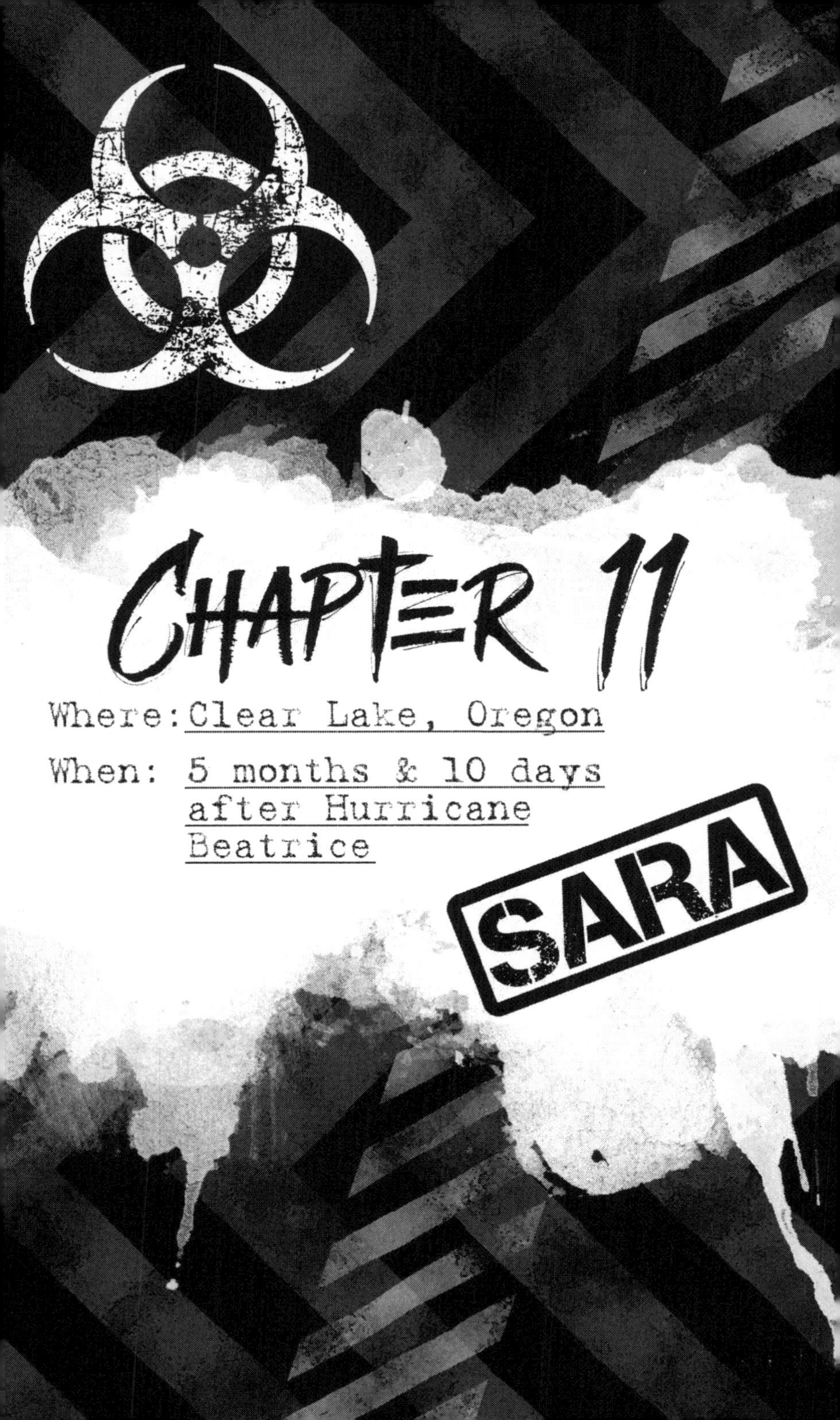
CHAPTER 11
Where: Clear Lake, Oregon
When: 5 months & 10 days after Hurricane Beatrice
SARA

SARA

Clear Lake, Oregon
5 Months & 10 Days after Hurricane Beatrice

"King me!" Freddie announced proudly, grinning up at Jonah, who pretended to be all indignant.

"I play winner," Janie called out, eyeing the checkerboard with a sharp, keen gaze.

Jonah was like an extra grandfather around camp. He'd taught the kids all sorts of "old-school games," as Derek called them. Backgammon, poker, checkers, dominoes, and even chess, which wasn't as popular as the others.

"Who taught you to be so good at checkers?" Jonah asked my son.

"Mom," he stated firmly.

"What?" Tina sang teasingly in my ear as we started to get the fire ready for dinner. "You mean there's something he knows that wasn't passed down by Jack?"

Laughing, I shook my head. "Uh, no. Jack's not allowed to play games. He gets way, *way* too competitive. Even Go Fish and Chutes and Ladders get him all riled up. Plus, it's the one game in which Freddie can truly beat his dad."

Tina giggled, shaking her head and shooting another glance at the table.

Freddie, Janie, and Mallory were getting a few games in before dinner. Martin had just finished with their schoolwork. Josh had been with them, but he'd left right after with Derek, Ivan, and Brody to check traps and get in a little hunting before it got too dark or started raining.

The camp was busy with as many people as we had now. Mose was still working on the spiked fence. Travis, Jesse, and my dad helped him, as did Brody occasionally. So far, it faced two sides of the tree line, but they eventually wanted it to go around the camp and portions of the lake. The Gold girls didn't mind laundry duty, though Margaret and Millie helped them.

Jonah took over the gardening, having set up several rain barrels around camp. It wasn't indoor plumbing, but it was better than no water at all. Derek and Josh kept us fed with wild game. Freddie, Janie, and my dad fished just about once a week. And we all had turns with security watches. We'd slowly settled into a routine. It wasn't perfect. It wasn't easy. But we'd learned to cope.

There had been the small pack or two, but nothing too big. We'd stopped it before it truly started. And the other survivors Derek had seen hadn't been spotted again.

I glanced up at the sky. The day was overcast, with much darker clouds rolling in from the distance. If I had to guess, the rain wouldn't hit us until later that afternoon or evening.

"Pretty ugly, right?" I heard behind me, and I smiled at Dad. "Let's hope it's just rain, yeah?"

"No kidding. Coffee?" I offered, pointing to the kettle on the fire.

"Sure, kiddo," he sighed, smiling when I handed him a cup. "This from that haul a couple days ago?"

"Yeah, I think so," I said, pouring myself a cup as we walked to my porch steps and sat down.

Derek and Josh had stumbled on a small cabin about ten or so miles from camp. The owners had obviously tried to settle in and hunker down, but it didn't work out. Derek had heard the growls, hisses, and clawing from inside the house, though he'd said the stench alone told him what had happened. Someone had to have been bitten before locking themselves inside. After drawing them out and killing them, he'd raided the cabin. All of it had been put to good use. Among the usual canned goods and supplies had been coffee, chocolate, beer, and whiskey. The two latter items may have resulted in the owners' demise, considering Josh had said empty cans had been all over the cabin, but that was just my opinion.

Dad and I were quiet for a few minutes, just letting the sound of the kids' laughter wash over us. Tina had joined in on the games, as had Martin, who was probably using it as a teaching tool.

"You know what I miss?" Dad said softly out of the blue, smirking when I looked over at him. "The diner."

Giggling, I leaned into him. I felt him press a kiss to the top of my head. "All of it? Or just the pie?"

"Oh, God. *Pie!*" he groaned like he was in pain. "I definitely miss pie…and ice cream. Cold beers at Shelly's while watching the game. Hot showers…"

"Hell yes, hot showers," I sighed, smiling down at my cup of coffee. "I miss…my cell phone." I wrinkled my nose at that but glanced up at my dad. "I do. It has videos and pictures on there I can't get back. Some go as far back as when Freddie was born; I just kept moving them over every time Jack would upgrade us or whatever. And everyone was just a text or phone call away."

Dad huffed a laugh. "Freddie being born…That was a day to remember."

Chuckling, I nodded. "I thought Jack's entire company would put the maternity ward on lockdown. Joel alone scared the nurses half to death."

Dad laughed, shaking his head. "Damn, I'd never seen a man so happy to be a dad, except maybe me." He wrapped an arm around my shoulders, giving them a squeeze. "And we both ran frantic the day our kids were born."

"He was," I said with a giggle. "Seeing me in pain…He couldn't take it."

"No…No, he couldn't," he agreed with a light laugh. He sobered quickly but shook my shoulder gently. "You still think…?"

I smiled sadly, shrugging a shoulder. It had been five months since I'd last heard Jack's voice in a panic on the phone. It had been even longer since I'd seen his face, been wrapped in his arms, and kissed his lips as he promised me he'd be home soon, that he'd be careful, and that he loved me more than anything.

"No, don't do that, Sare," he chided. "Don't give me the answer you think I want to hear. I know you hate the pity, kiddo. I know

I was out of line about Derek, that it's none of my business. Just… Tell me what you *think*."

"I think it's a long damn way from Florida," I stated simply, starting to get up, but he tugged me back down.

"Finish."

"I think it's a long way, and…" I sipped my coffee, but Jack's dog tags caught my eye, and I wrapped a hand around them. "I think…" I met my dad's gaze. "If *you* could survive, knowing what you know, then imagine what my husband and Joel and Rich and Dottie could do."

I expected pity from him, simply because anytime my husband or his family were mentioned, people reacted as if I was in denial, like I couldn't face it. I could face the reality that was around me, but I had more faith in my family than that. To just assume they were dead seemed like a slap in their faces, a disgrace to who they were. However, Dad simply nodded, kissing my forehead.

We both heard the sound of Jack's truck. I'd told Derek to use it because four people couldn't all fit with supplies and whatever they could possibly catch. Mose tugged the gate out of the way just barely in time for him to pull through. Derek was flying down the damn road.

The big black truck skidded to a stop, and Josh bounded out over the side, yelling, "We've been spotted…" He ran up to Dad and me. "They were on the same road and saw us. Two cars, dunno how many people, but they followed us."

Dad turned to me. "Get the older ones and the kids in the bunker. Now, Sara!"

I turned toward the table, calling Freddie and Janie. Jesse and Lucy were arguing, but I grabbed her arm. She was due any minute, so we couldn't afford for her to get hurt. Hannah shoved Mallory my way as well. I could hear my dad giving orders as I slammed open the door.

"Derek, Brody, you'll stand with me. Travis, I want you down and low on top of Jonah's RV, covering us. Mose and Tina, you'll take position at Sara's cabin; only show yourselves if you have to. Ivan, Margaret, Hannah, and Martin, I'll need you to cover us from the woods and my cabin. Josh, I want you with Sara."

Josh nodded, trotting up the porch steps as everyone else got into their positions. I gave the bunker a quick look as I followed everyone inside, making sure Millie and Jonah had made it down into the bunker okay, along with Lucy.

Before I closed the door, I said, "Stay quiet. We'll get you when it's clear."

"You be careful, Sara," Millie warned.

Nodding, I closed the trapdoor, rolling the rug partially over it. Joining Josh at the window, I watched as a car and truck pulled in through the gate.

"Sara, here," Josh whispered, shoving a rifle into my hand. "Take it. We'll cover them from here."

We both aimed through a space between the windowsill and the boards Derek had nailed to the outside.

Dad stood between Derek and Brody. Not one of them drew their weapons, but Derek's compound bow was strapped to his back, and Brody had his rifle the same way. However, my dad stood calmly, gun belt on, arms crossed, and completely emotionless.

There were six of them, from what I could see. Four men and two women. All of them got out of the vehicles, walking to my dad.

"This could go really bad," Josh sighed, shaking his head. His eyes didn't leave the scene on the campgrounds, but he kept talking softly. "See the girl…younger, with hair color like yours? And the guy with the blond hair?" he asked, giving me a quick glance. When I nodded, he said, "They're the ones I gave the rabbits to that day Derek and I caught that doe. Remember?"

"Okay…"

Josh tsked. "Derek came back to tell Hank about them. The reason we gave them the rabbits was because Derek didn't trust them any farther than he could throw them. He said something about them was off."

"Like how?"

Josh swallowed but turned to the window. "I don't know. He just said his gut told him not to bring them back here. I mean, we're all about keeping people alive, but he did *not* want them here."

The leader of the group seemed to be a middle-aged man with graying hair and broad shoulders. He had a slimy smile and an automatic weapon strapped to his back. In fact, all of them were carrying heavy weapons, almost military grade.

We couldn't hear what was being said, but I took in Derek's and my dad's body language. Both seemed calm but tense. The people started back toward their cars, but one guy near my truck pointed inside the bed.

"What's in the truck?" I asked Josh.

"We snagged four rabbits and a wild turkey," Josh said, grinning my way. "That bad boy is my doing."

Grinning his way, I gave him a high five. "Nice job."

Our celebration was cut short, though, when voices were raised and weapons were drawn.

"I think the answer is no, asshole," I heard Brody's voice growl.

Groaning, I shook my head but readied my weapon, as did Josh.

"Everyone needs to calm the fuck down," the leader ordered, standing with arms spread between our people and his. I noted he hadn't drawn his own weapon.

"You're not taking our food. We've already fed your people once," Derek told him, pointing between the couple. "There's plenty of woods, plenty of game, and it looks like you got weapons to hunt with."

"Oh, I don't think you understand, archer boy," the leader taunted. "We're not taking just your food. We're taking everything…"

When the leader pulled his automatic weapon to his front, my dad shifted, taking Derek and Brody with him. Bullets in rapid fire followed them all the way across the camp and underneath Jonah's RV.

Josh and I raised our weapons at the same time that Travis started firing. The girl with my hair color went down, and her boyfriend didn't take two steps before an arrow was lodged in his chest. I fired toward the leader, which made them all panic because bullets were coming at them from every direction. They scrambled for their cars, but I aimed for the leader again, finally nailing him in the leg. He hobbled to his truck, falling into the back as another guy got behind the wheel.

Two of their people were dead, and one was rolling on the ground holding his stomach, which had an arrow in it. The truck peeled out, almost backing into the lake, and the last remaining guy dove for the car. Bullets pinged off the trunk, shattered the back window, and destroyed a tail light, but it followed the truck out of the driveway.

"They just…left their people?" Josh asked, standing up.

"No honor among thieves, I suppose," I muttered, shaking my head. "If there's more of them, they'll be back, but not for their people."

"Revenge," Josh surmised.

"Yeah, or to finish what they started," I sighed, pointing to the trapdoor. "Check on them, but don't let them out just yet."

When I opened the door to the cabin, it was to chaos. There were calls of clear, but there were also calls of names that went unanswered. My only focus was Derek and Brody…and who they carried between them.

"Dad?" I yelled, leaping from the porch to the grass and running as fast as I could.

"Aw hell, Sara," Dad grunted, looking more pissed off than in pain, but there was blood staining the leg of his jeans. It was low, down on his calf, but still, it was red and seemed to be flowing freely. "I'm okay. It's straight through. It looks worse than it is."

They settled him down onto the picnic table. I took my knife from my leg, cutting his pants. Immediately, a rag was shoved into my hand, and I tied it just below my dad's knee.

"Get him into the cabin. We'll have Margaret look at him," I told Derek, who nodded solemnly.

The light was slowly leaking away from the day, giving a pale glow around us. The smell of rain weighed heavily in the air, wet and cool.

I stood up, turning to Brody. "We need everyone inside. Make sure to do a head count."

"We…um, lost Travis," he stated, rubbing the back of his neck.

Mose and Tina ran up from my cabin at the same time a piercing scream came from the woods.

"Shit, that's Hannah," Tina whispered.

"Damn it! Where's Ivan and Jesse? Weren't they with her?" Dad asked, wincing as he tried to stand when gunfire echoed out of the trees.

"I'm on it," Derek stated, smacking Brody's shoulder. "C'mon, Brody…"

"Hank," Mose rumbled, wrapping my dad's arm around his big shoulders. "Let's get you inside."

"Those bastards will be back. They're…" Dad groaned, pausing his steps for just a second. "He said they had about twenty…"

"Yeah, and he coulda been lyin', sir," Mose argued. "We've got to—"

Margaret's heartbreaking cry for Ivan and Hannah met my ears, and I knew what had just happened. She fought Jesse as he pushed her toward camp, and Brody and Derek were right behind them.

"We lost 'em," Derek said, pointing to Mose. "Get him inside. We've got a pack out there! The gunfire drew them in…"

Mose gave up guiding my father and finally just reached down and picked his ass up in order to get him into the cabin. The sounds of growls, snapping twigs, and groans made my skin crawl. Even worse was the sound of Margaret's utter heartbreak as she cried out for Ivan and Hannah again.

I could hear the pack breaking through the trees, and when I turned to look, about ten burst from the woods, some catching on Mose's spiked fence and some getting pushed around it. They found their mark in the would-be thieves, who were still lying in the grass, and Travis, who I now could see had fallen to the ground from his perch on the RV.

"There's only a handful. We could do this," Tina said, and I nodded.

Both of us raised our rifles, and Derek loaded an arrow. We took out the few that emerged from the trees, and we stopped the ones from feasting on Travis and the bodies the thieves left behind. A large hand landed on my shoulder, and I looked to Mose.

"Let's cover Travis. We'll bury him come morning. We'll also pile up those infected off to the side and burn them in the morning too."

"What about—" Tina started, but Jesse joined us.

"I'll help with Hannah and Ivan. We'll put them all behind Jonah's RV."

By the time we'd piled up the infected and covered our lost friends, nighttime was just about upon us and the rain had started to fall. It was light and misty, but I could feel it in the air that it would grow heavier soon.

We started for Rich's cabin, hearing my dad's curses, but Derek's hissed curse made me spin around.

"Headlights. Look," he whispered, pointing toward the driveway.

Bright lights flickered through dense trees, growing closer and closer.

"I want everyone inside. Lights out. Got me?" Derek ordered, spinning Tina and me around and pushing us up into the cabin. "We've got company comin'," he announced once inside. "I want lanterns out, candles out. Margaret, if you're workin' on Hank, take it down into the bunker. You can use the lanterns down there."

Once my dad was safely taken downstairs, I called Freddie to the trapdoor.

"Baby, I want you to watch over Grandpa while Margaret bandages him up. Okay? And make sure everyone stays quiet."

"Okay, Mom," he promised with a nod.

The trapdoor shut, killing the last of the light. Derek was at the window on the left; Mose and Brody were watching out of the window on the right. Jesse was pacing. Martin was by the back window with Tina.

I stood next to Derek, trying to see. Headlights beamed across the lake but didn't come far into the camp. It looked like three large vehicles plus a few people milling around. Two large silhouettes ran for my cabin, but I couldn't see much more from where I was.

"Oh, my sweet God," Martin muttered, and I spun to see that he was looking out the back window. "Guys, we have a pack moving through. And it's…huge."

Brody laughed. *Actually* laughed. "Well, maybe they'll take care of the assholes at the gate for us."

"They'll still smell us, you fuckwit," I snapped. "If you can't hear, the rain's picking up."

"Yeah, well, your loud mouth ain't helping, princess," he countered, turning to Josh and then Derek. "Just keep the bastards from breaking in."

The rumble of an engine and then rapid gunfire met my ears. I could hear yells and voices outside, not to mention infected meeting an end. But one voice rang out above the rest.

"Watch for friendly fire!"

My heart stopped.

"No…" I whispered, shaking my head. "Jack?" I barely breathed the name aloud before Derek's head spun to face me.

"You're one delusional bitch, Sara," Brody chortled, shaking his head and firing a round right outside the window. "That motherfucker's dead…and good fucking riddance."

"Brody, I will fucking kill your ass! I swear to God!" Derek snapped, bringing his gun up.

"Derek! Hold your fire!"

"Fuck me," Derek muttered, reaching for the door. "She's right." When Brody started to argue again, he yelled, "Everyone, *stop!*"

The door swung open, and guns aimed in every damn direction. Two pointed inside, and three pointed out, though Derek lowered his, giving Brody a glare. I was aware that the handgun pointed at Brody was Joel, but it was the other man stepping into the room who made me lose it.

I backed away a couple of steps as I took in the one thing I'd been hoping to see for the past five months.

Jack.

"Sara," he rasped, and the mere sound of his voice was my undoing.

The gun in my hands fell to the floor. Tears blurred my vision, and my legs trembled. Before I could fall, though, I was wrapped in the one set of arms I'd missed so damn much.

"Jack?" I cried, gripping him with everything I had.

He was leaner but stronger. His face was scruffy, his clothes wet from the rain and stained from fighting. But he was there. He was real and alive and beautiful.

"I knew it, I knew it…I knew you were coming…" I rambled, pushing back so I could see his face. "You're here. You're real."

His tired brown eyes watered, and he barely nodded, but he turned his face to kiss my hand as words tumbled out of my mouth and probably made no sense.

"Where's Freddie?" he asked.

I was just about to tell him when the door burst open. I struggled down to the floor just as a handful of infected tried to force their way in at the same time something outside exploded, lighting up the entire camp.

Jack fell forward when a piece of wood shattered from the door and hit his head. He shook his head as gunshots rang out, but I grabbed him as the guys tried to force the reaching pack back outside.

Patting the side of his face, I made him look at me. "Jack?"

"I'm okay…I'm okay," he chanted, squeezing his eyes closed and shaking his head, but he stood up.

"This door's not gonna hold!" Mose yelled, and even with Joel holding it with him, it was starting to bend forward, cracking down the middle where it had busted in.

"It *has* to fucking hold!" I argued.

Derek glanced over at me. "Actually, it doesn't. We can lead them away from here. They can't get at them." Another explosion rattled the windows. "Jesus, Jack…Did you bring hell with you?"

Jack grinned briefly, eyeing the trapdoor, but Joel merely nodded, saying, "Yeah, pretty much."

Jack ran to each window, looking out, only to go to the next. "Joel, the only way to do this is to let the door fall and then push our way out. They've got a bunch rounded up over by the lake."

"Got it."

Derek seemed to understand, and he turned to the rest of us. "As soon as that door falls, shoot every-fucking-thing you've got."

Grabbing up my rifle, I stood between Tina and Jack.

He leaned over and kissed me quickly, whispering, "Some welcome-home party, Shortcake."

Shaking my head and aiming my gun, I merely said, "Oh, this isn't the party, Jack..."

JACK

My ears rang with the blow I'd taken to the head, but I'd live. I felt almost giddy at the fact that Sara was standing next to me. I wanted to wrap her up, kiss her and never stop, but the timing was all fucking wrong. We were trapped inside my dad's cabin, and we needed to get out in order to clear the camp.

Derek's compound bow aimed out the broken section of the door, and he released it, loading another arrow and saying, "On three...Ready?"

He glanced around at us but then smacked the large black man's arm. I hadn't recognized him at first, but now I remembered him from Sandy. Moses. He and Joel looked to each other and then counted down, jumping back from the doorway.

Bullets and arrows assaulted the zeaks at the door, giving us just enough space to push through. Joel and Moses took the lead, using their strength and size to push the assault back. There had to be ten of us in my dad's cabin, and unfortunately, I couldn't focus past the fight.

When we all were able to spill out onto the porch, everyone split off in separate directions, and I took in the camp to see what my group had done. They'd thrown a few of our diesel-filled bottles at what looked like two different swarms, or maybe Sasha had split them up, but the fires burned, drawing in the idiot zeaks, which caused a few to spread the flames. It also lit up the camp bright enough to see.

"Hot damn, if that ain't helpful," Joel said with a chuckle, bringing his fingers to his lips and issuing a sharp whistle as one of the four-wheelers drove by.

It was my dad and Quinn, the former catching sight of everyone and smiling, but he turned to me. "Ruby and Lexie have the other four-wheeler. They've taken out a few with cocktails, but we've got more rolling in."

"Copy that," I grunted, taking out a fucker reaching up at me from the ground. "We've got to keep your cabin clear. And where's everyone else? Where's Sasha?"

At the sound of her name, my big girl bounded out of the shadows, teeth bared, head low, and growls shaking her entire body.

"Abe's got Olivia and the kids in the RV," Dad answered, and we both glanced over to see it surrounded by so many zeaks that the fucker was rocking.

Rain poured down in sheets, and I wiped my face. "I got it! Go… and keep this cabin clear!"

I spun toward our caravan in time to see my wife—which was so very fucking surreal—shoot three times, taking out three zeaks, only to take out a fourth with a knife. Something about that scared me and at the same time turned me the fuck on, but I realized I shouldn't be shocked that she'd survived this shit. Running by her, I tugged her shirt sleeve.

"I need your help, and…" I trailed off, but she didn't wait for me to explain. I wanted to tell her I couldn't let her out of sight for just that moment, but she seemed to understand without the words.

We stopped in front of my Hummer, and I reached for the rifle I'd set on top, engaging it.

"See that RV?" I told her, and she nodded. "We've got people in there. Kids…"

"Oh, damn, Jack," she breathed, reloading her weapon. "How do you—"

"Just wait," I told her, looking up. "Sasha!" I called, and suddenly, the big dog was standing in front of me. "Separate!"

"*Boof*," Sasha pushed out, taking off toward the RV. Snapping at them, she ran low, fast, and just out of reach of the zeaks all the way around the vehicle.

"As soon as she gets their attention, we'll have an easier time clearing them," I told Sara, who was watching with fascination. "Ready?"

"Yeah," she said, standing up as soon as Sasha had about a dozen zeaks all focused on her.

Another bright flash of fire lit up everything around us, which actually helped us, and we shot down the bastards around the RV.

I pounded on the door. "Olivia, Abe…You guys okay?"

The window flew up, and Abe's face loomed in it. "We're good, son."

"Good, then stay put for now. You're as safe as you can be, but take this," I told him, handing him my .45.

"Jack, wait!" Ava called. "Here!"

The door flew open, and my compound bow was handed out to me, complete with all my arrows.

"Half Pint, close it and stay inside!" I ordered, waiting until she did as I said, but I could hear the cries from Aiden and Sabrina inside.

The four-wheeler with Ruby and Lexie skidded to a stop in front of us, and Ruby hopped off. "It's a bitch to see out there. We need to get these headlights on…"

She rushed to my Hummer, turning on the headlights, and Abe followed suit with the RV. Lexie ran to my dad's truck and did the same. It helped tremendously. I could see that most of the east side of the lake was clear, with a few stragglers stumbling in, but the north side of the lake, the side the cabins were on, had some still wandering through. Gunfire popped off here and there, but I could tell it was slowing down. I heard people yelling at each other, working together to clear the camp.

"Lose the four-wheeler, Ruby. We'll work a sweep on foot," I told her. "We've just about contained it."

It seemed to take forever for the growls to stop, for the sound of bullets and yells to come to an end. We walked slowly around each cabin, finishing off zeaks that were still wallowing around on the ground. Someone had already started a zeak bonfire, which gave off enough light that we could kill the headlights of the vehicles.

Sara and I worked together, not saying much, but we were just about to make our way back toward my dad's cabin when three zeaks stepped from the shadows between our cabin and his. One caught Sara off guard, taking her to the ground, but I put an arrow through his head, yanking his ass off her. She rolled over, aiming my gun from my nightstand, the one I'd noticed was gone from the house in Sandy. Two shots, two thumps to the ground from behind me, and I smirked her way.

"Damn, beautiful. I needed you with me all the way from Florida," I told her, helping her to her feet.

As soon as we were upright, she wrapped herself around me. Suddenly, everything came pouring out of her. I backed us to the steps of our cabin and sat down, pulling her to my lap sideways as we stumbled over everything.

"I missed you so much..."

"I can't believe you're here. All of you..."

"I love you, Shortcake. Nothing could stop me; just ask any of them."

"I have so much to tell you. I love you...so much!"

"Me, too."

"*Boof*," Sasha chimed in from beside me, making me chuckle.

"Sara, I'd like you to meet the only other girl besides you who's stolen my heart," I said through a chuckle as Sasha licked my face and then Sara's.

"Oh yeah?" Sara asked, roughing up Sasha's big head as she sniffled and smiled at the same time.

"Yeah," I sighed, looking from the big dog to Sara. "She's saved my life more than once."

"Well, then, she's *most* welcome," Sara crooned, getting more licks as Sasha wriggled excitedly.

"Sara," I heard Derek call, and we all looked up to see him just as covered in shit as the rest of us. "I think we're clear. One or two may be out there, but they won't be a big deal. And the rain's letting up a little."

Sara nodded and stood up, grinning. "I'll be right back, then."

I wanted to follow her, but Derek stepped in front of me. "She...I... Sweet fuck, am I glad to see you guys!" he finally blurted out, pulling me in for a rough hug. "Goddamn, she never stopped thinking you were coming. I didn't..."

"It's good, man." I patted the side of his face. "I owe you...for her."

"Not just her, Jack," he said with a shrug, backing away as he smiled a little.

Behind him stood Sara, but it was the person at her side who made me fall to my knees. "Jesus, Freddie," I barely whispered, tears forming in my eyes.

"Daddy!"

My God, it was the sweetest sound—aside from Sara's voice—I'd ever heard. Even better was the feel of my son in my arms again. I stood up with him wrapped around me, and I buried my face in his neck. He still smelled the same but with sweat and dirt and little boy all over him. He was the sweetest smell in comparison to what was around us.

I felt arms go around me, and I pulled back to see Sara with tears welling up and falling down her face. I cupped her cheek, wiping away one set of tears, only to give up and kiss her.

"*This* is your welcome-home party, Jack," she whispered, grinning when I snorted and sniffled at the same time.

"I knew you'd come, Dad!" Freddie said, beaming at me like it was Christmas fucking morning. "Mom and me...we just *knew it!*"

I hugged them both, just relishing the feel of them, the smell of them. Pulling back, I kissed Sara again, whispering, "Sorry I took so long. I got a little held up."

Sara giggled sweetly, which was music to my ears, grabbing my face and kissing my lips roughly. "Late is fine, Jack. Better late and safe than not to arrive at all."

Suddenly, hands and arms encircled us, and Sara squealed at the sight of my mother and father, and they yanked Freddie from me, smothering him in kisses. Sara got swept up in a hug by Joel. There were new faces and some introductions, but it was damn late, and some shadows held back. However, those who were friends and family came forward. I felt a firm grip on my shoulder, and I turned to see Hank, looking older than I remembered.

"I'm glad you guys made it, son," he said, and I could see his eyes flicker to his daughter. He shifted on his feet, and I glanced down to see his leg was bandaged. "I didn't think you'd...Bah, it doesn't matter. We've got some things to go over, and we lost some people tonight, but it looks like we gained some new faces. Welcome home, son."

Freddie came back to me, and I scooped him up, only to wrap an arm around Sara. I glanced around to see everyone—my group and theirs—watching us.

"I'm sorry…for who you lost. We…lost people too along the way," I said, frowning. "We're here, and I'm not going anywhere, so…"

My dad walked up to Hank, reaching for his hand. "Just tell us what you need, Hank, and we'll do it."

Hank smiled a little. "Not now. In the morning. It's been a long damn day. We'll leave cleanup and stories for tomorrow."

Replies of, "Sure, Hank," were called out, and I nodded his way as Sara hugged me tighter when our boy yawned widely.

Freddie turned my head when everyone started to walk away. "I've got lots to tell you," he whispered, looking a little like Sara, which made me smile.

"Oh, yeah?"

"Yeah, lots!"

I kissed Sara's lips, then my son's forehead. "You know what, buddy? Me, too!"

EPILOGUE
Where: Clear Lake, Oregon
When: 5 months & 11 days after Hurricane Beatrice
SARA

SARA

Clear Lake, Oregon
5 Months & 11 Days after Hurricane Beatrice

"I've caught lots of fish, Dad," Freddie rambled. "And Derek taught me and Janie how to shoot. And Grandpa Hank showed up…"

I walked by Freddie's room with a bucket of heated water for the bathroom; Jack and I both needed to clean up a bit now that the fight was over. But I was barely able to contain everything I was feeling. It was late, there would be so much to do the next day, but to hear my son's happiness, to hear Jack's appeasing hums…It felt like a dream.

I set the bucket by the sink and then walked back into the living room to see Tina and Janie coming in the door.

"I didn't know if…" Tina started, grimacing a little.

Smirking at her, I shook my head. "Just because he's here doesn't mean I'm kicking you guys out on the street."

Tina chuckled but looked up when heavy footfalls thumped into the room. "I just wasn't sure, Sara. That's all."

"Jack, this is Tina and her daughter, Janie," I introduced. "They've been in the spare room since we got here."

I could see he was exhausted and probably a little overwhelmed, because I knew I was. But he smiled a sweet, soft smile, shaking their hands.

"I'm not here to disrupt anything," he said, shooting a wink my way. "There's plenty of room."

"Thanks," she whispered, telling Janie to go get ready for bed. She looked back to him. "I'm…um…I'm glad you made it okay. It's nice to finally meet you."

He grinned, and it was beautiful and kind. "You too."

She swallowed nervously, something that was rare with her, but tears welled up in her eyes when she met my gaze. "We lost Martin tonight. I didn't know until just now. Mose did a check, and I guess he got lost in the big fight, so they just found him…That makes four."

"Okay." I rubbed my eyes with the heels of my hands and nodded at the same time. "Damn it," I sighed, my voice breaking. I jumped when warm, strong arms wrapped around me, and I melted into Jack's embrace. "Four…"

"Shh," he hushed me. "I'm sorry, Sara."

I shook my head, hearing Tina's door click closed.

"I didn't think you lost so many…"

Pulling back, I sighed. "We lost three today…earlier, before you guys got here. We had some…bad people show up — survivors who were trying to take all our things. That's who we thought you were and why we were hiding. There was a fight, and it drew in a small pack."

"How many have you lost total?"

Snorting humorlessly, I said, "Now…six."

"Six?"

Sniffling, I swiped at my face. "Yeah, you only knew two of them. Travis…and Leo."

"Oh, damn," he groaned, gripping his hair and then rubbing his face.

"Jack, I…" I started, and he waited, looking down at me. His eyes were a warm, deep brown as his gaze seemed to rake all over my face. "I want to do this…this catching-up, trading-stories thing, but…"

He grinned, hugging me close and kissing my forehead. "Me too, but we need to clean up and get some sleep. Freddie fell out midsentence, midyawn."

"Oh, I'm sure," I said with a light laugh and then pointed to the bedroom. "I brought a bucket of warm water to the bathroom. It's all yours."

He shook his head. "You go ahead. I need to grab some stuff out of the Hummer."

I laughed a little. "Only you and Joel would steal an Army Hummer."

A crooked grin flashed quickly as he shrugged. "We had *two*." He held up two fingers. "Go on, Shortcake. I'll be right back."

Taking a lantern into the bathroom, I eyed myself in the mirror. There was filth and blood all over me. I stripped down, bathing with soap, the warm water, and a cloth, finally pulling on fresh clothes. When I stepped back into the room, Jack was sitting on the edge of the bed, and Sasha was asleep and twitching, as if she were already in the middle of a dream, on the floor under the window.

"You mind?" he asked, pointing to her. "She's…She usually stays with me."

"No," I said, smiling down at her. "I don't mind."

She was beautiful, big and black and sweet. But I'd seen her with him; she absolutely adored him, protected him fiercely. I'd give her anything in thanks for keeping him safe. A spot on the floor was a small, easy thing.

"Did…" Jack started but frowned down at the floor before standing up from the bed.

When he didn't finish and started for the bathroom, I stopped him. "Did I…what?"

"You haven't slept in here, have you?" he finally asked so softly that I barely heard him. "I just…It looks…"

"I did for the first few nights, but…no," I told him honestly. "I mostly slept with Freddie…or on the sofa."

His smile was sad but relieved too.

"I couldn't; it hurt too much, Jack. And no one else slept in here, either. Dad would sleep on the couch occasionally, but he stays in his own cabin most of the time."

Jack nodded silently, reaching down into a duffel bag to grab some clothes, and then he stepped into the bathroom. I slipped into the bed, smiling down at the dreaming dog. Her whiskers twitched, her feet shuffled, and her breathing picked up. She suddenly sat up, glanced around, and I scrubbed her head, toying with her ears, which she seemed to like.

"Thank you," I whispered to her, receiving a snuffling lick to my face before she curled up on the floor beside the bed.

I had to have dozed off at some point, because I snapped awake at the feel of the bed shifting and warm arms wrapping around me.

"It's just me," Jack whispered against my cheek.

Rolling over to face him, I smiled, reaching up to touch smooth, freshly shaven, clean skin, not to mention bare chest and lean, newly defined muscles. "Oh, *now* I remember you…"

He chuckled, pressing his forehead to mine as his hands roamed, cupping my ass a little over the boxers I was wearing. "You mean you didn't before? I was just some…stranger you were letting into your bed?"

"Meh," I scoffed, shrugging a shoulder, but I squirmed closer, tangling my legs with his. "You seemed familiar enough," I teased him, loving the easiness that had returned.

Long, calloused fingers slipped down my face, across my throat, to the chain around my neck. Even by low lantern light, I could sense the question, but I watched his face take in his name. The clink of metal as he turned the dog tags over in his hand was sort of loud in the room.

"Your son put those on me," I whispered, my eyes never leaving his face. "We'd had a bad day that day." I quickly told him about the pack and having to shoot Leo, one of our own, who had turned, and Freddie's meltdown after shooting an infected in order to save me. "So…everyone thought we were crazy or in denial, but we kinda stuck together. We kept our faith just between us."

"I'm sorry."

"Don't be," I said, laughing a little, which made him smile. "We were right. I'm kinda on cloud *I-told-you-so* nine right about now. There are one or two people I'd like to gloat to."

"Me too. I knew the possibility," he started softly. "The closer we came, the more we saw, the bigger the possibility was that you'd be…But I had to *know*. I had to get here to see for myself. And now, it doesn't seem real, and it's certainly not fair. I'm no better than anyone else out there who lost family, but I'm one lucky son of a bitch right about now."

"Shh, Jack." I placed my fingers over his lips, recommitting his face to memory. The tiny scar from the fight he'd had with Brody was still there on his bottom lip. There were deep purple circles beneath his pretty eyes from lack of sleep, not to mention stress and worry.

There was a brand new scar across his brow, following the arc of it, which caused me to frown a little as I traced a finger gently over it. There was another one just inside his hairline that was new to me too. "I think we're both pretty fucking lucky."

His hand that was still toying with the chain around my neck gave a gentle tug. My lips practically smashed into his, and what started messy and a little awkward slowly settled down into…us. The kiss was easy and perfect, and I'd missed it so much that my hands gripped him, my leg squeezed him closer—though never close enough—and tears leaked from my eyes.

"I missed you…so much," he mumbled against my mouth, sounding just as crazed as I felt. "To think of you…hurt, but I'd dream about you, about Freddie, anyway. And I'd wake up to the real shit…"

"I know. I get it. It's why I couldn't stay in this room," I said, rolling onto my back and bringing him on top of me as his lips never left my skin—my cheek, my neck, my mouth. He settled between my thighs, and I moaned at the feel of him…the weight, the warmth, and the bulge pressing always perfectly where it should. "God, I missed you…here."

I felt the sweet yet cocky grin against my throat when he pressed his hips into mine. "Where?"

A wanton moan combined with a breathy laugh escaped me. "Yeah…"

"Jesus, Shortcake…I want…"

Grabbing his face, I pulled at him almost forcefully in order to look him in the eye. "I'm not…protected anymore, baby." I wrinkled my nose a little. "There's not exactly birth control growing on the trees out there."

He grinned, and it was happy and silly-sweet. "Good thing Joel's a fucking horn-dog, then…"

He pushed himself up off the bed, and I licked my lips at the sight of him—boxer briefs tented sexily, his body all newly cut and toned but still lean and long, and the sweetest ass I'd ever had the pleasure of putting my hands on—as he bent to his bag to pull out a box of condoms.

My giggle couldn't be contained if I tried. "Seriously?" I whispered, trying to keep it down from the room next door. "Who? Which girl?" I tried to think of everyone I'd seen, but the night was a blur.

"Ruby," he chortled, rolling his eyes and shaking his head as he set the box on the nightstand. "The tall redhead. He's a ruined man. And these…" He held up one foil packet. "These are the easiest to find out there."

Jack slipped back beneath the covers, whispering, "Just like old times, Sara. We have to stay quiet." He brushed my hair from my face. "You're still *so beautiful*."

"I love you" was all I could get out before I had to kiss him again.

He kissed me fully, giving into everything. Jack tended to hold back until he felt like he could just…let go. Tongues danced together, tasting, relearning, reuniting. Hands grasped and pulled, pushed clothing away, and skimmed over places we knew by heart.

Jack reached for my shirt, tugging it off, but he trailed kisses up the chain around my neck. "I want you to keep these on. Always. I like my name on you."

Tears welled up and my chest constricted when I nodded. If he only knew that was the main reason I wore them, but I simply whispered, "Okay."

When we'd finally freed ourselves from underwear and shorts, I took the condom, ripped it open, and rolled it down over him, guiding him to me as he braced a hand beside my head.

"You have to stay quiet," he warned, his mouth quirking up into the lazy half smile I loved completely. However, it was Jack who moaned long and deep into my neck when he slipped fully inside me. "Christ Almighty," he ground out through gritted teeth. "It's been so fucking long since I felt this good."

My breathing faltered when he started to move. We kissed each other to stop sounds, smothered them against skin and lips and ears. The frantic feel dissipated, leaving slow, even thrusts. Jack's eyes squeezed closed as he drove into me in a steady rhythm, whispering about love and missing me as we slowly grew closer and closer to the edge. When he vowed that he'd never leave me again at the same time his fingers found my clit, swollen and sensitive, I had to bite down on his shoulder to keep from crying out. The release caused an overflow of emotions to erupt. Tears and sobs escaped me against his skin as I pulled him as close as I could. His own release was heavy, a string of hissed curses buried into my neck as he finally stilled.

When he pulled back, I saw his own tears had spilled, and I cupped his face, wiping them away.

"We're okay. You're home, Jack. You're home...It's okay."

Nodding, he rolled to the side, removed the condom, and tied it off before dropping it into the garbage can. Wrapping an arm around my waist, he pulled me close. He brushed kisses across my lips, nose, and forehead. "I'd do it all over again to get to you, Shortcake. You've always been worth the fight."

"You're here, Jack. That's all that matters."

He smiled. "Sleep, baby. I'll be here when you wake up."

Jack

Faint noises got my attention, some close while others seemed far, far away. The bedroom was still dark, though some gray, dreary light was squeezing through the boarded-up window.

The feel of smooth skin sliding against mine made my senses come alive. I glanced down to find the prettiest thing I'd seen in a long damn time. Long, deep-auburn curls spread out behind Sara, and my gaze fastened on creamy skin and pouting lips—lips still bruised from the night before. My old, expired dog tags clinked somewhere below the sheets, causing me to smile but wonder about them. I had a feeling there was more to it than just Freddie putting them on her.

Rolling to my side, I reached out to tuck a lock of hair back behind her ear. Just watching her sleep didn't even seem real. It felt like a dream. I'd busted my ass—and driven the entire group to the point of exhaustion—just to get to this place. The fact that she was alive, that Freddie was alive and healthy, was something I'd never, ever take for granted. I was a grateful man.

The sound of camp coming alive met my ears, as did the rumblings inside the cabin. I heard my son, up and raring to go, but Tina seemed to know we weren't ready, so she coaxed him outside with her and her daughter. She even let Sasha outside with them.

"She's a smart, smart woman," Sara muttered, her eyes still closed. "I love her even more right now."

I chuckled, leaning in to kiss her forehead. "We have to get up eventually, Shortcake."

"Mmhmm…Five more minutes," she mumbled into my neck as she snuggled in closer.

Grinning, I held her tight because "five more minutes" always meant at least thirty to forty-five minutes more. And I had a feeling Freddie wouldn't be held off for long. He never was, and this time would be no different, especially given how long it had been since we'd all been together as a family.

Inhaling deeply the scent of her hair, I noted it smelled different. It wasn't the fruity scent she used to use, but she still smelled like home.

"Where'd you meet her?" I asked softly, unable to keep my questions at bay. I wanted to know everything I'd missed, everything that had happened to keep her alive.

Sara smiled against my neck, pressing a kiss to the skin before pulling back to look up at me with sleepy-sweet eyes. "You want to do this now?"

Brushing her hair from her face, I settled closer to her. "I'd rather *we* do this now, just us, and then face everyone else and their questions."

It was how we'd always worked, especially when I'd been gone for tours overseas. We'd always escaped, talked it out, focused on us again after being apart.

"We found Tina and Janie on the 26 coming here. They'd been trapped for days; her husband had turned—he'd been bitten." She paused, shaking her head and reaching up to trail her fingers across my face. "Sandy got really bad about a month after you called me," she continued, wrinkling her nose a little. "I kept telling everyone we needed to go, but martial law had kicked in and they really weren't letting anyone out of the county. A couple days before we left, all of it fell. There were infected people everywhere. The soldiers had left or been turned, the streets were crazy, and we'd boarded up every window just to keep away from them. Derek and Dad were pretty adamant about staying, fighting. And they did for a bit, but I finally put my foot down and said I was leaving with Freddie, that I was keeping my promise to you.

"It caused a big fight between Dad and me, but the day before I was going to leave, he showed up at our house with Derek and a whole truck filled with supplies. He told me that Portland was on fire, that you'd been right, but that I wasn't to go alone." She paused for a second, and I kissed her lips just because I could.

"It was actually better that I didn't leave without them, because… we would've never made it just Freddie and me," she sighed, smiling sadly. "Dad sent me with Derek, Brody and Leo, Millie and Josh Larson, and Martin and Carol North."

"He didn't come with you?" I asked, and she shook her head.

"No, he couldn't. He wanted to, but he had a whole nursing home filled with patients he needed to take care of. He was hoping that someone would come to move them, but…" She shrugged. "There was no one *to* come for them. He stayed as long as he could. He's only been here a month or so. He brought who he could with him, though—about nine people, although we've lost some. Martin and Carol are gone. Leo. Travis. Ivan. Hannah. We lost Leo and Carol about a month after we got here. Maybe more. I don't know. Time seems…lost."

Her voice was soft, almost emotionless, but I understood it. She locked those sad, deep-blue eyes on me.

"I never stopped hoping you'd come," she finally said, her voice breaking a little. "I just…couldn't. And I had to stay strong, fight for Freddie. He was…Oh God, Jack, he's so smart and brave," she sobbed, shaking her head, but I wiped away her tears. "He was so damned determined to learn to shoot in order to be able to fight, to protect *me*. He's just…you all over. He actually got pissed off when I wouldn't let him have a gun. I'd wanted to wait until we got here… or maybe I was stalling. I don't know."

I sniffled and laughed at the same time. Her pride in him was palpable. Her love for us was practically glowing out of her.

She swallowed thickly, getting herself under control, before saying, "Anyway, we… We settled in here okay. Derek and Josh hunt for us, trap. Leo taught Janie and Freddie to fish the lake, and they've gotten damned good at it. Once Dad got here, he fished with them. Moses, Brody, and a few others started building fences. Jonah, this elderly gentleman…You'll love him. He and Ivan helped us with water. You know, rain barrels and stuff. Occasionally the boys will run across abandoned cars or cabins, and they'll salvage what they can. Dad brought more with him. Millie started a garden, but Jonah is the one who really works it."

"Your dad's in charge?" I asked, remembering how they'd looked to him last night.

"Yeah. It was Derek, really, at first, but Dad's just..."

I huffed a laugh. "He's kinda perfect to be in charge, really. It suits him, probably comes with the whole firefighter thing."

She grinned and nodded. "Yeah. He stays so calm too." Her smile fell, and she tucked her hair back, only to reach for my face. "I don't know what I'd have done without them. All of them. Derek...He... he kept me from going crazy. Tina too. One time, I completely lost my shit. I was glad Freddie didn't see it."

Gliding the backs of my fingers down her beautiful face, I asked, "What happened, Shortcake?"

"We were hunting—Derek, Josh, and me. A pack came through as they were dressing the deer. There was a soldier among them." Her eyes met mine as tears streamed down her face. "I flipped the fuck out, Jack. I shot him, and then...and then..."

"Okay, okay, okay," I chanted, pulling her completely to me. I wrapped my arms all the way around her. "I'm here. I'm okay. It wasn't me."

"That's what Derek said, that it wasn't you," she mumbled into my neck. "He...he *made* me look."

"Good, I'm glad," I whispered against her cheek. When she pulled back, I smiled at her, cupping her face. "You did amazing, Sara. With this place, with Freddie. All of it."

"I'm just glad you're here," she sighed, her forehead meeting mine before her lips dropped a soft kiss to my mouth. "I didn't think you'd...I had to believe. Otherwise, I'd have gone crazy."

"It was close," I sighed, settling her back to her pillow. "My turn, I guess, huh?" When she nodded, I kissed her—long and deep—simply because I wanted to remind myself that the journey had been so fucking worth it.

I took a deep breath and let it out. "I...Joel and I were sent to the base to give extra security. Mom and Dad went as medical volunteers, just in case. And boy, did they come through." I snorted, shaking my head. "The storm hit the state hard. Really hard. Especially on the west coast. The gulf. But the east side had tornadoes..."

I told her about waking up in the medical facility, that it was just the four of us. "Jesus, Sara...There was *no one* on that base alive, except for Sasha. And we found her in an apartment. Someone must've stashed her there to keep her safe, but..." I shook my head. "Joel and I came really close to getting ourselves killed that day, but where we were and how the wreckage fell saved us. Then my parents kinda quarantined us in a wing away from it all. And we had to heal before we could leave, so we used the time to stock up, plan…"

I curled a lock of her hair around my finger because I needed to touch her. "It took us over two weeks to get out of Florida alone. The place was insane. We were able to move a little easier once we started heading northwest. We found Ruby and her sister, Ava, just before we left Florida. The people they'd been with just dumped them off, leaving this kid, this young girl, inside a zeak-filled Wal-Mart."

"Zeak?" Sara asked with a chuckle.

"Joel. I'll let him tell you that word's origin," I muttered, rolling my eyes. "Anyway…Wal-Mart…" I snorted, looking to her. "You know, it wasn't much different in there than before the virus…"

Sara giggled, shaking her head. "Keep going."

Grinning, I kissed her nose and told her about making our way between big cities, avoiding major highways. "We found Lexie just before leaving Mississippi, inside this farmhouse. Her whole family had turned. She had a shit-ton of supplies—food and fuel, mainly—and gave it to us in trade to come with us." Grimacing, I turned to Sara. "She's…young, baby. She's…kinda mad at me too. She'll be an even more pleasant thing now," I muttered sarcastically. "She's…"

"Got a crush," Sara finished for me, smirking a little, but I could see the worry.

"Yeah, but I…" I shook my head. "I told her no repeatedly. Ruby thinks it's obnoxious, my mother said it's hero worship, and Joel laughs, although he knows I'm not trying to be mean, but…" My rambling trailed off. "I'm not making any sense, I know."

Sara cupped either side of my face, kissing me softly. "It's okay. I get it."

Narrowing my eyes at her, I asked, "Who?" When she didn't answer, I started guessing. "Brody?"

She snorted and then glared my way. "Uhh, hardly. He's just as *cheerful* as ever, and he blames me for his dad, since it was me who shot him after he turned. He saw me do it. He won't say it out loud anymore because everyone threatens him, but I see it in his face. He really blames me."

"If not him, then…"

"Jack, please..." she whispered, looking down at my chest. "I don't want trouble, honestly...This will be...Derek's developed his own crush, I think. I just...We stuck together through all of this, but...he's feeling...more. And I couldn't hurt him, but he...There would never be anyone but you," she finally sputtered out. "Even if something had happened and I knew or whatever...I'd only ever feel this way about you...It wasn't fair, and I told him that."

"Shh," I breathed against her lips, smiling a little. "He's always been attracted to you, Sara. I just beat him to the punch that night at Shelly's Bar."

"No!"

"Yes." I laughed, nodding a little. "I see we're still breaking hearts, Shortcake."

She sighed. "He loves you, Jack. And he would never disrespect you, but I could see...things changed with him. He fights it; I see it, but I honestly don't think it's *me*. I think it's just all this...shit."

Nodding, I sighed. "Maybe it's all this shit, but I don't know. God, baby...You're beautiful and strong and sweet. That's a hard thing to ignore. Trust me. I don't like it, but I *get it*. It's something I've learned to live with since I fell in love with you." My chest constricted before I asked, "Is there a problem? I mean..."

"No! No, Jack. I...I saw his face last night, baby. He's so conflicted. He wanted you guys back just as much as me, but then..." She groaned, rubbing her face. "I don't want trouble between you two. I love you...*only you*. I did everything to discourage it."

"Ah." I smirked, toying with the dog tags around her neck, and she nodded. "Aw, Sara. Look at me," I whispered, cupping her face. "I won't say anything, baby. Promise. Unless he steps out of line..."

"He won't." She narrowed her eyes at me. "Though, I reserve the same right, Mr. Chambers."

Laughing, I raised my hands in surrender. "Like I could stop you."

She giggled a little. "That's right. Now...Keep going."

Grinning, I saluted her. "Yes, ma'am. Okay, where was I? Mississippi. After we left Lexie's farm, we made it as far as Kansas before we needed supplies. Dodge City was...a mess. The town wasn't all that big, but apparently the virus hit all at once, so the streets were just swarmed. That's where we met Quinn."

I went on to tell her about Wyoming and the babies, which made her gasp and then smile. "You'll like Olivia," I told her. "She's a good mom, and those kids are just way too smart. Abe had been watching over them, but he's in his seventies, so he knew coming with us was the best thing. We also found another couple—Tim and Nikki—but we lost them in Boise."

I reached up to touch the scar over my eyebrow, and Sara gently pulled my hand away to trace it softly.

"I…I tried to save them, but…" I shook my head, looking away for a second. "Fuck, Sara, I honestly don't know who's worse…The zeaks or the survivors. It's like some people have lost all reason, you know?"

"The survivors should *know* better," she countered, frowning as she pulled my gaze back to hers. "The…zeaks…" She grinned when I chuckled at the word coming from her. "Well, they at least have an excuse for being…savages."

God, I couldn't stop from kissing her if I tried. My lips met hers roughly, but I slowed us down a little, only to pull back and just… look at her.

"I had…no fucking idea if you'd survived, if you'd come here like I'd asked, but I kept going. I kept pushing all of them. I hardly gave them a choice in the matter," I started ranting. "I…Shit, I hardly cared who came with us, but if they did, they knew we were heading here. End of fucking story."

She grinned, running her fingers deliciously through my hair. "That's my stubborn husband."

I shrugged a shoulder. "I finally caught a glimpse of hope at home. I stopped in Sandy."

Tears welled up in her eyes. "Did you…"

"Oh, I got your note. Jesus, just knowing you'd left the house okay, that you'd been alive there. That meant…*everything*. Thank you."

"How's it…"

I shook my head sadly. "Sandy is…no more."

"Hey," she whispered, kissing me lightly. "It's okay. Home is… here. Now. Home is where you are, where Freddie is, where all those people outside are. It has to be."

"I know," I sighed, pulling her closer, and then finally rolled onto my back with her on top of me. "I know, Shortcake. Believe me. I couldn't give a shit where we are. Just having you here, right here, is enough for me. I'm so fucking grateful."

"Me too." She leaned in to kiss me but grinned when the sound of the front door of the cabin met our ears.

"I'd recognize those footsteps anywhere," I said in a whispered chuckle. I patted her bottom. "C'mon. As much as I want to stay in this bed all day…"

"We can't. There's so much to do."

She kissed me once more with a sweet smile and soft laugh before getting out of bed. We used some of the water from the night before to clean up a little and to be able to flush the toilet. Sara was dressed and armed by the time Freddie's patience had completely evaporated.

"Dad!" he yelled, bursting through the bedroom door just as I finally strapped my gun to my thigh. "That dog you brought…She's so freakin' *awesome!*"

Grinning, I couldn't help but scoop him up and toss him over my shoulder. "I know. She is *really* awesome."

"We're keeping her?"

"Oh, yeah, we're keeping her."

Sara's giggle was soft, but I heard it. It was the happiest sound, one I used to live for, and I'd do the silliest shit just to hear it. I kept Freddie over my shoulder as we walked through the cabin.

We stepped out onto the porch, and there were more people milling around than I was used to, but they were all busy. The zeak cleanup was underway. Mose was driving my truck to load them and pile them up, and Joel was using the four-wheeler with the trailer. The tables were full. Some people were just talking, some were preparing food.

My mother was looking at Hank's leg, where he'd been wounded the day before, and he glanced up to see us, smirking a little but pointing our way.

"You know," he started slowly, "there'll be no living with her now. She was right that you were coming, so she's gonna hold that over our heads forever and a day."

Grinning, I slipped Freddie to the grass and wrapped an arm around Sara's shoulders. "That's my girl. *Who's* the stubborn one?" I asked in her ear.

She was wearing a wicked grin, and I loved it.

"I'll ease off in a month or two," she told her dad before kissing his cheek as he muttered under his breath. "How's the leg?"

"Sore, but Dottie's fixin' me up," he told her, smiling my mother's way.

Sara hugged my mother, and they exchanged whispers like usual, Sara nodding in answer to some question. Next she went to my father, who was eyeing a small garden with an older gentleman, and gave him a hug, as well.

Ruby's RV door opened, making me smile as Ava came out, sleepy-faced, with her Sabrina shadow right behind her, followed by Ruby and Olivia with Aiden in her arms. The only one I hadn't seen was Lexie.

"Sara," I called, waving her to me. "I'd like you to meet these ladies and the tiny gent."

"Okay," she said with a smile as they approached.

Ruby was the first to us. Forgoing any introductions, she wrapped my wife in a hug. "Omigod, it's nice to meet you, Sara. I'm Ruby."

Sara grinned. "You too."

"This is Olivia," I introduced, placing a hand on the woman's shoulder, and Sara shook her hand. "That crazy man is Aiden."

"Oh my goodness," she crooned. "Aren't you handsome?" When Aiden gave her his toothy-dimply grin, my girl was done for, just like I knew she'd be when I'd first seen the chubby boy. "And who's this?" she asked, kneeling down in front of Sabrina.

"Sabrina," she answered. "Jack talked about you."

Sara grinned at the laughter but nodded. "Yeah, well, he's talked about you too. All of you. Freddie and Janie are around here somewhere. They're about your age, so you won't be alone. Okay?"

"Okay," Sabrina said with a smile.

Ava was quiet, but I pulled her to me, saying, "Today you're shy, Half Pint?"

She shook her head but smiled Sara's way.

"It's nice to meet you, Ava," Sara said, looking to me.

"I'm..." Ava started but faltered and blushed a little. "I'm glad that you're okay. We came as fast as we could for you."

Sara crooned, pulling Ava in for a hug. "Thank you, sweetie." My beautiful girl looked at all of them, saying, "There's food and water. Maybe even coffee. You can make yourselves at home here."

Ruby nodded and thanked her, guiding everyone around the table, but her eyes met mine, flickering to the RV and silently telling me where Lexie was. I only nodded and shrugged.

Gazing around a little, I caught sight of Joel with Mose. They'd started a cleanup fire but had stopped, pointing to the fences. My eyes then fell to the far back corner of the camp. There were makeshift crosses, four graves in the process of being dug by Quinn, Derek, Brody, and a man I didn't know, and two mounds with grass growing. Six. They'd lost six damn people. And more from careless, guileless survivors than from zeaks.

"Son, sit," Hank stated, catching where my gaze had fallen. "I've got a feeling we're gonna have company again. We took out three of theirs before they ran out of here like a scalded dog."

"*Boof*," Sasha added, walking up to us, and I ruffled her fur.

"Nothin' personal, big girl," I told her but turned back to Hank, who snorted. "And that pack was the biggest I've seen."

"Me too. I think Portland is empty and they're hunting for food," he stated, which caught the attention of the few people around us.

My father sat down across from us, and my mother finished with Hank's bandage and then took a spot beside Dad. Sara leaned against me, handing me a mug of coffee.

Hank glanced between my parents and me. "I'd like to be prepared. I'd like these people prepared, armed, and ready. They only saw who we let them see."

"Which wasn't much, Hank," Tina stated. "They saw you, Derek, and Brody. They have no idea how many of us were shooting at them."

"Yeah, exactly," Hank agreed. "If they come now…" He gestured around the camp at all the people. "We have numbers."

"Numbers but way too many ways to get in here," Dad added, glancing around with a grimace. "Everything's so open. Those fences are great against the zeaks, but not…people." He pointed toward the fence line, where Joel and Mose were removing zeaks that had skewered themselves onto the spikes.

"You know, Brody's been talking about Klamath Lake, specifically Rocky Point," Josh piped up from the other table. "We've never had enough people to leave to scope it out, but…now we do."

Hank eyed him for a second but then turned toward the graves, giving a sharp whistle. "Brody, come over here for a second!"

"Well, this should be a joy," Tina muttered, making Sara snort and smack blindly her way. "What? He's just…At least he's not drunk; he's an absolute *peach* when drunk."

I chuckled but buried it into Sara's upper arm. I really liked the woman. She was going to get along with Joel perfectly.

"Brody, talk to me about Klamath Lake. What were you thinking?" he asked when Brody joined us, though he stood away a bit, leaning on a shovel.

Brody shrugged. "Really, for supplies. There are tons of hotels and lodges down there. It's not all that far, either. But... *heaven forbid* we leave the camp short."

The jibe hit the mark it was meant for, and Sara flinched.

"Brody, focus on someone besides yourself...just for a few minutes," Hank drawled, much to my amusement. "Can you do that?"

Brody sneered but nodded. "It would take a day or two and a rather large group, but we could scope out the area for supplies. Maybe even a safer location—a bigger place, bigger lake...Not that I'm not grateful for *Camp Chambers* or anything, but there's a group out there trying to take it, and this is open and easy to sneak in. There are so many of us that we won't fit in four small cabins and a few RVs much longer. A lodge, something big, something even gated..."

"You're free to leave *Camp Chambers* anytime you wish, Brody," Sara snapped, her lip curling in anger. "I think I told you that on the way here."

I chuckled, which only pissed the asshole off that much more, but he knew who was around him. He was outnumbered, outsmarted, and a minority with how he felt about us. If he said one derogatory word toward her, he'd be obliterated. And I honestly had no desire to hand him his ass my first day there. I was way too fucking happy to be home. Tomorrow? Maybe.

"Whatever," he sighed, rolling his eyes back to Hank. "It would need scouting first. I've only been there a couple times, and that was years ago."

Hank nodded, adjusting his baseball cap. "Okay... Well, we can't go yet, not until I'm healed. If we do this, then I'd like to go with the scouting party. Until then, we have work to do, and I'd like to start keeping a couple of people as patrols. Even at night."

"We can do that," my dad stated with a nod. "We did it on the road, so we can do it here."

I nodded in agreement. "Absolutely. And we have weapons."

"And you're trained," Josh added.

"Well, that too," Dad conceded. "Though, anyone can be trained in weapons and fighting."

"Even you, Brody," Derek drawled, slowly walking up to the tables. "You could use some discipline."

Brody bit his tongue, which I found interesting, until Sara leaned to my ear. "Derek punched him the hell out not long ago. My dad? He threatened to tie him to a tree. Same day. Right after my dad got here, in fact."

"Oh hell," I sighed, shaking my head, but I kissed her cheek and stood up. Looking to Hank, I said, "We'll talk about that scouting trip a little more, but after your leg is healed. For now, we'll do what you need here." Turning to my cousin, I held out my arms. "Where do you need me?"

He grinned his lazy-ass smile. "Christ, everywhere. The graves are just about done," he said, the smile slipping off his face. "But there are infected still left to burn, and the gate needs repairing. Oh, yeah, and more fencing…"

"There's laundry and water to boil," Tina added with a giggle.

"Traps to check," Hank piped up.

"Fish to clean." Sara grinned, kissing my lips. "Anywhere, Jack. Just…pick your poison."

Grinning and cracking my knuckles, I nodded. "Fair enough. I'll get started, then."

TO BE CONTINUED…

ACKNOWLEDGMENTS

I need to thank Jenny Rarden for always keeping me going, for cleaning me up, and for setting me straight. I'd also like to thank some of my friends who have pushed me to keep going, cheered me on, and helped me with the tiny details: Reina Latona, Pamela Stephenson, Sue Bartlet, Bethany Tullos, Jodi Parker, Inga Kaczmarek, and Melanie Moreland. And lastly, thank you to Coreen Montagna for the beautiful cover and all her hard work taking my words and making them into an amazing book.

And finally, I need to thank my husband, John, for putting up with something that once started as a hobby but turned into something different. Love you.

About the Author

Deb Rotuno was born and raised in central Florida, where she currently lives with her husband and four cats. She's worked in retail for almost seventeen years, but if she were able to do anything she wanted, she would be a full-time reader, writer, and fur-baby mom. She has always been a big reader, and writing was something she started late in high school, but she began to dabble in it again once she discovered fanfic in 2009. Since then, she's read and written plenty in her spare time, especially since she cannot watch a TV show or a movie without thinking about how she could write a story like it.

Website: www.debrotuno.com
Twitter: @Drotuno
Facebook: Facebook.com/drotuno
RR Books Website: www.rr-books.com
RR Books Twitter: @RR_Books
RR Books Facebook: Facebook.com/writers.at.rrbooks/

Made in the USA
Lexington, KY
06 November 2016